THE TALE THAT WAGS THE GOD

James Blish

edited by Cy Chauvin
introduction by John Foyster
bibliography by Judith L. Blish

ReAnimus Press
1100 Johnson Road #16-143
Golden, CO 80402
www.ReAnimus.com

© 2017, 1986 by James Blish. All rights reserved.

ISBN-13: 978-1542833356

First ReAnimus Press print edition: January, 2017

10 9 8 7 6 5 4 3 2 1

PREFACE by Cy Chauvin

James Blish (under the Name William Atheling, Jr.) has written two previous volumes of science fiction criticism: *The Issue At Hand* (1964) and *More Issues At Hand* (1970). These books are largely devoted to technical criticism of current magazines and books of the time; Blish's comments were intended primarily for the writer, although readers found his criticism fascinating as well. The essays in this collection, on the other hand, are more generalized and theoretical. The five essays in Part I are thematically linked, and present a mosaic picture of Blish's view of science fiction, and may help to place it in the general context of art, literature and life. Together, these essays seem to form part of the extended theoretical and historical work that many critics and writers wished Blish would write after *More Issues at Hand* was published. Some of the other essays reflect Blish's interests outside of science fiction. "Music of the Absurd," for example, concerns itself with the excesses of modern, serious concert music. But I think this article makes an interesting contrast to "The Arts in Science Fiction" and "A New Totemism?" The extremes of modern music which Blish describes make this music seem the product of an alien culture, not our own; the very oddity of our own culture contrasts with the blandness and paucity of the art depicted in sf, which Blish criticizes. In "A New Totemism?", Blish wonders how the encounter with intelligent aliens might affect the future of art, in particular the unconscious assumptions art makes about the nature of humanity; assumptions that even sf about alien cultures makes all the time. Similarly, other essays in this book illuminate each other. So while *The Tale That Wags the God* was never planned by Blish, I believe it is more than a mere compilation, or posthumous afterthought; I don't think this is due just to luck, but reflects the consistent nature of Blish's mind and his consistent critical principles and interests.

He did plan two other collections of criticism: *Dead Issues at Hand* and *The Agent as Patient: Seven Subjects With An Object*. The preface to the first begins:

The peculiarly uninviting title of this third Atheling volume rather accurately reflects its contents, I am afraid. For my subject this time is the historians (and, only secondarily, the histories) of science fiction; and my thesis is that most of them are pretty bad, and that the ground they purport to cover will have to be gone over again, unnecessarily and thanklessly. Thus, these *should* be dead issues, but they are still to hand...

Besides the preface, the book consists of four chapters corresponding to the four types of sf scholar: (1) Moskowitz: Light Without Heat; (2) Zwei Welke Rosen, Entsprungen; (3) Suvin Looks East; (4) Merril: Guesswork and Gush. Suvin[1] was to emerge as the genuine scholar. The four promised essays all appear to be projected from existing pieces, mostly *F&SF* reviews.

---

[1] Darko Suvin gave Blish some insight on a number of matters, notably on Blish's story "Surface Tension," the popularity of which puzzled Blish for many years. "In answer to my bafflement, Darko asked me to dig out of my library either of the two issues of the Aldiss-Harrison *SF Horizons* and look at its cover picture. 'That,' he said, 'is the central thrill of "Surface Tension," and what most of your serious work is about.' The picture is a woodcut showing a monk, on his hands and knees, crawling out of the familiar world through a break—which he seems to have made himself—in the Aristotelean spheres and looking amazedly at the totally different universe he finds outside them. This view of my central theme includes Damon Knight's view of it—'getting born'—but isn't nearly so restrictive for me, nor does it require the complex and admirable ingenuities of detail Damon had to resort to (about 'Common Time') to buttress it, or Darko's admittedly sometimes murky formalistic terminology.... In fact, what could be simpler?" This is taken from a letter published in *Cypher* 11, May 1974.

"Zwei Welke Rosen, Entsprungen," for instance, would have focused on Lois & Stephen Rose's *The Shattered Ring*, which Blish reviewed in *F&SF* in August, 1971. Alas, the expansions and revisions that would have been necessary to make the book publishable were never even begun, and the book only exists as a plan in the Bodleian Library's collection of Blish papers at Oxford.

The Agent as Patient is much more complete; all the seven essays which were to comprise this book are extant save one ("The Kafka Scandal"), although some revisions Blish apparently intended for at least two of the essays in this volume were never completed. In the book's introduction he wrote: "Critics clash frequently and noisily, over matters of detail, but it seldom happens that their performance is tested against their subject matter from a reasonable distance." Blish's subjects were artists, or artistic fields or genres, and the object of the collection "to winnow out contemporary critical reactions to these subjects, and test these reactions for viability." Among the subjects examined were James Branch Cabell ("The Long Night of a Virginia Author"), modern music ("Music of the Absurd") and science fiction ("The Function of Science Fiction")—all of which are included here. The latter essay, in a magazine appearance, was titled "The Tale That Wags The God," and I have taken this for the title of the book.

Other essays ("The Science in Science Fiction" and "The Arts in Science Fiction") were originally given as talks before the Cambridge University SF Society in England, and recorded and later published by Malcolm Edwards. "The Literary Dreamers" first appeared in *The Alien Critic* in 1973. "Poul Anderson: The Enduring Explosion" was published in the special Anderson issue of *The Magazine of Fantasy and Science Fiction* in 1971, which accounts in part for Blish's wholly laudatory discussion of this author's work. "A New Totemism?" and the somewhat tongue-in-cheek "Probapossible Prolegomena to Ideareal History" were both published posthumously in England.

I have also included two items of biographical interest: "A Science Fiction Coming of Age," which is a largely unpublished piece of autobiography (focusing mostly on Blish's childhood), and a conversation with Brian Aldiss recorded at a British sf convention in 1973. The latter is the most revealing interview Blish ever made—it reveals the emotion behind the man and his fiction, as well as his intellect.

John Foyster's introduction was originally published elsewhere, and read by "William Atheling Jr." while he was still alive and well, and a practicing critic. I know of no one who has better pinpointed Blish's strengths as a critic, or explained more completely why his criticism is of such value to science fiction. The essay is especially useful if read with a copy of *The Issue at Hand* alongside for reference.

Blish, along with Damon Knight, was one of the first truly informed critics of sf, but he also wrote for the literary quarterlies (where two of the essays in this book appeared) and filled other roles in science fiction as well. He bridged many of the gaps in sf: between writers in America and England (he was an American transplanted to England); between the new generation of writers and the old (he encouraged such new writers in the 1960's as Thomas Disch and Joanna Russ, and older ones such as Poul Anderson); between routine commercial fiction and that which attempted to be literature (he wrote the first *Star Trek* book series and *After Such Knowledge*); between literature and science (he knew both); and, of course, between writers and critics. I know of no one else in science fiction who was a bridge between so many. This perhaps was his most important achievement.

I hope you enjoy his book.

— Cy Chauvin
April, 1984 Detroit, Michigan

INTRODUCTION, by John Foyster

William Atheling, Jr.: A Critic of Science Fiction

The critical function consists in saying what you like and why you like it: less often it is a matter of dislike which is involved. No one, however, who has any pretension to critical skill could care to leave it at that, for while it is a relatively simple principle it may be applied in many ways. Furthermore, since many human beings are inclined to pretend that they are so much above their fellows that their judgment is impartial, we also have a class of critics who relate their work to absolute "objective" standards.

In practice a critic does in fact simply state his likes or dislikes: but since, thanks to John W. Campbell, Jr., not all opinions are of equal worth the critic seeks to demonstrate that *his* opinion is a reasonable one, based on criteria which have wide acceptance. The skill with which critics do this varies greatly. On the one hand, amongst critics of science fiction, we have those who simply assert that such-and-such is a great sf novel because

(i) the critic likes it, and

(ii) he has read a hell of a lot of sf and therefore knows what he is talking about. (The extreme forms of this disease occur when the critic adds that the work in question may be added to the "sf canon.") On the other hand we have those critics (few though they might be) who attempt to appeal to wider sensibilities. And at the extreme and most remote from our near-sighted canoneer we have William Atheling, Jr.

It would be pleasantly simple if everyone could agree on just what constitutes reasonable grounds for liking a work of art, though it could be a trifle boring. As it happens, it is rather difficult to find much more common ground than my broad assertion above that one has to do more than *claim* that the work of art is "good." In *Warhoon* 25, Robert A. W. Lowndes took a minimal line and suggested that criticism "consists of three elements: reporting, interpretation, and evaluation." To a certain extent this is true (even though, as I stated above, it is practically minimal), but the following might be noted. *Reporting,* as Lowndes implicitly defined it, incorporates almost all of what is currently accepted as "criticism" in the sf magazines. For Lowndes suggests that this is just a matter of telling the reader what he will find in the book *provided* that he "can read with any degree of proficiency." Since Lowndes admits that this is an area in which almost every critic shows weaknesses on occasions, it is clearly not as simple as it superficially appears. Atheling makes a good fist of this kind of work, particularly, for example, in his discussion of "The Weather Man" (pages 101-103 [115-118] of *The Issue at Hand*[2]). This is not to say that this is all there is to that particular review, but it is an excellent piece of "reporting."

Interpretation and *evaluation* are closely linked. If the critic's interpretation is incorrect, then almost certainly his judgment as to whether the work is good or bad will be incorrect. As it happens, Lowndes singled out Atheling's article on his own *Believers' World* for considerable praise, so it is hardly necessary to repeat the exercise. But let me add that the piece following the article on *Believers' World* in *The Issue at Hand* (pages 62-70 [68-79]) seems quite a *tour de force* on the interpretation side.

---

[2] *Editor's note:* Page references are to the first edition of *The Issue at Hand*, followed by the equivalent reference [in square brackets] to the second edition (printings from 1973 onward).

In his essay "Literary Criticism and Philosophy" (in *The Common Pursuit*) F. R. Leavis gave a short formula, but one which is perhaps harder to interpret: "The ideal critic is the ideal reader." By this Leavis means the reader who fully appreciates what the writer had done, and is able to perceive the relationship which this work holds with the rest of the works of literature. Atheling seems to fulfill these conditions rather well. He has certainly read widely in science fiction; he is not unlettered when considered against the larger realm of general literature. Furthermore he shows himself to be able to appreciate both sides of any piece of science fiction—as science fiction, and as literature. As an example we might take Atheling's well-known review of Arthur Zirul's "Final Exam." As Atheling himself puts it:

To begin on the most elementary level, Mr. Zirul's prose contains more downright bad grammar...

—an instance of Atheling as schoolteacher or, as he suggests himself, as the editor that Zirul should have had. Then, on page 85 [97], he moves off into slightly higher realms to discuss the approach Zirul has taken in writing this story ("the author is omniscient"), something which few editors and (almost) fewer writers appreciate, at least in science fiction, so that we may suggest without stretching the point too far that here Atheling is acting as rather more than an average sf critic, and that he is endeavouring to take a larger view. And finally Atheling the sf fan reveals to us that Zirul's plot is really old-hat. I have deliberately chosen this unpromising story to show how Atheling *could* apply himself to even the meanest story. I *don't* suggest that Leavis had this sort of thing in mind when he wrote "Literary Criticism and Philosophy"—merely that, viewed within the sf framework, Atheling seems to meet some of Leavis' requirements.

At the risk of becoming even more boring, I'm going to see how Atheling measures up to the strictures of yet another critic: Marcel Proust. In a footnote to his essay "In Memory of a Massacre of Churches" (superficially about Ruskin) Proust remarks that the critic's first task is to make "some... attempt to help the reader feel the impact of an artist's unique characteristics." This is one of Atheling's strengths, though it can so easily be a weakness, a mere pigeonholing of each author which results from overlooking the word "unique." Even when reviewing Garrett's parody (pages 74-76 [84-87]) Atheling fastens onto the "unique" characteristics of George O. Smith and Anthony Boucher. This sort of critic is worth ten of the fellow who merely says that "A is like B." But in his book Atheling goes rather further than this, and says rather careful things about writers like Bester, Budrys, Kornbluth, and Shiras. These are the names which occur to me first, but I am sure the list of careful characterisations is much longer. But Proust asked for something more, and if I can boil down a sentence of over 150 words accurately, he also wanted the critic to investigate the writer's vision of reality (*cave* Philip K. Dick?). This is not something which can easily be done in science fiction, where the writer's vision often stops at 3c a word, but Atheling attempts it, and the subject is, as might almost be predicted blindfold, Robert A. Heinlein. Whether Atheling succeeds in his attempt is another matter, and one upon which I cannot comment: my interest in Heinlein is so slight that it hardly seems worth the effort.

Now Atheling is no Leavisite, and he does not seem to me to be likely to be much of a fan of Proust. Yet it is pleasing to note that his criticism manages to at least be consistent with what these two very different writers thought about the nature of criticism. He is speaking the same language, and in this he is almost alone amongst writers on science fiction.

More important than Atheling's performance as measured by others is the extent to which he manages to live up to his own standards. Atheling has never been reluctant to say what he is trying to do, and this makes our task much easier. Let us begin at the beginning.

If science fiction is really growing up (a proposition that could use some defining), however, it is going to need a lot more criticism than it's been getting. The nature of the criticism will be determined by just how far science-fiction readers would like to see the idiom grow. (Page 11 [5-6])

When Atheling wrote this (1952), sf criticism was really limited to the writings of Damon Knight: beyond that was chaos, consisting largely, however, of rather unscrupulous puffs.

Since then there have been no new major critics of sf: in a moment of weakness Atheling listed Anthony Boucher (a fair middle-of-the-road reviewer), P. S. Miller (good at cataloguing), Frederik Pohl (???), Lester del Rey (only moderate), and Sturgeon (whose reviews were characterised by little thought and lots of writing). Later enthusiasts might add the names of Alfred Bester and Judith Merril: I blush for them. So, apart from Atheling and Knight, sf seems to be totally lacking in good professional reviewers. Among the amateurs have been some writers of more or less the same class as Knight and Atheling (Arthur J. Cox being the most obvious example), but there has not been this "lot more criticism." There has been, in fact, a swing away from this towards a deification of sf writers, though no one, to my knowledge, has gone so far as to claim that they are above suspicion. Criticism of J. G. Ballard, for example, has tended towards either of two extremes: that Ballard is *great* because he is Ballard, and that Ballard is *bad* because he doesn't write like the other fellers. Neither of these two arguments, which have consumed vast quantities of paper and time, constitute what Atheling had in mind when he wrote of "more criticism."

In this early piece, Atheling develops his argument: that science fiction, to advance, must shake off the bonds of being a ghetto literature, and try to establish itself as literature without any modifiers whatsoever. And it is here that Atheling first describes the critic's functions. It will be noted that they are rather different from the criteria that I have quoted already. First, he writes (page 12 [7]), the critic must bring to the attention of editors and writers *reasonable* standards to be observed in the writing of sf. Secondly, he must explain to his readers what these standards are.

Atheling makes no grandiose claims for what he is to write: his intent is clearly to try to improve the writing of science fiction by getting down to the wordsmith level. This he does consistently throughout his career, but *also* attacks the problem at higher levels, as I have indicated above. The technical criticism, Atheling continues, will be essentially destructive, at least at first glance: but its intent is constructive in the long run. In this prediction Atheling was completely correct: he did tend towards destructive technical criticism throughout his career. But on many occasions Atheling was constructive and even interpretative: there is little in his review of *Stranger in a Strange Land* which is destructive or even anything which would suggest that Atheling was capable of such blasting as Zirul received. The chapter, "A Question of Content," is entirely constructive, although little has come of it.

Atheling continues by asserting that "every science fiction editor operating today is flying by the seat of his pants" and that this explains the publication of much of the poor sf of the period. But a commercial editor *must* operate in this way to maximise profits. Campbell's great success stemmed from his willingness to bend in whichever direction his reader response suggested would increase sales most while at the same time giving the impression of being the most immovable man in science fiction. Atheling's point may well be true when considered in absolute terms, but a science fiction editor is not hired to publish good fiction; he is hired to publish stories which will sell large numbers of copies of his magazine(s).

This is the one possible flaw in Atheling's position: that of half-pretending that science fiction is not commercial (or even hack) literature. This is no great fault, for Edmund Wilson had the same trouble when he wrote about detective stories and the writings of H. P. Lovecraft. The sales of both of these forms indicate that Wilson must have missed some inherent enchantment (me too, by the way), and though his criticism remains sound and thoughtful it is not very helpful to fans of Agatha Christie or HPL. Atheling's attitude is by no means as extreme as Wilson's and as the prophets of science fiction continue to claim its impending (or now past) maturity it is probable that more and more science fiction stories (and perhaps even, in some remote heaven, science fiction editors) will meet the most exacting standards.

Nevertheless, most, if not all, of Atheling's criticism is directed towards faults which are as grave in commercial fiction as they are in fiction which claims a little more for itself: that the faults are so common in the fiction that appeared in *New Worlds* suggests that although Moorcock headed in the right direction he had by no means arrived. Thus, on pages 18-20 [13-16] Atheling is able to list some fairly common faults of science fiction—phony realism and "deep purple"—and still find them around many years later. I suspect that there is more of the former than of the latter in today's science fiction, probably because it is more difficult to recognise. But there is still a lot of deep purple in Zelazny's writing, for example, and Atheling's words have clearly not yet reached all the important ears.

Atheling's aim, as he has indicated right from the start, was to improve science fiction by working on those best placed to perform the task of *really* improving it: the editors. This is discussed at some length in the chapter "A Sprig of Editors." But later in the book (page 76-78 [87-89]) Atheling discusses the editor who regards himself as the perfect judge of writing and who insists on "helping" writers. It is terribly true that there have been many such pests, but as Atheling indicates elsewhere, sf does need strong and demanding editors. This difference between the editor who muddles in affairs that he knows nothing about and the editor who directs a wayward author onto the correct path is something that Atheling never seems to have investigated at length: indeed, to do so would have required more space than Atheling ever had in fanzines. Instead he concentrated on particular instances (Zirul and McLaughlin, and on Crossen/Wolfe). This makes for lighter reading but there's also a slight laziness about it all.

Atheling's chapter on negative judgments does reveal his preoccupation with this aspect of his craft. Here his attention is concentrated on it, and yet he still manages to be constructive (as in his provision of information about a *good* chess story by Carl Gentile, or in his giving Algis Budrys a pat on the back) in an apparent orgy of destruction. Though his intent is harsh, Atheling sees light at the end of the tunnel and cannot help but be softened by it.

A major failing of sf critics in general is the tendency for them to examine the "science" which may or may not be present in any given novel or short story. To some slight extent this is justified *if the fault in the science interferes with one's enjoyment of the story*, and it is possible, after all, to enjoy a story in which the science is dubious. Atheling almost puts this point of view (page 116 [133]) when he writes about the unpleasant practice of allowing sf reviewers to review popular scientific works or even more serious books. As Atheling remarks, one goes elsewhere for that kind of review. But he does not extend this argument to those who criticise "science" in novels or short stories. Perhaps he feels that an sf reviewer will react in much the same way as the average reader towards scientific bloopers. I don't think this is quite the case, and sf critics have fallen on their faces (say, into a bowl of water?) in overextending themselves. Perhaps Atheling had this partly in mind when he wrote of "expertitis" on page 52 [56], There's only one really gruesome example of Atheling in this role: his review (page 24 [21]) of a story by Dean Evans. He devotes some five lines to detailing the horrid errors in chemistry and pathology by Evans, though he never gets around to saying just how these hamstring the story. He *does* go on to make it plain (though only in passing) that these errors are less important than the problems concerned with the writing itself. Further on (page 46 [48]) Atheling has listed himself has having been on the side of "science" (as against "fiction"), but he now indicates that he has changed sides (or rather that the "sides" have merged toward the left): in the same paragraph he makes the following remark, which probably expressed a feeling that he had been harbouring for some time: "Bradbury writes stories, and usually remarkable ones; he is of course a scientific blindworm, but in the face of such artistry, it's difficult to care." There is no need for me to underscore the importance of this passage: for Atheling, as for every critic worth his salt, it is writing first, frills afterwards. The advent of Bradbury undoubtedly lowered the relevance of science to science fiction (though it never *really* mattered) and Atheling here acknowledged a fact which many have not yet become aware of. Science is *needed*. Yes (see Sturgeon, page 14 [9][3]), but it is *not* all-important and perhaps should not even be considered unless it becomes very obtrusive (in which case it is at fault anyway).

Science *was* obtrusive in Clement's *Mission of Gravity*, and this was made rather worse by the publication of "Whirligig World" in *Astounding,* which Atheling discusses in the chapter on editors already mentioned. Atheling was then suggesting that

---

[3] Atheling quoted Sturgeon from memory: "A [good] science-fiction story is a story built around human beings, with a human problem, and a human solution, which would not have happened at all without its scientific content."

Campbell would back *science* against *fiction:* this deplorable tendency was observed in action far too often in Campbell's later years as editor of *Analog/Astounding*.

Though science *per se* is not all-important in science fiction it is necessary in the context of Sturgeon's rule, which Atheling finds a useful scale. His discussion of Kornbluth's "The Goodly Creatures" is instructive. He demonstrates fairly clearly that a story which science fiction fans may like, even like for its supposed scientific content, may not be science fiction at all. Assuming, that is, that you hold to Sturgeon's rule. Of course vast quantities of modern science fiction fit into this category but Atheling's time has always been limited.

Atheling touches lightly on the connections, if any, between art and science fiction. In discussing *Stranger in a Strange Land* (in which art is conspicuous by its absence) the subject is naturally raised, though not in a way disparaging to Heinlein. Reviewing Miller's "The Darfsteller" Atheling manages to make some approaches to the subject, but the major statement on the subject remains James Blish's anthology for Ballantine, *New Dreams This Morning*. Perhaps Atheling felt that the connection was tenuous and not yet ready for any full exploration: the situation has unfortunately scarcely changed.

The ability to sum up all the flaws in something is a rare quality: Atheling did this for science fiction when he wrote, "Failure to grapple thoroughly with the logical consequences of an idea is one of the most common flaws in science fiction, as it is in all fiction." Even with that last phrase, which tends to weaken the whole idea, Atheling has succinctly made the point which, though it has remained true enough through all these years (as might be expected of so general a statement), has as yet had little impact on thinking about science fiction. This approach, which applies to science fiction so much more than to other forms of fiction, is of such grave import that it should be blazoned on the walls of all who think they know where sf is at, right up there with the quotations from Chairman Mao. He had something to say on the same subject, naturally, but let's not range too widely.

Sadly, Atheling's most important ideas have not borne much fruit. Though he was often brilliant, perceptive, and articulate, as I've tried to indicate, he was too often far ahead of his time. His major points have been forgotten in favour of Judith Merril's asides, the steady drone of P. Schuyler Miller, and the ugly squawks from elsewhere. It is hardly surprising, then, that Atheling's gift to the future has also fallen by the wayside.

Two of the chapters in *The Issue at Hand* are not fanzine items: "An Answer of Sorts" has to do with bread-and-butter matters, and "A Question of Content" is rather more important. It is unquestionably Atheling's *magnum opus*. While his indictment of the fumbling of sf writers, mentioned just above, is important, it pales into insignificance besides Atheling's insight into the somewhat plainer problem besetting science fiction: nothing ever happens that is worth worrying about. "Look," says Atheling, "if we want anyone to take science fiction seriously then we must have authors who are *saying something*." Of course we also need the writers to grapple with the logical consequences of the "something," but unless a novel has *some* "content" it is not worth considering. Many science fiction novels are overloaded with message: this we have seen too often. But very few actually have something embedded in the story (as opposed to "grafted on") that is worthwhile. Atheling lists a few: *1984, Player Piano, Limbo, Brave New World,* and *Star of the Unborn*. Would he add any to that list now, many years later? The number still remains small: authors prefer to fake a background by having the *action* important. Little Billy is the first man to Mars, Jack Barron (isn't he a tv makeup man anyway?) is a powerful personality in popular entertainment, the harlequin draws the attention of the whole world to himself; now I am Prince, Immortal, discoverer or editor of an sf magazine. Yet they are all empty, these novels;

they have no content in the way that Atheling suggested. There is no advance beyond *The Skylark of Space* in any but the most trivial fashion.

Was Atheling wasting his time, after all? Will science fiction ever become worthy of the kind of criticism he was able to bring to it? Will it ever reach the maturity he urged upon it?

Now read on:

— *John Foyster*

Part I

1. THE FUNCTION OF SCIENCE FICTION

Not every man would have the daring to title a story of his own "The Finest Story in the World," but Rudyard Kipling knew exactly what he was doing. If there is any short story in English which deserves to be called the finest on all counts—for characterisation, for perfection of language and structure, for emotional power and depth of implication, and in many other departments—I would nominate James Joyce's "The Dead" as the front-runner; but this is not at all what Kipling meant to claim by his title, which I think he would have retained even had he been in a position to know Joyce's piece and share my assessment of it. He was talking about Story as Tale—the kind of story which is so intensely interesting in itself that it hardly matters how it is told, and the best examples of which have survived many retellings and will survive many more.

It should not be surprising, as C. S. Lewis points out in *An Experiment in Criticism*, that almost all such stories are fantasies; nor should it be surprising that Kipling's exemplar of the type is a science fiction story. Many readers and almost all writers in this field know that Kipling was one of the finest of all science fiction writers.

What *should* be surprising, but unhappily is not, is that this fact about Kipling is unknown to the vast majority of teachers and scholars of English literature—and to the few that do know it, it is a source of embarrassment.

This is a specific example of a general situation. In the nineteenth century, virtually every writer of stature—and many now forgotten—wrote at least one science fiction story. Edgar Allan Poe wrote several; so did Ambrose Bierce, and Fitz-James O'Brien, and Edward Everett Hale, and Jack London, and many others. As an example of such a production from an author unknown now, let me cite *The Last American*, by J. A. Mitchell, which was published in 1889 by Frederick A. Stokes & Brother, and went through ten editions in the succeeding four years. Additional examples from this period may be found in a volume edited by Sam Moskowitz called *Science Fiction by Gaslight.*

Jules Verne, in short, was just plain wrong in assuming that he had invented a whole new kind of story. It had been in existence for decades; indeed, it was almost commonplace, and widely accepted. Poe's life, let it be remembered, was cut short in 1849. By about 1860, the science fiction story was a fully formed and highly visible literary phenomenon in English; Verne was merely the first author working in the form in another language to catch the public eye.

These writers did not call what they did "science fiction," or think of it as such; the term was not invented until 1929. When H. G. Wells published his early samples of it in the 1890's—and in the process showed that such pieces could also be works of art—he first called them "fantastic and imaginative romances," and, later, "science fantasy" (a term which has now been degraded to cover a sub-type in which the science content is minimal, and what little of it is present is mostly wrong). Most of its producers, however, never bothered to give it a label, nor did editors feel the lack; it was considered to be a normal and legitimate interest for any writer and reader of fiction. Indeed, the Utopian romance, such as Butler's *Erewhon* and Bellamy's *Looking Backward,* was a prominent feature of that literary landscape.

This assumption crossed smoothly into the twentieth century and gave every sign that it was going to continue undisturbed. Guy de Maupassant wrote science fiction; so did Joseph Conrad; so did Lord Dunsany (especially in his five Jorkens books). Science fiction novels, mostly by Carl H. Claudy, appeared regularly in *Boys' Life*—which was not an innovation either, but only a continuation of the dime novel tradition established by the Frank Reade series. There was so much of such work by about 1926 that when *Amazing Stories,* the world's first science fiction magazine, appeared in that year, it sailed for a considerable time almost entirely upon reprints, including some from German sources.

And it is still possible in 1970 to say that there are few writers of stature, from Robert Graves all the way down to Herman Wouk, who have not published at least one science fiction story, even if one rules out of the definition of "writers of stature" all those who have made their reputations almost entirely inside the field itself (e.g., Isaac Asimov, Ray Bradbury, Arthur C. Clarke, Robert A. Heinlein).

Yet there has been a significant change in attitude toward such material, which I have exemplified by the ignorance of or embarrassment toward Kipling's science fiction which is endemic among most teachers and scholars who are not specialists in science fiction. An even more specific example of the new attitude may be found in Graham Greene's "The End of the Party." This story is science fiction in an almost chemically pure state—though its subject, telepathy, is still regarded by most scientists as being too unlikely to reward serious study—but Greene goes out of his way, inside the story itself, to reject the label, as though his tale would somehow seem less plausible did he not repudiate the form in which it is cast. The attempt, of course, only calls attention to the fact Greene wanted to sweep under the rug, and in this he is fortunate, for if people interested in pigeon-holes (and there are people with legitimate professional interests in pigeon-holes, such as librarians) cannot call the story science fiction, they will have to call it fantasy, which would be *more* destructive of its credibility.

Greene is not alone. Consider the case of Kurt Vonnegut, Jr. He has been published in science fiction magazines; he has attended one of the ten-day sessions of the annual Milford (Pennsylvania) Science Fiction Writers' Conference; he was for a while a member of Science Fiction Writers of America, the field's sole professional organization; he has testified to his admiration for science fiction, and his attendance at Milford, in one of his novels (*God Bless You, Mr. Rosewater, or, Pearls Before Swine)*; and almost all of his work is science fiction. But both he and his publishers now take the most elaborate public pains to deny and/or ignore these plain facts, as though they were somehow pejorative, like a criminal record.

Another case: When Walter M. Miller, Jr.'s *A Canticle for Leibowitz* achieved hard-cover publication, his publishers denied on the flap copy that it was science fiction, a tack that was obediently followed by most of its reviewers. (That is to say, by reviewers in the American press, most of whom still will not review a science fiction book unless they are so assured that it is somehow some other kind of thing.) Yet it had been first published, serially, in a science fiction magazine; all of Miller's prior and subsequent production has been science fiction, and has appeared in those same magazines; and the novel itself won a "Hugo" award (which it deserved) as the best science fiction novel of its year, an award accepted by Mr. Miller with no show of protest.

Still more recently, both Thomas M. Disch and Brian W. Aldiss, science fiction writers virtually since birth and important innovators in the field, have shown preliminary signs of repudiating their creche at their first success outside it, as though, again, their past work was somehow discreditable. One of America's most recent major publishers of science fiction will not actually label their books science fiction because they fear the label will limit sales; another tries to have the best of both worlds by describing it coyly as "partly science, partly fiction, and just a little beyond tomorrow's headlines."

These examples could be multiplied, but I think the point is clear. Most mainstream reviewers and critics seem happy to follow its lead, which has, indeed, become a sort of critical syndrome. Kingsley Amis has struck it off in an epigram:

"Sf's no good," they bellow till we're deaf.
"But this looks good." — "Well then, it's not sf."

And Theodore Sturgeon has summarized the situation in more usual critical language, though just as tersely:

Never before in literary history has a field been judged so exclusively by its bad examples.

To this, I will add, never before in literary history has so sharp a change in critical attitude taken place without anyone's taking any notice of it, let alone wondering how it came about.

Yet had anyone thought that question worth asking, the answer would have been immediately to hand. One needs only to look at the dates, and to think, briefly and indeed quite superficially, about the recent history of any kind of genre fiction.

The villain of the story, as any political theoretician could have postulated *a priori*, is a social invention; in this case, the invention (by the American publishing firm of Street & Smith) of the specialized fiction magazine, that is, the kind of magazine which publishes only love stories, or only detective stories, or only cowboy stories. This invention, as it turned out, was malign; in literature, it is almost a pure obverse of Mussolini's discovery that the way to raise the birth rate is to fail to supply electricity to housing projects. Every such magazine ghetto—with one highly significant exception—killed off the literary sub-type it attempted to exploit. The first such to die was the love story, which had been rendered superfluous by magazines like *True Confessions* (though these were not to last much longer). The sports story followed; by 1944 there were pulp magazines so specialized as to publish nothing but stories about a single sport—baseball, mostly, but football, hockey and even basketball also had their monomaniacal journals, as I remember only because I wrote for them, out of financial desperation and in an agony of boredom. The sports story is now utterly dead. The Western or cowboy story was the next victim, followed by the formal detective story. There are hardly any such magazines any more, except for a few detective magazines and a lot of science fiction magazines; indeed, there are no longer any other magazines of specialized fiction, for the penultimate member of the line, the "women's magazine," survives today only upon recipes, interior decoration and sex advice, and publishes as little fiction as it can possibly manage.

The significant exception, as noted, is the magazine devoted to science fiction (and marginally, to fantasy), of which there are still quite a number, though they are now threatened by another social invention, the paperback book. These magazines have managed to change with the times, and indeed offer a startling example of adaptation to social invention which brings one back directly to Mussolini's discovery. During their early history, they thrived side by side with magazines devoted to what the literary historian would call the Gothic tale (though it was quite unlike the product now being marketed under that label, such as the works of Daphne du Maurier): magazines with titles like *Weird Tales, Horror Stories* and *Terror Tales*. The once-enormous popularity of ghost stories now seems puzzling until one realizes that they were utterly dependent for their effect upon the uncertainty and shadowiness of all sources of artificial light prior to the general installation of electricity, which did not become universally available in the West, even in the United States, until well after World War I. Once one can dispel a shadow by touching a button, belief in ghosts is doomed, and with it the literature of ghosts. (There is, to be sure, a vigorous modern revival of interest in witchcraft and demonology, but its roots lie in eschatological realms which have almost no bearing upon this argument.) Today, magazine fantasy is chiefly allegorical; the brief Gothic excursion is almost forgotten, although the nerve, as *Rosemary's Baby* showed, can still sometimes be touched by invoking much more powerful and essentially irrelevant fears. (For example, Ira Levin's novel is much closer to the women's-magazine convention than it is to the Gothic; its two central fears are "Suppose my baby should be born deformed?" and "I think the neighbors don't like me." The witchcraft is only a paranoid top-dressing. Fritz Leiber's *Conjure Wife*, a much better book and one much more knowledgeable about the essentials of magic, nevertheless is also paranoid at bottom; it exploits the common fear of the ineffective male that women are members not only of a sex, but of a conspiracy.)

For the survival of its specialized magazines, however, science fiction paid a heavy price. An all-fiction periodical—and all one kind of fiction, at that—demands to be filled periodically; if good material is not available, bad must be published. (Television is now suffering the same kind of attrition.) The pulps, furthermore, never did pay well, and the rates for science fiction were particularly low up to about twenty-five years ago; Horace Gold, a veteran of that era and later one of the field's best editors, once described them as "microscopic fractions of a cent per word, payable upon lawsuit." As a result, the field became dominated by high-production hacks, so that what was to be found beneath the lurid covers was often quite as bad as the covers suggested it was. (In mitigation, it should also be noted that new writers raised in this school did learn one art which is almost extinct in mainstream fiction today: tight plotting.)

How seriously this segregation has hurt the field may be seen in almost any of the critical excursions into it undertaken by mainstream critics, for it invariably turns out that what they are discussing in such excursions is the pulp era, not modern science fiction. One such article which appeared in *The Saturday Review of Literature* (before that title was truncated) about a decade ago was even illustrated with magazine covers from the early 1930's; and an article by the eminent French critic Michel Butor which was published in the Fall, 1967, issue of *Partisan Review* mentioned not a single living author of science fiction but Ray Bradbury (whose work offers a splendid example of what we now mean by "science fantasy").

This, however, may be no more than an example of cultural lag, like the familiar one between painting and music. In his significantly titled *A Century of Science Fiction*, Damon Knight, who is almost the inventor of serious criticism in science fiction, wrote in 1962:

By and large, the hostile critics have fallen silent. When s.f. is mentioned by a respected literary figure today, his comments are likely to be informed and friendly—an unheard-of thing twenty years ago.

At the time, this was really only a hope, for if challenged to cite such friends, the only ones Mr. Knight could have adduced were Kingsley Amis and C. S. Lewis (and the latter was after all virtually an insider, having written three science fiction and eight fantasy novels, and published short stories in one of the U.S. science fiction magazines). But it was an informed hope, for it was based in large part upon another social change which Knight, like all his colleagues, had long known to be absolutely inevitable: the advent of space flight. How great an influence this has had toward making science fiction respectable can be estimated from the fact that of the many millions who watched the first lunar landing on television or heard it on the radio, hardly any could have escaped exposure to two or three interviews with science fiction writers.[4]

But the reason for the trend back toward respectability goes much deeper than this. Let us recall to mind that, in the teeth of modern critical scorn, science fiction has been popular with readers *and writers* over a long period — more than a century — during which the very possibility of space flight, atomic energy and other staple subjects of such stories was discounted by almost everyone.[5]

What explains this popularity, under such handicaps? Knight suggests (in the same preface quoted earlier):

Science fiction is distinguished by its implicit assumption that man can change himself and his environment. This alone sets it apart from all other literary forms. This is the message that came out of the Intellectual Revolution of the seventeenth and eighteenth centuries, and that has survived in no other kind of fiction.

This is a valid and critically useful insight; but were the factor it describes the only one in operation, readers could obtain the message equally well from the accounts of actual space flights and other wonders which they find in newspapers. (And this is in fact now a fairly widespread assumption: All of us in the field

---

[4] This was an international phenomenon. I was in Venice at the time, where I heard myself being quoted over Rome Radio.
[5] When Robert H. Goddard began his rocket experiments in the early 1920's, he was rebuked editorially by the *New York Times* for wasting his university's money. The possibility of space flight was rejected with scorn alike by theoreticians like H. Spencer Jones, the then Astronomer Royal (in a book with the misleadingly science-fictional title *Life on Other Worlds*), and practical engineers like Lee de Forest, inventor of the thermionic valve without which radio and television alike would have been impossible. These examples, too, could be multiplied, *ad nauseam*.

have now been asked, "Now that they've really landed on the Moon, what do you guys have left to write about?" One writer confronted with this question replied with justifiable irritation, "For Christ's sake, lady, there hasn't been a moon landing story published in fifteen years"; but though the question does show the usual ignorance of science fiction, what is more important is that it shows a rather frightening continued ignorance of the boundlessness of the realm opened by the Eagle landing.) Yet sales figures for science fiction last year were at their highest in history.

In addition, therefore, I propose that—in an age which has seen the decline of religion as an important influence on the intellectual and emotional life of Western man—science fiction is the only remaining art form which appeals to the mythopoeic side of the human psyche.

This proposal brings us full circle back to what Kipling meant by a Story. In *Fiction and the Unconscious,* Simon O. Lesser makes the point formally:

Like some universally negotiable currency, the events of a well-told story may be converted effortlessly, immediately and without discount into the coinage of each reader's emotional life.

A related argument is proposed by Susanne K. Langer in *Philosophy in a New Key,* that music calls to our attention a class of conceptual relationships which also includes, and therefore is usefully analogous to, the emotions (a most difficult idea to paraphrase, but luckily not without helpful antecedents, particularly in the work of Kenneth Burke). Later, in *Feeling and Form,* she proposes more generally that art, like science, is a mental activity whereby we bring certain contents of the world into the realm of objectively valid cognition, and that it is the particular office of art to do this with the world's emotional content.

In comment on this latter proposal, George Richmond Walker adds:

> Even scientific theories are accepted or rejected because of what can only be called an aesthetic preference for clarity, simplicity, elegance and generality. It is the function of the arts to make us widely and deeply aware of our affective experience, to help us to know and understand what we feel.

In support of Walker's first point, it is useful to remember that the fundamental aesthetic rule by which scientific ideas are judged, which is usually put as "The simplest theory which accounts for all the facts is the preferable one," was formulated by William of Occam as "One must not multiply entities without reason"; it is a product of the logic of medieval scholasticism and therefore vastly antedates the scientific enterprise *per se*; it is often called "Occam's Razor." The obverse of his second point is that science concentrates on helping us to know and order our sensory and operational experience—the external rather than the affective.

There has always been some overlap between the two. The mathematician Michael Polanyi noted:

> The affirmation of a great scientific theory is in part an expression of delight. The theory has an inarticulate component acclaiming its beauty, and this is essential to the belief that the theory is true.

This is not perhaps, very happily put, but the meaning shines through. More colloquially, C. P. Snow has testified that the act of scientific discovery includes an aesthetic satisfaction which seems exactly the same as the satisfaction one gets from writing a poem or novel, or composing a piece of music. I don't think anyone has succeeded in distinguishing between them.

Most psychiatric theories, the Freudian most markedly, seem to depend for their continued life almost entirely upon their effectiveness as artistic constructs, since none of them makes a good match with sensory and operational experience, and their record of medical effectiveness is no better (and no worse) than that of other forms of faith-healing—and we shall see below that faith is also a question of some importance.

Science fiction at its best serves all three of these avenues to reality, and in this it is unique:

(1) It confronts the theories and data of modern science with the questions of modern philosophy, to create "thought experiments" like that of Einstein's free-falling elevator which may in themselves advance science. The most striking example of this, of course, is space flight itself, for which science fiction both provided the impetus and prepared the public; but scientists themselves have lately turned to using science fiction to propose thought experiments dealing with the social effects of what they do, as may be seen in the story "The Voice of the Dolphins," by the late Leo Szilard. Obversely, most such thought experiments posed by today's philosophers unconsciously fall into science fiction form. Here is an example by George Richmond Walker:

Suppose there were beings on another planet who were organized differently from us, with different sense organs, different brains, and different logic and mathematics. Their views of the universe would necessarily be very different from ours. Would the universe then be what they say it is or what we say it is?

(2) Like all the arts, science fiction adds to our knowledge of reality by formally evoking what Lord Dunsany called "those ghosts whose footsteps across our minds we call emotions."

This is what makes it an art; as Walker says, a true knowledge of understanding of affective experience is the basis of wisdom; it is what distinguishes the civilized man from the savage, the adult from the child, and the sane from the mentally ill. But unlike any other art, science fiction evokes for the non-scientist the basic scientific emotions: The thrill of discovery, the delight in intellectual rigor, and the sense of wonder, even of awe, before the order and complexity of the physical universe.

(3) Science fiction creates myths in which, because the authority of modern science is invoked to back them, modern man can believe (though whether or not they are worthy of belief is the subject of another essay altogether). As the worldwide reaction showed, the emotional experience of watching the first lunar landing was primarily a numinous one, thoroughly secular though the facts of the event might be described to be. Again, too, there is a supporting obverse phenomenon: Whereas the mass psychoses of the past derived their assumptions and trappings from religion (for example, the chiliastic panic of 999 A.D., or the witch-craze of the sixteenth and seventeenth centuries), today their form is science-fictional (the Church of Scientology, the flying saucer mania). It will be observed that this mythopoeic function is one which cannot be fulfilled by even the very best fantasy, for here there can be no question of belief; indeed, of all the arts, fantasy requires the greatest suspension of disbelief, a sophisticated intellectual exercise which is outright inimical to the will to believe.

If this hypothesis is valid—as necessarily I believe that it is—then we are unlikely to see any decline in the popularity of science fiction in the foreseeable future. It further follows that the appearance of any such decline would have implications reaching far beyond the apparently tiny corner of recent literature occupied by science fiction. As Robert Conquest put the heart of the matter in *For the 1956 Opposition of Mars:*

Pure joy of knowledge rides as high as art.
The whole heart cannot keep live on either.
Wills as of Drake and Shakespeare strike together;
Cultures turn rotten when they part.

[I am indebted to Brian W. Aldiss, Harry Harrison and Robert A. W. Lowndes for suggestions and citations.]

2. THE SCIENCE IN SCIENCE FICTION

It was suggested to me that I talk about the science content of science fiction, and I suspect that there are at least a few people in this room who think that such a title could properly only be followed by an hour of dead silence. And I'm prepared to agree that most of what we call science fiction—even "hard" science fiction—is technology fiction at best. The scientific content, as a scientist would understand the term, is quite invisible.

However, we do play around quite a bit with what we think of as scientific facts—or what we *hope* are scientific facts—and this gives us our cachet for using the label which Mr. Gernsback hung on us in 1929. Now a lot of the science content (such as it is) in present-day science fiction is deplorable, as we all know; but I would like to look back for a moment to the pre-glacial era when I began to read this stuff. I'll give you a few examples of the things I learned about science from science fiction.

For one thing, there was a convention among the authors of those days that since the solar system lies approximately in a flat plane (the plane of the ecliptic), the only way you could get from one planet to another was by traveling along that plane. This meant that if you were attempting to go any distance beyond the orbit of Mars, you were involved in an awful lot of banging and clashing about among the asteroids. My favorite example of this comes from a somewhat later period—a story by Sam Moskowitz in which the hero, in order to reach Saturn, finds himself necessarily banging and clashing his way through the planet's rings. Now, if there is a more avoidable astronomical object in the solar system than the rings of Saturn, I do not know what it is! But there was this flat plane convention; and we were stuck with it. It took me a long time to learn from science fiction that space happens to be three-dimensional, and that in order to avoid the asteroid belt all you need is a slight expenditure of fuel and you can go over it!

Another thing I had to unlearn was that at least the major asteroids were inhabitable. There was a marvelous moment in a story by Harl Vincent called "The Copper Clad World," which appeared in *Astounding Stories* in September 1931, in which the hero's ship passes close enough to Vesta—or another one of those large rocks—so that he can see its steaming volcanic jungles and a gigantic waterfall! I don't know whether he actually saw any aborigines or not...

We also learned from primitive science fiction that atoms were solar systems and electrons were planets. As it happens, one of John Wyndham's first stories (then sailing under his original name of John Beynon Harris) was a novel of this kind. The hero found himself dwindled down on to an electron and found it very much like a sort of Cretaceous Earth. This novel won the praise of H. G. Wells—I couldn't understand why then, and I still can't today. But my first encounter with the idea was a short story in *Astounding* of January 1932 by one Francis Flagg, called "The Seed of the Tock Tock Birds."

Another convention of that time which is, as a matter of fact, still with us goes under the name of "the crushing gravity of Jupiter." I encountered this first in a story by Paul Ernst—"The Red Hell of Jupiter"—in *Astounding,* October 1931. Now, it is probably no news to most of you that the "crushing gravity" of Jupiter is approximately 4G. And if you were to stop and think this out for a moment—think of your actual weight and then say, "Suppose I weighed four times what I weigh now: would I be crushed to the ground, never to rise again?" — well, of course you wouldn't. It's still around, however: Howard Fast is peddling this one in his latest book.

Nowadays the situation *is* somewhat better. We have with us a number of writers who either had scientific training or have made it their business to try to pick up some accurate information. When you read a story by Poul Anderson, Raymond F. Jones, Hal Clement, Arthur C. Clarke, or Larry Niven, you can be reasonably sure that when they say such-and-such is a scientific fact to the best of our knowledge, they are not leading you up the garden path; it's not something you're going to have to unlearn later, with great pain.

We have also two other groups in modern science fiction whom I shall have to mention, simply because I'm forced to, although they don't really form part of the subject of my talk. One is the group of people who are largely scientifically illiterate, but write very well indeed. They like to say that what they do is speculative fiction rather than science fiction. Well, their originator — grandfather, perhaps — was Bradbury; today we have J. G. Ballard, Harlan Ellison, and the whole *New Worlds* school. The stuff is often very well worth reading, but not for its scientific content.

Secondly, we still have the fossilised remains of the old school of science fiction writers who knowingly peddled scientific garbage, didn't care that it was garbage, and whose work furthermore has no redeeming literary qualities — or any other qualities that I can see. Here I shall only mention two Englishmen, in deference to the fact that I'm a guest here: Charles Eric Maine, who hasn't been with us recently; and John Lymington, who unfortunately has.

But even among the group of writers whom I consider scientifically responsible, even if not scientifically formally educated, we have a group of acceptances in modern science fiction which are impossible by current scientific standards. I'll give you a very short list; I'm sure you could multiply these examples endlessly: telepathy; faster-than-light travel; time-travel; anti-gravity; force-fields or force-screens. You will find writers like Poul Anderson, Isaac Asimov, Larry Niven, Ray Jones—all of these people I have named as responsible writers—taking these things for granted and using them. And the readers sit still for it. This seems odd; but it also seems to me that it is philosophically rather easy to defend—and here I'm going to drop into a few generalities.

Thomas S. Kuhn wrote a famous and highly recommendable book called *The Structure of Scientific Revolutions.* He points out that, whatever we might like to think, and whatever the mythology of the history of science tells us, new ideas are *not* accepted as soon as they come along, as soon as the evidence makes it clear that new ideas are needed. Actually, science progresses in a series of convulsive hiccups, during each one of which the attempt to suppress the coming convulsion is the strongest feature of the landscape. There is always a body of conservatism which is defended to the death before the actual overthrow takes place. He calls this—the characteristic feature of this body of conservatism—*paradigms,* and he defines them as follows: "universally recognised scientific achievements that, for a time, provide model problems and solutions to a community of practitioners."

Now these paradigms can be various. They can go all the way from the turtle that supports the elephant that supports the sky in Indian mythology down to what we have to sit still for in classrooms today. The one thing they do have in common is that the scientists of their time hate to see them overturned. I quote again from Kuhn: "Copernicanism made few converts for almost a century after Copernicus' death. Newton's work was not generally accepted, particularly on the continent, for more than half a century after the *Principia* appeared. Priestley *never* accepted the oxygen theory, Lord Kelvin the electromagnetic theory" and so on. To this I will add a few examples of my own.

The motions of the moons of Jupiter, which was an early Renaissance discovery, was doubted as late as the middle of the seventeenth century in very august quarters. The last recorded denial of the motion of the Earth itself can be dated 1823. This occurred in an edition of Newton's *Principia* which was edited by two learned Jesuit astronomers who said, in a footnote, "Of course, to make sense of all this, one must accept Mr. Newton's assumption that the Earth moves in space, although our faith teaches us this is not so." Well now, in a sense they may have been right: what moves in space is, of course, a relative proposition. But I do think it would be awfully inconvenient if we had to go back to the Ptolemaic epicycles at this late date!

It took twenty years to establish special relativity. This is now apparently nailed down to the ground very firmly on all four sides, and I shudder to think of what would happen to the whole body of present-day assumptions in theoretical physics if we had to do without special relativity now. But there were people who doubted it very, very much, and for a very funny account of the "back to Newton" movement I recommend a book to you by the very gifted Martin Gardner called *Fads and Fallacies in the Name of Science.* He devotes a whole chapter to the movement, and it is very funny, and at the same time very sad reading. We still have, in general relativity, a theory that is widely doubted (by me among others). Part of the reason for this is that evidence for it is so slight and so hard to come by. But it is gradually gaining acceptance, and it is something that we might describe as a *coming* paradigm.

I return to Kuhn for a moment. Before I do, the question naturally arises, what is actually the reason for this convulsive movement? Why does science *have* to proceed in a series of revolutions rather than smoothly, as the mythology says it should? Well, Kuhn says, scientists do not treat anomalies as counter-instances, though, in the vocabulary of the philosophy of science, that is what they are. Once it has attained the status of a paradigm, a scientific theory is declared invalid only if an alternate candidate is available to take its place. Initially, only the anticipated and usual are experienced, even under circumstances where anomaly is later to be observed.

I'd now like to point out the apparent size that an anomaly has to be before we can overturn a paradigm.

We have before us now a phenomenon called the quasar—a name which expresses absolutely nothing except that we do not know what it is. It has been violating the laws of special relativity hand-over-fist, backwards, forwards, and sideways. We do not know whether they are distant objects or far objects; whether they are exploding galaxies or some condition of matter about which we know nothing as yet. The whole thing is up for grabs. One thing is for sure: that as relativistic objects they put us into a great deal of trouble.

Now, thirty years ago or more, the great British astronomer E. A. Milne (not to be confused with the author of the Pooh books) exposed something which he called dynamical relativity. I am neither physicist nor mathematician enough to go into this at any distance whatsoever, but I do know something about its reputation. It was quite elegant mathematically, and the general reaction of astronomers and theoretical physicists to it at the time was: well, yes, it is quite convincing, and there seems no way to attack it; but it is so far-reaching that nobody can think of any way to test it either. As a matter of fact, Milnean dynamical relativity makes Einsteinian general relativity look like a blackboard exercise. Nevertheless, it seems to me, intuitively, that these things are behaving in a very Milnean way indeed; and we may eventually find ourselves referring to somebody whom we would then be calling "poor old Einstein"! Or quasars may eventually be explainable in Einsteinian terms; my instinct is to say they can't be. But here is a huge anomaly that cannot be ignored, and it's got us into serious trouble, and we may need a new paradigm for it.

Now let's get back with a sigh of relief to science fiction, and to my list of scientific impossibilities which sf writers and readers nevertheless accept. I think that in this light we can understand them a little better.

Telepathy, for instance, is in trouble with the scientific community for one main reason: it is in complete conflict with that paradigm we call the electromagnetic theory. We do know, of course, that across the skulls of every one of us race minute electrical currents; and the movement of electrical currents produce radio waves. However, these have been measured by Rolf Ashby, Adrian Walter and Grey Walter, and one can now say that if the nearest person to me has a radio receiver in his skull, his chances of picking up the radio broadcasts from my skull are about as good as his chance of making an audio recording of a smoke-signal. So that kind of transmission is out. Telepathy is therefore impossible.

When we look, however, at the evidence which has been gathered, and we make the temporary assumption—as we must—that some of this evidence has been honestly gathered, and honestly reported, and *may* represent real instances, we find also that it is characteristic of telepathy that its strength of reception does not vary over distance—even over long distances. Now we are in trouble with something much greater than the electromagnetic theory: we're in trouble with the inverse square law itself. To me this means one of two things. It means either that telepathy *is* impossible, by *two different* paradigms, or else it tells us that the electromagnetic theory is the wrong paradigm to apply here. Now I have no idea what the right one might be; and one of the problems of telepathy is that nobody who has ever worked seriously in the field, and is respected as honest and responsible, has himself ever managed to come up with a decent model for how it works. There is no altering this paradigm to the ones we know *don't* work in order to account for this evidence.

This field also offers a lovely example of the kind of resistance Kuhn was talking about in his book. One scientist approached on this subject said, "In any other field, I would grant the reality of a phenomenon on one tenth this much evidence; in this one I would not be convinced if there were ten times as much." My favorite example of the open mind!

Now, I could go back to my little list here of our other impossibilities—and I will, just briefly. Faster-than-light travel is forbidden to us by special relativity; anti-gravity is forbidden to us by general relativity. I uttered the heresy that, so far as special relativity is concerned, if it was wrong it would not be the first time that Einstein was wrong. You'll recall that he crowned his career by publishing a unified field theory, which he discovered he could not defend, and had to withdraw. So far as anti-gravity is concerned: this depends upon a whole series of highly metaphysical assumptions in general relativity, and general relativity still does not have the status of papal dogma in science yet. There may be a way around this one too.

Time travel? Well, all right, let's play both sides of the street on this one. Supposing general relativity is in fact right, and we all live on the surface of a hypersphere. If you make the slight additional assumption that the hypersphere is rotating in four dimensions, round its unimaginable center from which it is expanding, time travel into the past becomes instantly possible— all you have to do is drag your feet a little. How much energy it would take to drag your feet I am unable to tell you, but this has been seriously proposed. It could be done. Again, nobody knows in the first place whether the universe is a hypersphere or not, *let alone* whether it's rotating, so we are in no position to say with great positiveness that time travel is permanently impossible.

Force fields or screens? Well, again, they climb in the face of the electromagnetic theory. You can't make the expanding wavefronts of a wavefront stop expanding. No. Well, telepathy tells us that perhaps there is something wrong with the electromagnetic theory—or at least that it may be the wrong paradigm to apply to that particular problem. So again, let's not hear so many doors slammed around here, please.

Now here's where I'm about to get myself into trouble. I mentioned three classes of science fiction writers. I'm now about to take my first class, and sub-divide that into three more. I'm talking, remember, about science fiction writers that I consider to be responsible to what they consider to be scientific fact.

Most of such people, however, only extend the consequences of our present-day paradigms into the future. There are some who present futures in which new paradigms obviously prevail. Most of them do this unconsciously, but whenever a writer tosses out a reference to working telepathy, or working faster-than-light drive, he is talking about such a future—and of one thing we may be *very* sure: the future *will* offer us new paradigms. We may kick and scream and have to be dragged into them, but they will be there.

There are also a very few modern science fiction writers who do this consciously. I'll give you two examples only. My favorite one is Lester del Rey, who quite often writes about faster-than-light drives, and who has made a game out of the fact that every time he introduces a faster-than-light drive in a story he has a new and different explanation for it!

Raymond F. Jones—who hasn't been around lately, I'm sorry to say—did this in a story called "Noise Level," in which he proposed what was essentially a new method of scientific investigation. You lock up a group of scientists in a room, with a whole mass of dubious and not-so-dubious evidence that something impossible can in fact be done, and you don't let them out until they do it! To do this, you must expose them to as much garbage as possible. You don't give them all the standard accepted references on what gravity is, and why anti-gravity can never work, and so on. Instead you pile in all the occult books you can find on levitation. You introduce, if possible, a fake film showing a man actually going up with an anti-gravity pack on his back, and tell them it's real. You do everything possible to increase the noise level with which a scientist is surrounded, tell him that it has, in fact, been accomplished, and that for the protection of his country or whatever he's got to duplicate it. And see what they come out with.

This is a lovely notion. It is obviously a new paradigm of sorts. Jones recognised it as such; in fact, he thought of it as a law of nature, and his later stories in the series degenerated into an argument as to whether or not it could be patentable under U.S. law, which is a distinct side-issue. But that's a fault in the writer, not in the idea. The idea is obviously a paradigm which *might* be of considerable force. Who knows?

So my final expression is this: in my opinion—in my profoundly *religious* opinion, I might add—it is the duty of the conscientious science fiction writer not to falsify what he believes to be known fact. It is an even more important function for him to suggest new paradigms, by suggesting to the reader, over and over again, that X, Y, and Z are possible. Every time a story appears with a faster-than-light drive, it expresses *somebody's* faith—maybe not the writer's; but certainly many of the readers'—that such a thing may be accomplishable, and some day will be accomplished. Well, we have a lot of hardware—including, I'm sorry to say, a couple of old beer cans—on the moon right now, to show us what can be done with repeated suggestion. I think it can be done philosophically on a far broader scale than we have ever managed to do before.

So I come down now, having prepared my retreats as best as possible, to my conclusion, which surprised me as much as it may surprise you. It seems to me that the most important scientific content in modern science fiction are the impossibilities.

3. THE ARTS IN SCIENCE FICTION

The subject of the arts in science fiction might seem at first to be a nonsubject—science fiction began, after all, as a pulp magazine medium where the only arts the writers were interested in were those involved in constructing one cliff-hanger after another, and if possible keeping the story moving by dialogue rather than anything else, because they had no faith in the reader's ability to follow more than three sentences of description. But this, of course, is not a question of art at all; it is simply a question of minor technique. Actually the subject has several sub-divisions: one of them being the role of the arts in sf proper; then the effects of the arts on sf; and finally—though this may really be a nonsubject in truth—the influence of sf on the arts.

The fact of the matter is that, until very recently, few of the arts were mentioned in sf, and certainly not in commercial sf. It's quite commonplace in realistic fiction to find references to painting, to other people's writing, to music, and so on. In sf there is a tremendous dearth of this, with one exception (and probably not to Kingsley Amis' surprise)—there has been quite a lot of writing about jazz in sf. And it's still going on: the May 1972 *F&SF,* which is devoted to sf in the universities, contains a rather extended comparison between jazz and sf by Philip Klass (who writes sf under the name of William Tenn). Kingsley Amis made a similar comparison in *New Maps of Hell;* and in a number of different stories Theodore Sturgeon has described, or attempted to describe, the effects of jazz.

But when you try to survey the field as a whole since, say, 1926 (when magazine sf began) you really find very little reference to the arts at all, and when you *do* something very curious crops up—you find that the artistic tastes of the future are decidedly worse than our own. One of my favorite examples of this is Sturgeon's *Venus Plus X:* a thoroughly experimental novel, done in a series of slices, or alternate takes. The alternative slices are pictures of contemporary suburban family life in the United States, each of them designed to show the blurring of the traditional roles of the sexes in modern America. We have now seen that taking on a rather more revolutionary color, but at the time this novel was written (1960) it was more or less subterranean, and Sturgeon was very interested in it. In between these slices are pictures of what appears to be a utopia, far in the future. The secret of this utopia is that all of its inhabitants are hermaphrodites: the blurring of the sexes has gone all the way down to the physical level, with everybody both male and female at the same time, playing both roles. In describing his utopia Sturgeon also took some pains to describe what its artistic life was like, and it consisted of gauzily-clad children doing folk dances, statues in the quasi-heroic, or late-Mussolini, style, and buildings apparently designed on the same order (except that these were only public buildings; everybody else appeared to live in huts of some kind, out in the forest, cracking nuts and making pottery—I couldn't quite figure out if they had reinvented the potter's wheel or not). The whole thing has a rather dated quality, as the kinds of art Sturgeon was pushing in this ostensibly future utopia were the kinds of thing that the Southern Agrarians had been pushing back about 1925—surely quite unsuitable unless Sturgeon was trying to tell us that things had backslid a great deal by the time his utopia came up; and I don't think that's what he meant. The gimmick of the novel is that the utopia is also in the present; it's just geographically isolated from the rest of the world, and these hermaphrodites have been created by surgery. So perhaps it isn't at all surprising that their artistic taste doesn't appear as advanced as that of Utopia ought to be. Now bear in mind that I'm not prepared to say what the artistic taste of a utopia ought to be like, but I do not think it would be either Southern Agrarian or Socialist Realism, and this peculiar combination is what Sturgeon gave us in this novel.

This is not an unusual sort of blind spot in sf. You find it in Heinlein; for example, *Stranger in a Strange Land.* Among the many other theories that are included—or advanced as fact—in *Stranger in a Strange Land* is a considerable swatch of the aesthetic theory. And Heinlein, in the course of telling us what he prefers through the omniscient Jubal Harshaw, makes it very plain that for Heinlein the absolute epitome of any art-form is the narrative, or storytelling, art. This means that he has no use for the abstract, not only in fiction and poetry, but also in music and painting. He likes paintings which tell a story. As a matter of fact, Rodin's "Fallen Caryatid" is his type-case of the perfect work of art. The poor girl has been trying to hold up the corner of a Greek building for two thousand years, and finally it has been too much for her, and she has fallen down. But she is bearing up bravely and trying to push that corner of the building up again. This, to Heinlein, is a perfect piece of storytelling, and just exactly what he likes to see in graphic arts. Similarly, when he treats a piece of music one will find that all the music Heinlein discusses, in this and other books, is program music. He doesn't know very much about that either. Nevertheless, he has a general bias for narrative; no other kind of art appears to exist for him.

Heinlein goes on, in discussing the graphic arts, to repeat the old canard that abstract artists paint the way they do because they never learned to draw. A little knowledge of the early histories of some abstract painters, including some of the most famous—Picasso in particular—would have shown him that they began by being very good draughtsmen, and only those who we speak of as Primitives became abstract artists without having a good deal of preliminary training or skill in this field. This has often made me wonder if Heinlein would carry this analogy over into music and say that composers of string quartets or piano sonatas or things of that kind became such because they couldn't "*plot*" a piece of music? Or perhaps, even worse, couldn't carry a tune? In any case, the bias is there, and it is very strong.

But, this is not limited to Heinlein. For example, a routine story called "The Face of the Enemy" by Thomas Wilson, which appeared in *Astounding S.F.* (August 1952), takes place on an alien planet, and in the course of it the hero discovers an extended musical composition written by the aborigines. The account in the story makes it very clear that this too is program music; as a matter of fact it appears to be a historical composition describing how one tribe triumphed over another and how beautiful towers arose thereafter. All this comes very clearly to the hero's mind, despite the fact that even the most sophisticated Terrestrial music lover, encountering a piece of Terrestrial program music for the first time, will be very lucky if he can tell you whether it describes a battle or a love affair. I have seen this experiment performed with a Richard Strauss composition, and to a fresh audience which had never encountered it before and knew nothing of its reputation, a good half of the listeners didn't even detect that it was intended as comic, let alone what the incidents were that were supposed to be going on in it. So how our hero, listening to a piece of musical composition whose artistic conventions are utterly and completely alien to him, can worry a piece of elaborate tribal history out of this thing is a mystery to me. I'm sure it was a mystery to Wilson too. This is the kind of attention, or non-attention, to the arts that has been the norm in sf until very recently.

There have been some honorable exceptions. Among others I would mention Jack Vance, who is apparently an instinctive anthropologist with a good aesthetic sense. He never fails to describe an alien culture and make you *feel* that it is alien, and to invent two or three art forms—not just try to transform Earthly ones—and to do so with great color, élan and flair. It is a pleasure to read even a bad Vance story—of which there are not very many—simply because of the intricacy and flamboyance and consistency of the way in which he invents art-forms. I'll mention one example: a story called "The Moon Moth," in which the art is mask making, and the masks were worn as a matter of social convention. What mask you wore presented you to your society as the kind of person you wanted to be taken as. If you wore the wrong kind of mask, or if you behaved in a way which was inconsistent with the mask you were wearing, you might find yourself involved in a duel, or dumped in a river, or asked to do something for which you had no training whatsoever. The masks themselves are elaborately described, and although I am no anthropologist—and no artist either, I should add—I have never seen any description of Earthly masks, in any culture, that bore the faintest resemblance to the masks that Jack Vance devised and described in this story; they were simply a marvelous invention.

The only sf story that John Ciardi ever wrote to my knowledge, had to do with an art vaguely related to jade feeling, which is a Chinese art totally devoted to the sense of touch. Jade pieces are carved, dipped in water to make them slick, and the aesthetic pleasure comes from feeling the delicacy of the contours. In the Ciardi story this had become a high art on another planet, and involved not only jade but all other kinds of objects: where we have pictures, music and so on they had these things. The one in the story turned out not to be a work of art at all, but a snare, a hypnotic device for trapping one's prey. But this came as a surprise in the story, and its beauty for me lay not in the fact of the snapper but in the fact that Ciardi here built up a whole art form, only slightly connected to Chinese jade feeling, and really made the reader feel that it had an immense history behind it and was the product of a whole culture.

The invention of new art forms for the future on our own planet have been equally few and far between. The most familiar example is probably George Orwell's invention of novel-writing machines in *1984*. Plainly, Orwell didn't know how they would work, nor did he care. The heroine of the story first appeared with her arm in a sling because she had been tending one of these machines and a lever had come loose and swung around and broke her arm. One doesn't have to be a computer technologist to know better than to expect a novel-writing machine to have a swinging axle, or anything of that kind. Really, Orwell didn't care. But there is a good possibility that novels could be written by machines. There has already been a certain amount of computer-generated poetry, some of which makes a certain minimal amount of sense. It is surprising that Orwell did not instead have music-writing machines, because at the time he was composing *1984* music *was* being written on machines. During World War II there suddenly appeared on the American market a slide-rule-like device with four wheels on it. It was made of pasteboard and operated by hand, and enabled anybody who could read one stave of music—just a simple melody, in other words—to compose an indefinite number of popular songs. According to *Time* magazine a great number of these things were sold, and one grateful customer wrote in to *Time* and said, on the recommendation of your story I bought one of these machines and, by God, I've sold the first song I wrote on it! It is much more likely, in other words, that music could be composed by machine than a novel or a poem. But I suppose that will eventually be done; I've been reading novels lately which look as if they've been written on such machines.

So, there are a few notable exceptions; but in general the arts of the future, as they are depicted in sf, very much resemble the terrestrial arts of the late 19th and early 20th centuries. They are

The Tale that Wags the God

what I might very generally term late Romantic narrative—the Holman Hunt/Richard Strauss type of thing. Occasionally you may hear of, for instance, performed symphonies, but although something like that is sometimes mentioned casually, little attention is generally paid to it. I once became interested enough in this to edit a collection of stories about the future of the arts, *New Dreams This Morning*. It made a rather slim haul; as a matter of fact I was forced to include two of my own stories because it was so hard to find anything in science fiction that dealt with the arts in a responsible way and showed any real knowledge of them.

The arts involved are themselves interesting. There was an Asimov story ("Dreaming Is A Private Thing") about the art of dream-composition, which is quite a feasible sort of art. We have had stories about recorded dreams which go back to Fletcher Pratt's "City of the Living Dead" in 1930—in which everybody got trapped in the Hall of the Dreamers, and the lazy attendants even stopped changing the records, so that they were all dreaming the same dreams over and over again.

The Asimov story, however, is not simply about the *recording* of dreams, but about the *composition* of dreams. This has become a creative art form in itself. It turns out to be not only about this particular technological innovation, but to contain quite a good credo for the arts as a whole, and for the essential loneliness and privacy of the creative act. Asimov just used this invention as a vehicle to make his point.

There was a story of my own about music, "A Work of Art." I included the hit machine and a great many other gadgets that I actually borrowed from my own time, just like Jules Verne. The story did not contain any innovations or inventions of my own in the art of music: they were all things I knew about that were going on at the time the story was written. In fact, the only innovation the story actually contains in this department is a workable musical typewriter. People have been struggling to evolve one of these things for years now, and as far as I know one still doesn't exist; but that is a pretty minor innovation. One element of the story that seemed most radical was the composition of musical soundtracks by drawing on the soundtrack beside the film. No instruments are involved; no musical notes are actually written down; but the man who does this has become a sufficiently superb sound technician that he can make sound waves on the film, and make the end result come out sounding just as he wants it to sound. I don't know that this has become perfected either; but at the time I was writing the story somebody was experimenting with this and producing a certain amount of (no doubt primitive) noise. Again, what I was discussing was not innovation in the art form itself, but the whole of the creative process. The art form which, as it turns out, is more central to the story, is one of which I am rather proud. This is the creation, for aesthetic purposes, of artificial personalities. You take a perfectly ordinary man, who may or may not be a volunteer for the experiment, and a group of psychologists and electroencephalographists resculpture him into a new human being. He has a complete set of memories—all of them false; but nevertheless he believes them to be true—and the climax of this art form is the exhibition of this artificially sculptured person to an audience, putting him through his paces. In the story it is a dead composer who is brought back to life, as it were.

There was also a story by Harry Harrison ("Portrait of an Artist") which I took great pleasure in including, partly out of iconoclasm. The art form involved is the comic strip; it is simply the story of an elderly comic strip artist who is eventually eliminated by a machine. He is working in partnership with a machine to begin with, and a new machine appears which eliminates him entirely. The story, however, despite the apparent triviality of its subject, is not comic. The man feels his replacement *very* deeply; and the fact that the art involved is minor, and of no consequence, is one of the things which makes the story as poignant as it is.

Damon Knight, in "The Country of the Kind," makes the very radical proposal that if you eliminate violence in the human heart—the very *impulse* to violence: not as in *A Clockwork Orange*, where you simply condition the man to be repelled by it—then the creative spirit will go with it. This is a highly debatable proposition, but one Knight puts forward with great persuasiveness. The only artist left in the world in this story is an artist who has committed a murder and has been made intolerable to his fellows by having a bad smell. He is entitled to approach anyone, do any violence he likes; they will not fight back. But his agony is not that people will not associate with him; it is that he is the only remaining creative man in the world. He keeps putting little statues in niches for people to find and leaving messages saying: if you can understand this, pick up a stone and strike, pick up a knife and stab. It's easy: try it. And nobody will listen to him, nobody will pay the slightest attention because, Knight proposes, violence and the artistic impulse are two sides of the same coin. It's a horrifying thought.

Then there was "With These Hands," a too-little-known story by the late C. M. Kornbluth. This is also a story of the replacement of the artist by the machine. In this case the artist is a sculptor, and the import of the story is almost the same as the Harrison piece, although the art form is of more importance. It is also an extremely poignant story, with the man preferring death among works of art formed by real human hands to a very lucrative position he has been offered operating a sculpture machine. "The Music Master of Babylon" by Edgar Pangborn is one of the very few knowledgeable sf stories about music I have ever encountered. The hero is a composer and Pangborn makes you *believe* in the man's ability as a composer, and even in his compositions. These are described at some length, and sound like real pieces of music. I have only once seen that done before, in Thomas Mann's *Doctor Faustus,* which is about the life of a composer. Mann has the daring to describe many of his major compositions, and with several of them I still retain the impression that I have heard them somewhere. This is not easy to do, but Pangborn brings it off.

The final one, "A Man of Talent" by Robert Silverberg, deals with a possible variant on the artists' colony, where a number of colonists go off to organise their own planet. They discover in the end that since they are all artists their lives have become meaningless, because there is no audience.

The reader will have noticed that the one thing all these stories have in common is the *disappearance* of art in one way or another. Replacement by the machine is a very common theme; replacement by barbarism — which is what happens in the Pangborn story: the Music Master of Babylon is the last musician in a barbaric world — is another; or the death of the artistic impulse by one means or another, such as Damon Knight's story of educating violence out of the human race. And these are all good stories in that they are all knowledgeable about the arts they are discussing. They are also uniformly pessimistic. And I began to wonder why this was so. I think there are two reasons: they are very disparate and probably have no connection with each other whatsoever.

One of them is Marxist. It is — or was — a commonplace of idealistic Marxism that art was essentially an aberration of the socially maladjusted individual who was seeking in art the ideals and the satisfactions which he could not find in the society that was grinding him down; and that when Utopia did arrive, the impulses which art satisfies for us now would be satisfied in reality by perfect social conditions, and that art would therefore no longer serve a psychological purpose. Of all the contributors to *New Dreams This Morning* I know of only one who had any real contact with idealistic Marxism, that being Kornbluth, who soon repudiated it. Nevertheless, this threat of the disappearance of art with the coming of Utopia—or at best the mechanization of art—is very, very common in sf even today—so common that it is hard to find any other kind of story about the future of the arts.

As I said, there is a second reason. Every period, with a few exceptions, believes it is on the edge of artistic anarchy. The one major exception I can think of was during the heart of the eighteenth century—the old age of Haydn and the whole life of Mozart. Musical norms then were so settled that nobody really felt there was any sort of revolution going on. Everybody understood the music that was being produced; nobody was upset by it. I call your attention to the fact that these very conservative composers, who we now know as belonging to the Classical Age, were revolutionaries in their time. They really upset the Baroque composers who preceded them—such as Bach and Telemann, who were the last of their line in the Baroque school. The Romantics were certainly archrevolutionaries to the Classic composers—Beethoven's music was regarded as a vast mass of cacophony to his contemporaries.

I am no expert on painting, but speaking from my position of vast ignorance it seems to me that painting and the graphic arts have reached a point where anybody who thinks he sees any meaning in them is a faker—and I deliberately take this philistine position to emphasize my point. This is a very common feeling in all the arts. Music—about which I do pretend to know something—has gotten so far away from the concert hall audience that composers who consider themselves modern have to organise themselves into societies and play to each other. They are not drawing the audience any more: the last truly modern composers to do so were the twelve-tone composers—Berg, Schoenberg and so on. These people won their way only after a tremendously hard struggle. They still do not have a very wide audience, but they are gradually winning acceptance, while the people who flock to hear John Cage or Stockhausen, or people who compose *musique concrete,* can hardly be described as hordes. With modern poetry the common complaint has been that it has been out of touch with its audience for decades, compared to the period when poets like Tennyson and Browning could count on being best-sellers. Nowadays, for every Eliot who has what might be described as a mass audience, you have fifty people who appear to be writing only to themselves or the next guy. Poetry has reached the stage now of isolated letters on the page. I think this is called concrete poetry; I am not sure. In any event I make no attempt to follow it.

It seems to me that this very conservative attitude—which has nothing to do with Marxism whatsoever—also prevails among sf writers. They look around at the arts they see now, and to them it appears to be complete anarchy. Their appreciation only extends as far forward in time as the things they grew up with. In music, for example, this would mean Wagner, Richard Strauss, maybe Prokofiev and early Stravinsky if they were lucky. That far they are willing to go. And their predictions are either for complete disintegration or for a return to some previous norm. They never seem to consider that for most generations the normative, artistically, is always in the *past,* never in the present. Except for a very few perceptive people, what is going on *now* in the arts always looks like chaos—and this is a very general attitude in sf.

I think this leads logically to the question of what the effects have been of the arts on sf. The answer is, very little, until quite recently, and the only arts that appear to have had much effect even upon recent sf are the literary arts. Some attempts have been made to use pictorial effects—typographical tricks and so on—to create pictures on the page in the manner of George Herbert, or some of the seventeenth century metaphysical poets. But the effect of advances in painting and music on what goes on in sf has been very little.

What has been happening in the literary sense has been quite interesting. I suppose we must call this the New Wave, for want of any better term. What is happening now, and has been happening for the past ten to fifteen years, is that sf has caught up with the movement that used to be known as the Modernists: John Dos Passos, Virginia Woolf, James Joyce, and a few lesser figures of that period are suddenly popping up all over the place, in the sf novel in particular, and to a lesser extent in the sf short story. I find this particularly interesting because the Modernist movement, after all, was principally a phenomenon of the late '20s and '30s, the time when sf was going through its blaster and BEM phase and did not know the rest of literature existed at all. Also I find it interesting that the New Wave began, and is still primarily sustained, in England, and has been going on while the realistic novel in England has entered upon a decidedly anti-Modernist phase, best illustrated by John Wain and Kingsley Amis and people of that stripe who are going back to very direct narrative forms and completely eschewing all the experimentalism which used to be such red-hot stuff. Now, just at this juncture, people like John Brunner, Philip José Farmer and others—epitomised by the new, new *New Worlds* magazine—have suddenly discovered that it is possible to arrange words on the page in something other than the traditional order, and are adopting with great enthusiasm these techniques of the '30s—to what effect we do not yet know.

In some cases it has been highly effective and very well used, although not entirely within the sf fraternity as we know it. Joyce, for instance, has had a tremendous effect on one British sf novelist who has been one of the very few men not only to *use* Joyce—which I would have thought impossible out of hand— but actually to assimilate him, and make Joyce his own. I refer to Anthony Burgess, who is from time to time an sf novelist, and a very good one. The influence upon him of Joyce, particularly late Joyce, which is hardest to assimilate, is very evident indeed, particularly in *A Clockwork Orange* but also in some of his non-sf novels.

Then we have Brian Aldiss's *Barefoot in the Head*—a very effective novel in itself, and in its technique a sort of child's guide to *Finnegans Wake*. Once you have read *Barefoot in the Head* you will be able to tackle *Finnegan* with absolute impunity, and very probably even get through it, which would be very good for you. *Finnegans Wake* is, I think, a masterpiece, although not such a masterpiece as *Ulysses*. Aldiss assimilated this technique and used it in *Barefoot* to his own purposes, and it worked out very well.

Moorcock is one man who has adopted some of Dos Passos's techniques, particularly in the Jerry Cornelius stories; and several other people have written those as well, including Brian Aldiss, James Sallis, and several of the *New Worlds* crowd. I have mentioned Burgess and Aldiss in connection with Joyce; there is also Farmer, who has shown a strong affinity for *Ulysses*. Aldiss also wrote an anti-novel which started out to be a perfectly straight anti-novel, but turned into another sandwich novel: alternate episodes of anti-novel and straightforward sf story. This was *Report on Probability A*.

I think it was an interesting experiment, although in some respects a failed one. The most interesting part about it is that it shows the most recent literary influence I have yet detected in sf. There are all those other people employing Dos Passos, Joyce, Faulkner and so on; but the French anti-novel is, after all, quite a recent development and here it is showing up. Just to show that he is not immune to the same prejudices as the rest of us, however, Aldiss is also very much hooked on narrative art, and in that novel the late Victorian painters, particularly Holman Hunt, have had quite an obvious influence. A Holman Hunt painting, "The Hireling Shepard," plays a part in the book. The painting is a highly symbolic affair in which a young gallant is diverting a shepherdess from her sheep by capturing for her a butterfly. The pattern on the butterfly's wing makes a death's head. It is a very typical Holman Hunt painting, the kind of thing which presents a suspended moment of a story that makes you want to say, "yes, and what happened *next?*" One can see how an interest in the anti-novel would lead one to be interested in that kind of painting as well, because the anti-novel just sits there. Nothing moves. Everything is done by implication. There is no plot; it just sits. It may be that what little plot the story has was introduced because of the publisher's interference. But it is an interesting combination: late Victorian painting and the French anti-novel.

With poetry the connection is not quite as bad as it was years ago. There used to be very little poetry in sf, and equally little notice taken of it. We used to have people who wrote reams and reams of flowery, unselective prose—particularly the fantasy writers, of whom my favorite horrible example is Abraham Merritt—and quite often you would encounter a writer who made the mistake of quoting some of his poetry.

I am told upon reliable authority that Robert Heinlein is firmly convinced that the works of the blind poet Rhysling are real good stuff! Robert E. Howard wrote quite a lot of bad poetry. Lovecraft, as you probably know, wrote many, many yards of it, some of it under the title "Fungi From Yuggoth," which was a sonnet cycle. It does not suggest that what underlies the title is any more promising than the title itself.

We do now, however, have some genuine talents and some genuine practicing poets in this field. I can document this: I have had a considerable volume of poetry published in little magazines both here and in the United States—and even in Hungary. But taking me out of the picture, we still have people like Aldiss, John Brunner, Thomas Disch, who are not only very sensitive writers of prose but also produce a considerable volume of poetry on the side, much of it very respectable stuff. Edward Lucie-Smith has edited a collection of sf poetry: *Holding*

Your Eight Hands (1969). True, it contains some dubious or outright bad specimens, but even the bad ones are bad in unexpected ways; only two are horrible fanzine verse, both of them by H. P. Lovecraft. John Robert Colombo, for example, is represented by a verbatim quotation from Mary Shelley's *Frankenstein,* rearranged as free verse. I deduce from his biographical note that this is something he calls "found poetry," but I call it plagiarism. Adrian Henri is included with three brief snippets dedicated to Lovecraft, Bradbury and Bester which do nothing but push about pieces of these authors' preoccupations, making them sound a good deal sillier than their originals. There are several quite long pieces which are actually one-punch short stories, and one of these, by Peter Redgrove, is not even set up as a poem; the other, by Edwin Morgan, is; but I can't see why — but both are pretty good stories. Kenneth Koch's "The Artist" is also a story, a satire on the current mania for gigantism in the plastic arts, which *is* also a poem in the same sense that William Carlos Williams' "Paterson" is: a welding together of journal entries, headlines, honest verse, half-bricks, broken bottles and old bones which does in the end turn out to have a coherent vision.

Far at the other end of the spectrum is George MacBeth's "Circe Undersea," which is a narrative poem told in a series of seven sonnets, with marginal glosses; a tour de force of beautifully visualized, unconventional material worked with apparent ease into a rigidly conventional frame. Another MacBeth poem, "The Crab-Apple Crisis," succeeds in making Herman Kahn funny, which I would have thought impossible on the face of it.

Quite a few of the poems belong to a class which, lacking any standard critical term for it, I call the rhymed editorial. Most of the work of W. H. Auden is of this kind, and it makes me acutely uncomfortable the more I agree with its content; while I sympathize with almost all of Auden's attitudes, I can see no more compelling reason to call most of his verse "poetry" than I can for the short story which has been broken up into what purports to be verse. Nevertheless, most of the work in this collection which falls into this class shows that the writers know Auden exists and that they have learned from him.

There are also some epiphanies—moments of intense realization, intensely expressed, and implying some previous situation which the poet does not tell you. The epiphany is the heartland of poetry, but it is not surprising that there are even fewer lyrics, and almost *no* single lines which you are likely to remember. In fact, the only irruption of outright song that I could find is abstract and Eliotian: "...our lives and days returned to us, but / haunted by deeper souvenirs than any rocks or seeds. / From time the souvenirs are deeds" (Edwin Morgan). This is fine in the same sense that "After such knowledge, what forgiveness?" is fine, but it is a bloodless sort of lyricism not far removed from the prosy; Poul Anderson has tossed off lines just as good in straight stories (e.g., "Time is the bridge that burns behind us"). Ah, well, it is no doubt a little early in the game for good sf lyrics.

But this interaction between sf and poetry is a hopeful sign; and it may also be a sign that modern poetry may after all recapture some sort of an audience. Sf seems to be becoming a mass medium (although possibly the smallest mass medium in history) and if a certain amount of poetry can be infused into it, and a rather modern sort of poetry—unlike "Fungi From Yuggoth"—we may have an audience to be reeducated, very much as the tv show *Star Trek* converted a lot of people to sf who wouldn't touch it with a ten foot pole before, because to them sf meant monster movies, and *Star Trek* taught them that this wasn't entirely true. The two phenomena are not, I must admit, closely comparable; but I do think there is some connection.

There has been a lot of rock lately in sf. Norman Spinrad's "The Big Flash" is the example which springs immediately to mind. Just as Sturgeon quite frequently attempted to describe the effects of jazz, so many of the younger people of the Ellison-Spinrad group are talking quite a lot about the effects, emotional or otherwise, of rock. I must confess these are inaudible to me; but plainly they are audible to younger people, so I obviously have a tin ear in that department.

On the whole it would seem to me that one of the rather big changes we see taking place in sf now is an increased consciousness of the existence of other arts besides pulp narrative, and of the fact that what is going on in contemporary art is *not* necessarily chaos and is not necessarily to be looked upon with pessimism. If it is taking sf writers a little while to catch up with the '30s so far as technique is concerned, well, please bear in mind what they were *doing* in the '30s: they were writing "Monsters of Mars," "The Revolt of the Machines," "Hell's Dimension," "The Exiles of Time." They were paying no attention to Joyce and Dos Passos and those people at the time they were writing. They were writing fiction for which they were being paid what Horace Gold once described as "microscopic fractions of a cent per word, payable upon lawsuit," and they had absolutely no time, or inclination, to keep up with what the literary giants of the period were doing. Furthermore, had they done so they would probably have said just what almost everyone else was saying at the time: this is utter chaos; literature can break down no further than this; we have reached the end. I remember at that time reading a book called *A Doctor Looks At Literature* which had a chapter in it on *Ulysses* beginning: "I am probably the only man in the world to have read *Ulysses* through twice." The rest of the chapter was devoted to demonstrating just why it was that *Ulysses* represented the absolute breakdown of all form and control in the novel, and said that from now on we could expect absolutely nothing of the novel. Forget it—the form was dead. Now, of course, we know that *Ulysses* was one of the most over-controlled novels ever written, so there is hope.

At the time, I am quite sure that had the sf writers turned to *Ulysses,* much less to *Finnegans Wake,* they would have seen chaos, just as we see chaos in John Cage and Stockhausen; and they would certainly have seen no possibility of adapting any part of it for *Astounding Stories of Super Science* or *Weird Tales.* So I think they can be excused for being forty years behind the times: forty years ago they were not behind any times, they were nowhere, not aware of what was going on at all.

Now comes the most interesting part, it seems to me, and that is the influence of sf on the arts — and there is some.

I have already mentioned Burgess, who has clearly been influenced by sf. The Argentinian writer Borges has obviously read a lot of science fiction too and has been influenced by it. His work shows it very strongly (and now it's beginning to feed back, to influence sf writers in turn). John Barth, an American novelist, has written one sf novel, *Giles Goat Boy,* and it would not surprise me at all to see him turn out another. Another American novelist, Thomas Pynchon, has written a massive encyclopaedic novel, simply titled *V,* in size if not in structure rather reminiscent of *Ulysses,* which is quite science fictional, in parts; and another, a shorter one, *The Crying of Lot 49,* which is a van Vogtian conspiracy story from the ground up, very funny and very ingenious.

There has been a lot of sf influence on music, most of it in rock. Rock groups have given themselves science fictional titles; they have written songs with sf lyrics. It has also had a considerable influence on what I suppose we must still consider as serious music. There now exists an sf opera called *Aniara.* It takes place entirely aboard a spaceship which has lost its course and is on a long journey to nowhere. Musically, it is a thoroughly eclectic opera: mostly twelve-tone, but also containing some neo-Romantic music, some *musique concrete,* some taped music of electronic sounds — all of which, however, is beautifully integrated. The poem is by Harry Martinson, who is one of Sweden's greatest poets; it was adapted from a long narrative poem. The opera has been highly successful, not only in Sweden but almost everywhere else it has played, and has been recorded as well.

When it comes to modern painting, quite a bit of influence has come from either sf or from the space program—I cannot exactly tell which. A fair amount of modern painting that I have seen reproduced in magazines is suddenly full of astronomical symbols, usually of pretty good accuracy. It is as though Chesley Bonestell, at his advanced age, has suddenly crept into the forefront of at least some part of modern painting. This is an interesting phenomenon, and one which, I suspect, will continue to develop as we go farther into space and find odder things than we ever dreamed of on the covers of pulp magazines—such as what we have recently discovered on Mars. Artists may seize upon this material for imagery, and may also draw more and more from the stories themselves, now that the audience for the medium is spreading.

So on the whole, though I thought that what I had here was a non-subject, there does actually seem to be quite a bit to be said about it—and, what is probably a great deal more important, quite a bit to *watch for*. We are standing effectively at the beginning of the invasion of sf by the arts, and the invasion of the arts by sf—these are two complementary processes. Where it will all go only God knows, but I think it is an extremely interesting process, and it is something that I am watching with great fascination.

4. A NEW TOTEMISM?

The imminence of manned spaceflight, though it may answer many questions, brings us to the verge of being posed anew one of the oldest and knottiest questions of iconography: What is the shape of the soul?

The connection between the two subjects is not immediate, but it is direct. We suspect that life of some sort exists on at least one other local planet, Mars. We know that at least two other suns beside our own, both relatively nearby, have at least one planet apiece. The implication is strong that planets are normal in the life history of a star; and that many stars must have planets like the Earth. The most conservative estimate published thus far puts the number of Earthlike planets in our Milky Way galaxy alone at 100,000.

We already suspect unEarthly life in these gulfs; in due course, we may find intelligent life.

It is not likely to look much like us. A frequent argument is that something very like the human shape presents so many advantages for an intelligent animal that that shape cannot help but evolve independently, parallel to our evolution. For instance, two eyes (at a minimum)[6] are essential for depth perception—hence for survival—and if they are to function at their best they must be reasonably close together and as high up on the animal as possible. An erect posture is necessary to free the

---

[6] Not a frivolous aside; early terrestrial reptiles had three; the human pineal gland is a relic of the third.

forelimbs for tool-using; the brain is best located in the head, in close association with the sense-organs; and so on.

To this argument, which is logical but suspiciously unimaginative, is opposed a school of thought whose spokesman is the eminent University of Pennsylvania anthropologist Loren C. Eiseley. It is his position that man as we know him is a product of an enormous series of evolutionary accidents, most of them so delicately poised that man must necessarily be alone in space. His poetic summation is worth quoting:

Lights come and go in the night sky. Men, troubled at last by the things they build, may toss in their sleep and dream bad dreams, or lie awake while the meteors whisper greenly overhead. But nowhere in all space or on a thousand worlds will there be men to share our loneliness. There may be wisdom; there may be power; somewhere across space great instruments, handled by strange manipulative organs, may stare vainly at our floating cloud wrack, their owners yearning as we yearn. Nevertheless, in the nature of life and in the principles of evolution we have had our answer. Of man elsewhere, and beyond, there will be none forever.

It is a positive wrench to think that a man who can assume so pure an apocalyptic tone might be wrong, but it will be a greater wrench if he is right—and his opponents are right, for the question will probably resolve itself into, What degree of approximation of the human form are we prepared to accept as manlike? Sophisticated minds will be unlikely to rebel at a giant spider with intelligence, or at any of the other zoological idiocies with which the movies lately are trying to frighten us; but if the Other Intelligence we first meet is vaguely manlike yet at the same time obviously not a man, all our training since the Dark Ages, when teratology was the most highly organized branch of medicine, will whisper to us: "A monster!"

How an artist depicts a man is in some sense—and probably the important sense—how he sees the indwelling spirit. This is visible even in totemism; if the divine is thought to reside in the animal, then the animal will be painted in idealized form, the man reduced to a pursuing stick-figure, as in the Spanish caves. The Egyptian deities glorify both the human and the animal at once, but in neither element of the mixture is there any pretense of depicting a visible surface drawn from experience. Greek and Babylonian totem-human mixtures shade off into forms apparently all human, but clearly labelled Love, Power, Thievery, Healing, Wine, Earth. The age of anthropomorphism spans the whole history of the transformation of the invisible, beardless, nightgownless Jahweh into somebody's grandfather, and his subdivision into such creatures as Raphael's angels.

Some residues of totemism still remain, in the West in the dove as the symbol of the soul; in the East in the doctrine of metempsychosis, and in the serpent, as Krishna saw it issuing from the dead body of his half-brother Balarma, as the symbol of Vishnu. The virtual extinction of belief in the soul itself in a scientific age might be read into the mystic animals of Morris Graves, such as his "Bird Caged by Moonlight," which seem to be in the process of disappearing into the elements of the earth and the air.

In the universe we are about to enter, even the nobility of Michelangelo's hand of God may be utterly irrelevant, and our whole iconography of the demonic and the divine become blurred beyond redemption. The first intelligent extra-solar race that we meet may be wiser and nobler than we are, and look all the same like something out of Hieronymous Bosch. The wisdom and nobility may not be there, but we are not going to be able to judge it by looking at the physical form and reading it as though it were a hieroglyph for "good" or "evil." The situation is comparable to a first encounter with African artworks, where no insight is possible until we realize that what seem like distortions to us are symmetries in a culture where our norms do not prevail.

Modern art may moderate the shock somewhat, at least that part of it which has not abstracted itself entirely into light, composition, texture and other wholly painterly matters and left the forms of experience behind. We have seen so many special versions of the human form now that it is perhaps hard to imagine one that is capable of upsetting us. Nevertheless, there is always something shocking about the real (to use this word in its most limited sense); the reactions of the man who encounters a *live* mermaid or chimera are yet to be written down. But the time may be coming.

The artists who are likely to be of service to us at that moment will be the Bosches and the Dalis rather than the Picassos, the Klines and the Klees. Paintings like those of the Cubists, or like "Caprice in February," in this context are not true distortions of our image of the human soul, but instead are hieroglyphics for it; indeed an excellent case could be made for this idiom as a form of writing, half picture and half word. With a few signs—a figure 7, a one-syllable visual convention for "hat," a stroke indicating motion—Klee gives us not only a windy street and a blowing newspaper, but also something we know to be a nose, and know it so well that we have no trouble in seeing the man attached to it, though Klee gives us nothing else but his feet and the ghost of his overcoat. The gaiety and warmth of this idiom are not in question, but it depends utterly upon many centuries of comfortably expectable bodies, however idealized or abstracted.

We will never meet a creature like Klee's except among ourselves. Our counterpart on some possible Earthlike planet of Alpha Centauri or 61 Cygni is much more likely to be constructed of something more like boiled beans, as in Dali's "Premonition of Civil War," and quite as tangible; and for this, only biomorphism can prepare us.

It will be interesting to see if the calligraphic artists, who are now generally higher in our esteem than the biomorphists, will hold their place in so vastly expanded a universe of discourse. While it may well be true that a rational soul, the *hnau*, remains the same regardless of its bodily clothing, the visual arts have seldom so regarded it. By the time the new point of view is fully assimilated, the totem will surely be back among us, and perhaps to stay.

5. PROBAPOSSIBLE PROLEGOMENA TO IDEAREAL HISTORY

In this essay (which means "trial") I propose to do five things: (1) Define science fiction; (2) Show why it arose when it did; (3) Explain why it is becoming steadily more popular; (4) Demonstrate that just as it has thus far produced no towering literary masterworks, so no such work can be expected of it in the future, and (5) Place it as a familiar phenomenon in world history.

Nothing so much gratifies the critical temper as criticising other critics, regardless of the subject-matter they are all ostensibly examining.[7] To put my readers at their ease, then, I shall begin in this enjoyable mode.

ARCHAIC ZELOTYPIA AND THE ODIUM TELEOLOGICUM

As others have noted, both historians and creators of science fiction are often unusually eager to claim for it respectable ancestors, working backwards through Voltaire, Swift and Cyrano de Bergerac to Lucian of Samosata. Most recently, Peter Nicholls has carried this process probably as far as it can be made to go, by including in science fiction's family tree the epic of Gil-

---

[7] V. Nabokov vs. Wilson, superficially about Pushkin's *Eugene Onegin*.

gamesh, which seems to have been composed a considerable time before the Sumerians discovered that they could produce serviceable laundry lists by biting spoiled bricks. It should be noted, however, that Mr. Nicholls' ongoing critical history is a sophisticated one, so that his examples are not primarily ancestor worship or fake genealogy; among other things, he is instead out to show certain traits and states of mind findable throughout literary history which, put together like puzzle pieces, united to form works we call science fiction. (If there is any real objection to his approach, it is that we most successfully define things by their centers, not their edges, in Dr. Jack Cohen's telling formulation.) The formidable Prof. Darko Suvin, the only formalist critic of science fiction known to me, is not an ancestor hunter either; but his definition of science fiction as "the literature of cognitive estrangement" eliminates family trees by permitting the inclusion of more ancestors than all the others put together (including some not intended as fiction at all), like an international convention of everybody named Smith—Smythes, Psmiths, Blacksmiths and Blacks also welcome.

The critics in apparent opposition are equally numerous and cover as wide a spectrum. Among these we may safely pass by the group exemplified by Judith Merril, to whose members science fiction is simply the Now Thing and Where It's At. The central, general tenet of this school is that science fiction was impossible before, and coincided with, the advent and rise of science and technology. The position is attractive and has the merit of relatively hard edges; at the very least, it does not throw into despair the prospective student who cannot read medieval Latin or Linear B. Like its converse, it has its megalomaniac extremes: for instance, I subscribe to it; and the late John W. Campbell maintained that science fiction *is* the mainstream, of which all other kinds of fiction are only backwaters. A more reasonable representative is Heinlein's claim that science fiction is more difficult to write than contemporary or historical fiction, and superior to them both. I disagree with every word of this, but I can see no possible argument with his immediately preceding point that no fiction, written in a technology-dominated era, which ignores technology can claim to be realistic. Kingsley Amis, throwing out of court any form of cultural aggrandisement, and admitting—as so few critics do—that a major function of science fiction is entertainment, sees it as an exclusively Twentieth Century form of social satire (though with the unavoidable and richly earned inclusion of H. G. Wells). This is perhaps *too* narrow, leaving out other *kinds* of science fiction, e.g. as thought-experiments, as early warning systems, as generator of paradigms, and so on. Brian Aldiss's history casts its net far wider, but also holds that science fiction cannot sensibly be said to have existed before science; his earliest allowed starter is Mary Shelley, a consistent choice and admirably founded and defended.[8]

But these two schools, despite their apparently fundamental opposition, are simply two sides of the same balloon; take the best of the first school (Nicholls), turn him inside out, and you have the best of the second (Aldiss); topologically they remain identical. (In some of the lesser possible pairs you will have to let quite a bit of gas out first.) There is an important sense in which Gilgamesh, Grendel & Co. indeed do belong in any history or theory of science fiction—though it is not a sense either advocated or rejected yet by either side. If I can establish this detail, the five theses in my opening paragraph will follow almost automatically.

PANOPTICAL PURVIEW OF POLITICAL PROGRESS AND THE FUTURE PRESENTATION OF THE PAST

---

[8] In this summary I have made everybody sound as solemn as owls, but many of these critics are witty writers; see particularly Aldiss, de Camp and Nicholls.

Somewhere around ninety per cent of the central thesis of this essay—which I haven't stated yet—is not mine at all; I stole it from Oswald Spengler. This is something more than the usual acknowledgment of a debt, for the fact itself is a supporting datum for the thesis.

However, it also requires some definitions, since for the sake of brevity I shall use a few Spenglerian terms. Because these words are also in common use, considerable confusion would result without prior notice of the special senses Spengler attaches to them; hence I place a glossary here instead of in the usual place.

Culture: This word has no anthropological meaning in Spengler's hands (as, for instance, we might refer to the Navajo culture, the culture of the Trobriand Islands, etc.). Spengler's cultures span many centuries and many countries; for example, his Classical culture extends from pre-Homeric times to the fall of Rome. In this view, only Chinese, Indian and Egyptian histories lasted long enough to develop into independent cultures with definite geographical boundaries.

Civilization: There are essentially only two kinds of historical philosophy, the linear (or progressive) and the cyclical.[9]

Marxism and Christianity are familiar linear theories; both believe that events are marching (or zigzagging) toward some goal. The cyclical theorist believes that history repeats itself. (Toynbee tried to believe both at once, resulting in eight volumes of minutely documented bewilderment.) Spengler's theory is cyclical, on an enormous scale. For him, civilization is but one of the phases every culture must go through unless disrupted by outside forces—and not one of its best phases, either. Since we are now living in the garbage dump of just this phase of his Western culture, I shall have more to say about this later.

---

[9] I omit the accidental or meanwhile-back-at-the-corral accounts of most school and popular histories; since they see no pattern to events, they cannot be said to have a philosophy.

The Tale that Wags the God

Contemporary. In the ordinary sense, I am contemporary with everyone who lived through a majority of the same years I did. Spengler means nothing so trivial. In his sense, one man is contemporary with another if each plays a similar role in the corresponding phases of their cultures. For example, Sargon (Babylonian), Justinian I (Classical) and Charles V (Western) are eternal contemporaries—"late springtime" figures whose careers are similar because they had to be; the choice for each was either to play this role at this time, or be nobody. Hence the fact that I am alive during most of the same decades as Richard M. Nixon is meaningless; his true contemporaries are Lui-ti[10] and Caligula. My own, necessarily, are some Hellene one of whose lost 140 plays placed last in the Games in a bad year, and a subpriest trying to make sense of the chaos Amenhotep IV's experiment in monotheism made of Egyptian religion.

I have drawn these examples of contemporaneity to illustrate as well another striking principle of Spenglerian history, which is that it is cyclical only at the intercultural level; history does *not* repeat itself on any smaller stage, let alone moment by moment in fine detail as in Nietzsche's "eternal recurrence."[11] Hence it would be futile to seek parallels between, say, King Arthur and Napoleon, though some can be forced; both were Westerners in sharply different phases of that culture.

It follows from this that Spenglerian history, since it is not rigidly deterministic, allows for considerable exercise of individual free will, within the role as appropriate to the cultural phase or season. In 1975 we live late in that era of civilization he calls Caesarism. In such a period he would not counsel a poet to try to become an army officer or courtier instead; but he might well say, "Now it is too late to attempt writing a secondary epic;

---

[10] "Ti" is an honorific meaning, roughly, "the august"; and the first Chinese emperor to so style himself was, by no coincidence, contemporary in the Spenglerian sense with Caesar Augustus.

[11] Nevertheless, Nietzsche was one of Spengler's two chief influences, the other being Goethe. He acknowledges them both at the outset and refers to them frequently thereafter.

in Milton the West has already had its Vergil." The incompletion and overall structural failure of Pound's *Los Cantares* would have been predictable to him from the outset.[12] On a broader scale, most of Spengler's predictions for the Twentieth Century after 1921 have come to pass, and in the order in which he predicted them, a good test of any theory. He did fail to foresee that they would happen so fast; but he set the date for the utter collapse of the West at around 2200, which is just about as much time left as the Club of Rome gives us, and for the same reason — insanely runaway technology.

GNOSIS OF PRECREATE DETERMINATION

It now remains to place science fiction within this scheme. This requires a further short discussion of the nature of our own times in general.

Spengler's view of history is organic rather than causal, and so is his imagery; as previously implied, he compares the four major periods of each culture with the four seasons. The onset of civilization is the beginning of autumn. At this point, the culture has lost its growth-drive, and its lifestyle is codified — most particularly in architecture, with the building of great cities or cosmopoloi which both express the culture's highest spirit and drain it away from the countryside. Here, too, law is codified and history is written (*all* history is urban history); and the arts enter upon a period of attempted conformity to older, "standard" models, like the Eighteenth Century in Europe, when it

---

[12] There is a grimly interesting real example of this in Spengler's own lifetime. Hitler was contemporary with Wu-ti (119-124 A.D.) and Trajan, but utterly failed to sense the spirit of the time — though some of his councillors did, most notably Hjalmar Schacht. At the beginnings of the Nazi movement, Spengler in his only public lecture told the cream of the Hitlerjugend that they were doing the (historically) right thing at the right time, but that their leader had it all balled up and that it would end in disaster for the entire West. The leader of a national movement, he said with grisly humor, ought to be a hero, not an heroic tenor. In 1933 he expanded the speech into a 160-page book, *The Hour of Decision*. The Nazis banned the book three months after its publication (as well as forbidding all mention of his name in the press — luckily he was too famous to shoot), but by that time it had already sold 150,000 copies.

became increasingly difficult to tell one composer or playwright from another.[13] In the West, civilization began to set in about the time of Napoleon.

Civilization may last for centuries and be extremely eventful; Imperial Rome is a prime example. At first, too, great creative works remain possible; I have mentioned Vergil, and in the West we have had Milton, Goethe, Joyce, Mozart, Beethoven, Wagner, Einstein. (Spengler would unabashedly add himself to such a list, I think justifiably.) But autumn ends, and a civilization becomes a culture gone frozen in its brains and heart, and its finale is anything but grand. We are now far into what the Chinese called the period of contending states, and the collapse of Caesarism.

In such a period, politics becomes an arena of competing generals and plutocrats, under a dummy ruler chosen for low intelligence and complete moral plasticity, who amuses himself and keeps the masses distracted from their troubles with bread, circuses and brushfire wars. (This is the time of all times when a culture should unite—and the time when such a thing has become impossible.) Technology flourishes (the late Romans were first-class engineers) but science disintegrates into a welter of competing, grandiosely trivial hypotheses which supersede each other almost weekly and veer more and more markedly toward the occult. Among the masses there arises a "second religiousness" in which nobody actually believes[14]; an attempt is made to buttress this by syncretism, the wrenching out of context of religious *forms* from other cultures, such as the Indian, without the faintest hope of knowing what they mean. This process, too, leads inevitably toward a revival of the occult, and

---

[13] A charming work called the Jena Symphony was long attributed to early Beethoven because one of the orchestral parts had his name on it, though some musicologists suspected Haydn. It turned out to be by somebody no one had ever heard of.

[14] *Vide* the Eisenhower religiosity: "Everyone should go to the church of his or her own choice, I don't care which it is."

The characteristic spirit of the West, which Spengler calls Faustian, is inherently linear.

here science and religion overlap, to the benefit of neither. Economic inequity, instability and wretchedness become endemic on a hitherto unprecedented scale; the highest buildings ever erected by the Classical culture were the tenements of the Imperial Roman slums, crammed to bursting point with freed and runaway slaves, bankrupts, and deposed petty kings and other political refugees. The group name we give all this, being linearists by nature,[15] is Progress.

Given all this, it is easy to deduce the state of the arts: a period of confused individual experimentation, in which tradi-

---

[15] *Note by Peter Nicholls:* Meng-tse, the only Chinese philosopher besides Confucius to have his name latinized—as Mencius—emphasized the ruler's duty to the people, advocated social welfare, and amplified the Confucian concept of 'magnanimity.' Nagarjuna, philosopher-monk and convert to Mahayana (Greater Vehicle) Buddhism, founded the 'Middle Path' school whose clarification of the concept of 'emptiness' (sunyata) is seen as a peak of intellectual and spiritual achievement in Indian thought; and wrote several critical analyses on views of the nature of reality, the means of knowledge and the origin of existence. Amenhotep IV (better known as Akhenaton; his wife was Nefertiti) reigned from 1379-1362 B.C. and besides advocating new intellectual and artistic freedom of expression, was the first monotheist known to history. Abandoning the old gods of Egypt for a single god of love and switching capitals from Thebes to his new city, Akhetaton, his neglect of practical politics prevented his reforms from surviving. Michael Psellus, philosopher and politician, headed the philosophy faculty at the new imperial university in Byzantium, initiating the renewal of classical scholarship by reversing the Aristotelian predominance in favour of Platonic thought and advocating a fusion of Platonic and Christian doctrine, thereby prefiguring the Italian Renaissance. The Abbassids were the second great dynasty of the Muslim Empire of the Caliphate (750-1258 A.D.), the Magian period being the mystical decadence of this. The *individuals* here aren't themselves villains of the piece; rather, it is the piece in which, and against which, they were historically forced to participate which is properly 'villainous'—as the following (abridged) quotation from Spengler indicates: "Contemporary with the 'positivist' Meng-tse there suddenly began a powerful movement towards alchemy, astrology, and occultism. It has long been a favourite topic of dispute whether this was something new or a recrudescence of old Chinese myth-feeling—but a glance at Hellenism supplies the answer. This syncretism appears 'simultaneously' in the Classical, in Indian and China, and in popular Islam. It starts always on rationalist doctrines—the Stoa, Lao-tse, Buddha—and carries these through with peasant and springtime and exotic motives of every conceivable sort... The salvation-doctrine of Mahayana found its first great herald in the poet-scholar Asvagosha (*ca.* 50 B.C.) and its fulfillment proper in Nagarjuna. But side by side with such teaching, the whole mass of proto-Indian mythology came back into circulation... We have the same spectacle in the Egyptian New Empire, where Amen of Thebes formed the centre of a vast syncretism, and again in the Arabian world of the Abbassids, where the folk-religion, with its images of Purgatory, Hell, Last Judgment, the heavenly Kaaba, Logos-Mohammed, fairies, saints and spooks drove pristine Islam entirely into the background. There are still in such times a few high intellects like Nero's tutor Seneca and his antitype Psellus the philosopher, royal tutor and politician of Byzantium's Caesarism phase... like the Pharaoh Amenhotep IV (Akhenaton), whose deeply significant experiment was treated as heresy and brought to naught by the powerful Amen-priesthood..." Spengler, *The Decline of the West* (tr. C. F. Atkinson, London: Allen & Unwin, 1971), Vol. 2, pp. 312-313.

tions and even schools have ceased to exist, having been replaced by ephemeral fads. Hence the sole aim of all this experimentation is originality—a complete chimera, since the climate for the Great Idea is (in the West) fifty years dead; nor will nostalgia, simply an accompanying symptom, bring it back. This is not just winter now; it is the Fimbulwinter, the deep freeze which is the death of a culture.

We can now define science fiction; and against this back ground, see why it arose when it did, why it is becoming more popular, and why we can expect no masterpieces from it, *quod erat demonstrandum est,* in the simple act of definition.

AGNOSIS OF POSTCREATE DETERMINISM

Science fiction is the internal (intracultural) literary form taken by syncretism in the West. It adopts as its subject matter that occult area where a science in decay (elaborately decorated with technology) overlaps the second religiousness—hence, incidentally, its automatic receptivity from its emergence to such notions as time travel, ESP, dianetics, Dean Drives, faster-than-light travel, reincarnation and parallel universes. (I know of no other definition which accounts for our insistence that stories about such non-ideas be filed under the label.) It is fully contemporary with Meng-tse (372-289 B.C.), the Indian Nagarjuna (150 A.D.), the Egyptian New Empire after Amenhotep IV, Byzantium in the time of Psellus (1017-1078 A.D.), and the Magian Abbassid period[16]—we have lots of company, if it's ancestors we're looking for.

It is not a Utopian prospect—Utopia being, anyhow, only a pure example of linearism in a cyclical world—but neither need it be an occasion for despair. I repeat, we have free will within our role and era, as long as we know what it is and *when* we are.

---

[16] Published in paperback as *The Makeshift Rocket* (Ace Books, 1962).

Even without any background, or belief, in Spengler, many of us have already sensed this. When a candidate for the presidency of the Science Fiction Writers of America made "fighting drug abuse" part of his platform, most of us felt almost instinctively that he was making a fool of himself; and Harlan Ellison's call to turn science fiction into a "literature of the streets" met with dead silence. Nor has there been noticeable response to the challenges of Philip José Farmer, Michel Butor, George Hay or British Mensa to turn science fiction into fact (and the Stalinist-oriented Futurians who published exactly this challenge thirty-five years ago gathered no following, either). It was this situation which led me to say six years ago that if an artist insists on carrying placards, they should all be blank.

The last words must be Spengler's:

... our direction, willed and obligatory at once, is set for us within narrow limits, and on any other terms life is not worth the living. We have not the freedom to reach to this or to that, but the freedom to do the necessary or to do nothing. And a task that historic necessity has set *will* be accomplished with the individual or against him.

Decunt Fata volentem, nolentem trahunt. [The Fates lead the willing, they drag the unwilling.]

Addendum: I wrote this in hospital with no reference books to hand but the second volume of *The Decline of the West*. I now find that Spengler's 1924 speech was not his only public appearance; he also delivered a lecture in Hamburg in 1929. The substance of the second speech, however, was exactly the same as that of the first.

Part II

6. POUL ANDERSON: THE ENDURING EXPLOSION

Some statistics first:

Poul Anderson made his first appearance in a science fiction magazine as an author in 1944, and in the Day Index (which reaches only through 1950) he has 17 listings. In the four NESFA Indices which I own (1951-1968), there are 210 more, plus 10 as "Winston P. Sanders" and one as "A. A. Craig." This comes to 238 pieces—many of them novels—in 25 years. This may be a record; its only close competitor is that of Robert Silverberg, who rolled up 190 listings (plus 19 as "Robert Randall") over a considerably shorter period. It certainly compares well with the record of that proverbial demon of prolificness, Henry Kuttner, whose lifetime science fiction output came to 170 titles. (All three men, of course, also wrote outside our field, and I haven't made any attempt to take this output into account.)

After the counting is over, there remains the question of quality, and here the Anderson record is unique. There may be a few poor stories among those 238-plus, but they would be hard to find, and I am not about to point any out here, either.

It's my opinion, which I suspect is widely shared, that Anderson is the only surviving writer of the Golden Age of *Astounding* who is still writing sf whose work has not gone steadily (or jerkily) downhill. But even this is a negative way of putting the matter. The positive side is that Poul Anderson the scientist, the technician, the stylist, the bard, the humanist and the humorist—a nonexhaustive list—is completely immune to any changes in fashion. He is, in short, an artist.

Once upon a time, I made an unfortunate attempt to label the kind of thing Poul writes as "hard copy"—work so deeply felt and so carefully crafted that it looks solid no matter from what angle you view it—and I asked for more of the same from other people. Everyone instantly assumed that what I was talking about was sf in which the science was correct, and thus inadvertently was born our present usage of "hard science fiction."

Well, Anderson writes hard science fiction in this sense as well. He has a degree in physics, and he uses the knowledge; the scientific and technological underpinnings of his sf are thoroughly worked out in advance and are as accurate as the present state of knowledge permits. No innocent is ever going to come away from an Anderson story believing that an electron is a little planet or that "forces" come in "orders" or that there is a steaming jungle on Vesta. Work of this kind is becoming increasingly rare and deserves all the praise we can give it.

In his novel *Tau Zero*, the scientific problem is deceptively simple: What happens when an interstellar vessel, accelerating at a steady one gravity, is damaged in such a way that it can't stop doing so? Furthermore, no violation of relativity is allowed—no passing the speed of light—and the technologies described must all be achievable from scientific knowledge as of 1967 (when this novel, abridged, first saw magazine publication).

Stated this baldly, the idea looks too confining to be worth a short story, let alone a novel. We have all been educated so thoroughly in the vastness of the distances between stars that one G of acceleration sounds like the veriest crawl; and in any event, a ship limited to sub-light velocities couldn't get very far in any useful period of time, could it?

Well, a little simple doodling with the basic equations of motion will show that at one G, an object can attain 99 per cent of the speed of light in less than a year. And as for "useful" time — if you are talking about the people on shipboard; they become subject to the Lorentz-Fitzgerald effect, which means that shipboard time becomes slower and slower than Earth time.

The eventual consequences of this seemingly modest and constricted set of assumptions are so staggering as to make the intergalactic epic of E. E. Smith, Ph.D. (who made up all his "science") seem in retrospect like a trip with mommy to the corner grocer. They lead, for example, to passages like this:

The ship quivered. Weight grabbed at Reymont. He barely avoided falling to the deck. A metal noise toned through the hull, like a basso profundo gong. It was soon over. Free flight resumed. *Leonora Christine* had gone through another galaxy.

It has become something of a joke to call a science-fiction story mind-boggling, but if that paragraph doesn't boggle you, you're unbogglable. It occurs on page 179, and what Anderson has waiting for you in the remaining pages strikes me as the second biggest boggler conceivable by the human mind.

The biggest, by far, is the one that hits you after you close the book, and it is this: *It is almost all completely possible.* Only at the very end does the author pull a rabbit out of his hat, and it seems like a rabbit *only* because of the scrupulosity of the rest of his argument: He makes two cosmological assumptions, one of which is in good odor among many reputable astrophysicists, the other a conjecture which, to say the worst of it, nobody is ever likely to prove wrong.

Anderson has not failed to populate his starship with interesting people with complex human problems, and the hero, the above-mentioned Reymont, is especially well realized. There are many moments of genuine emotion (as well as a few of facile tear-jerking). But nobody but a Dostoevsky could have given this novel a cast that would not be overshadowed by the grandeur of its events. Its flaws are mostly the consequences of its strengths. Overall, it is a monument to what a born novelist and poet can do with authentic scientific materials.

As a literary craftsman he is, as was Kuttner, a born technician, whose gifts in this area were refined back in the days when the one thing the pulp magazines absolutely demanded of a writer was that he know how to plot. In general, he is not as flamboyant about his mastery of structure as was Kuttner (who once confessed to me a temptation to write a story entirely in footnotes, a trick to be turned much later by Vladimir Nabokov in *Pale Fire)*; most of his work is simply unobtrusively well made. When he does show off, however, the results are sufficiently spectacular to make fellow practitioners turn white with envy. Consider, for example, *The Day After Doomsday*. What other writer would have the temerity to build the reader up for scores of pages toward a crucial space battle—and then attempt to tell it in terms of a ballad written many years after the event?

Not only does he attempt it, but he brings it off, which leads us naturally to Anderson the bard. He retains a deep and indeed scholarly interest in his Scandinavian ancestry, and it shows, usually to advantage. When he wants to give a story an epic quality, he starts an immense step ahead of the rest of us: he thinks of (or feels like) the *Elder Edda* instead of *The Skylark of Valeron*.

To be a bard is not necessarily the same thing as being a poet, but Anderson is both. Even the clichés on sundials ("It is later than you think") in his hands become living metaphors ("Time is the bridge that burns behind us"). Here is another case: An Anderson hero is contemplating an apparently placid society which seems to work well only because the people have no deep emotions, and he wonders how they would react if confronted with something like *King Lear*—or with a real tragedy, such as that of the man who "broke his regimental oath, and gave up wealth and honors and the mistress he loved more than the sun, to go and tend his mad wife in a hut upon the heath." (I deliberately quote this from memory; I haven't thought of that line since 1963, but I'll bet I don't have it far wrong all the same.) Of course the "real" tragedy is as invented as is *King Lear*, but I at least instantly felt that the bare bones of the one would not have been unworthy of the language of the other. Here the bard and the poet are united.

The sense of tragedy is also extremely rare in science fiction. To Poul Anderson it is a living entity. For him, it does not inhere in such commonplaces as the losses of old age, the deaths of lovers, the slaughters of war or Nature; as a physicist, he knows that the entropy gradient goes inexorably in only one direction, and he wastes no time sniveling about it. For Anderson, the tragic hero is a man like the one whose saga I have quasi-quoted above: the man who is driven partly by circumstance, but mostly by his own conscience, to do the wrong thing for the right reason — and then has to live with the consequences. A fully fleshed-out example is "Sister Planet," in which the hero, foreseeing that a friendly alien race whom he loves are going to be ruthlessly exploited by man, bombs their Holy Place to teach them eternal suspicion. His exit line is: *Oh God, please exist. Please make a hell for me.* And in a way, the prayer is answered, for when the man's body is found much later, he is carrying a Bible in which Ezekiel 7:3,4 are marked. Look it up.

I have never reread that story; it tore me to pieces the first time, and that was enough. But I am the richer for it. And I can only stand in awe of a man who could not only entertain the insight, but write it out. It is utterly pitiless, as genuine tragedy must be; very few writers, and almost no sf writers, know the difference.

The other side of that shield is comedy, and Anderson has written a lot of that, too. Most readers probably remember *The High Crusade*, in which a medieval army is carried off in a spaceship and winds up laying successful siege to a culture about ten centuries in advance of it technologically. I am not so fond of the "Hoka" stories Poul wrote with Gordon R. Dickson, but nothing can dim my affection for "A Bicycle Built for Brew,"[17] in which Anderson constructed a spaceship powered by beer and made me believe it would actually work.

Very few Anderson stories are solely adventure, gimmickry, tragedy, or any other single thing. They are wholes, and this is the source of his endurance. And it is mostly self-conscious and deliberate (the exceptions are the ideas, which come to him, as to all of us, from we wish we knew where). He has noted rather frequently, for instance, that in each scene he makes it a policy to appeal to at least three senses, to increase the reader's feeling that he is actually *there*. But though this is good policy, it is also only an indicative technicality. The real wholeness goes much deeper.

At the Detention (the 17th World Science Fiction Convention, Detroit, 1959), where he was Guest of Honor, he made an appeal for what he called a "unitary" approach to science fiction, in which philosophy, love, technology, poetry, and the minutiae of daily living would all play parts concomitant with their importance in real life, but heightened by the insight of the writer. You will note, I think, that this is more than just a prescription for good science fiction. It is a prescription for good fiction of any kind.

And Poul Anderson is his own best example of it.

---

[17] Cabell's *Jurgen* has its title character appeal to an "Artemidorus Minor" (Chap. 8) for whom James P. Cover's *Notes on Jurgen* offer three Artemidorii; but surely it would be the dream authority to whom Jurgen, himself in the grip of an elaborate dream, would appeal here. In Chap. 32 of the same novel, the priest of Sesphra cites five other authorities in a row straight out of Burton, as Cover later points out.

7. THE LITERARY DREAMERS

In an Author's Note to a neglected novel called *Smirt,* James Branch Cabell declared his intention of following "the actual and well-known laws of a normal dream"; laws which, as he saw his predecessors, only Lewis Carroll had previously followed (given two small exceptions) with "scientific exactness." Scientific exactness about dreaming was unattainable in 1933, let alone in 1862, for there was virtually no scientific knowledge available about the process before 1953.

Up until 1899, the most respected authority was the *Oneirocritica* of Artemidorus, who lived in the second century A.D.; he was a close observer who recorded dreams which are still common today, explaining their meaning by association on the theory that a skilled diviner ought to be able to make more of a given dream than the dreamer could. Cabell, like most modern Classical scholars, seems to have encountered Artemidorus through Burton's *Anatomy of Melancholy*[18] Burton evokes Artemidorus twice in his discussion of sleep and dream; he also has an alchemical theory of his own to propose, which seems quite incomprehensible now, but was the standard product of its age, a good long time after Artemidorus.

Popular dream-books aside, nothing further in oneirology of scientific importance occurred until 1899, the year of publication of Freud's *The Interpretation of Dreams.* Like Artemidorus, Freud interpreted dreams by association; but unlike the Daldian,

---
[18] See "The Long Night of a Virginia Author."

Freud handed back to the dreamer, rather than the interpreter, the job of divination. The explosive impact of this book needs no documentation; but it is not often noticed that Jung and his followers continued to cling to the Artemidorian method, in that they imposed the meaning of the dream upon the dreamer rather than vice versa.

For the Jungians, dreams are particular expressions of Platonic archetypes, which are supposed to reside in a "collective unconscious." No scientists, as Weston LaBarre has observed tartly, know where the collective unconscious might live in the physical brain; but it is worth pointing out also that Freud's Super-Ego, Ego and Id have never been localized, either.

Up until the 1800's, it was also possible to argue whether or not dreams come from God, like the prophetic dreams of the Old Testament. Aristotle firmly maintained that they did not, with his usual cool common-sense. The medieval Schoolmen, though they were united in believing that prophetic dreams were divinely inspired, were also equally divided on the source of what Cabell (who believed in magic) calls "normal dreams."

The question seems to have been resolved by Albertus Magnus—in his time a much more influential figure than his pupil Thomas Aquinas—who came down on the side of Aristotle. The moment was well chosen, however inadvertently. The ban on the teaching of Aristotle at Paris in 1210, which was directly responsible for the founding of Oxford University, was lifted gradually from 1241 to 1244 while Innocent IV was too busy hiding from the Emperor Frederick to give much thought to papal matters like curricula.

Thereafter, Aristotle's opinions on virtually every matter reigned supreme until at least 1600, the year of the burning of Giordano Bruno. Even Kepler, whose cosmology replaced Aristotle's and is still alive today, was expressing his earlier radical notions in Aristotelean terminology in 1596. As one result, the main *literary* tradition of the dream became its use as a vehicle for the exposition of otherwise unacceptable ideas, including, of course, political satire.

A type case is Kepler's own *Somnium*, which describes a trip to the Moon which Kepler well knew to be impossible then. (Kepler played it safe three ways: He wrote of dreaming not of the trip itself, but of reading an account of such a journey by another man — and *Somnium* was published posthumously in 1634.) This tradition persisted well into the 19th century, as witness George du Maurier's *Peter Ibbetson*, in which a potentially adulterous affair is carried on only in dreams.

What Cabell calls naturalism in the fictional treatment of dreams is thus a very late development in a field previously dominated by mysticism on the one side (e.g., John Bunyan) and editorializing on the other. It was to be expected, too, that the Artemidorus/Jung approach would be preferred to Freud's by subsequent artists; Jung's influence is everywhere apparent, for example, in *Finnegans Wake*, surely the most important of all dream novels, and in the fiction (*Seven Days in New Crete*) and the theorizing *(The White Goddess)* of Robert Graves. The reasons for this are apparent; it is a case of one predominately artistic construct supporting another. As C. S. Lewis observes, Jung explains the effect of stories of the marvelous by producing "one more myth which affects us in the same way as the rest." (He adds mildly, "Surely the analysis of water should not itself be wet?")

Lewis Carroll's dream tales are not based upon any visible psychological system, have no mystical content, and seemingly have no moral to drive home by allegory, though they contain much implicit criticism of how affairs are ordered in the waking world. In this sense, then, Cabell is right in calling them naturalistic; they resemble real dreams captured by a close observer, and do not exist for some more important literary or philosophical purpose. Cabell notes the correspondences:

These books alone did preserve the peculiar, the unremittent movement of a normal dream, and the peculiar legerdemain through which the people one meets, or the places visited, in a normal dream, are enabled unostentatiously to take visible form or to vanish, quite naturally, without provoking in the beholder's mind any element of surprise; just as these books preserved, too, the ever-present knowledge, common to many dreamers, that, after all, they are dreaming...

Its deliberately hypnotic cadences aside, the description is as matter-of-fact as Aristotle's, and as closely observed.

Cabell goes on to fault the Alice books for including the senses of taste and smell, which he believes are always absent in dreams; at present there is no evidence for or against this stricture except introspection and testimony. Cabell adds some other observations of his own: His dreamer's vision was circumscribed:

... a sort of mistiness pervaded matters, driftingly, unpredictably. And besides, at times, one or another visual detail would seize upon the attention, obsessing it, somewhat as though, from a shrouding fog, this particular detail... had been picked out by a flashlight. In consequence, you did not ever obtain a leisured and complete view of any person or of any place... Moreover, there was in his dream no perception of time... Everything happened, as it were, simultaneously, now that events, and many persons too, merged swiftly and unaccountably, into yet other events, or yet other persons... and space did very much the same thing. He did not often go to any place in this dream, for the sufficing reason that the place... came to him.

(Later, in *An Experiment With Time*, J. W. Dunne was to maintain that the dreaming mind was *in fact* liberated from time and space. Dunne's 1953 book, currently a fast-selling paperback in England, is a fascinating non-fiction exercise in introspection.)

Smirt conforms throughout to these conditions and restrictions. In addition, it includes a preoccupation with the dreamer's waking affairs which is also visible in the Alice books (as it is in *Finnegans Wake*), and some matters they do not include which nevertheless are often met with in dreams — for example, a sense of dread, a feeling of uniform hostility against the dreamer, the sensation that he is about to be supplanted or to die, and some moderately explicit sex scenes (all also present in the Joyce novel). Furthermore, *Smirt* went on to become a trilogy called *The Nightmare Has Triplets,* whose central volume, *Smith,* shows the dreamer as little more than an observer; the adventures happen to his imaginary sons.

The final volume, *Smire,* contains the most powerful suggestions that this is all, after all, "only" a dream, and the concomitant awareness on the dreamer's part that he is about to wake up. The outside volumes also include considerable consciousness of a clock in the dreamer's bedroom, plus several of its other fixtures. (Again, similar features are present in the Joyce work; however, I shall not pursue the comparison further, since I have already done so elsewhere.[19])

We must not suppose that Cabell knew anything more about the nature of "scientific exactness" than he did about the atmosphere of the Moon; he employed both metaphorically. However, he had thought long and hard about the virtues and vices of naturalism (as is particularly evident in his *Beyond Life),* he was a careful reporter when it suited his purposes, and insofar as the scientific knowledge of 1933 went, his account of the underlying conditions of dream is quite as good as anyone else's;

---

[19] A good popular account of all this work is *The Science of Dreams* by Edwin Diamond, who was for years the editor of the "Space and the Atom" section of the magazine *Newsweek*. A more condensed but at the same time less well organised version is distributed through Brian W. Aldiss' semi-autobiographical *The Shape of Future Things;* this version has the advantage of having been passed upon by Dr. Evans. Mr. Aldiss's book also suggested the present essay to me.

nor does it contradict the very few introspective records of previous writers on the subject or testimony collected by them, Freud included.

Hence I do not think it unfair to compare his observations — and by implicit extension, those of other literary dreamers — with present scientific knowledge.

Beginning in 1953, Nathaniel Kleitman and Eugene Aserinsky reported a series of researches showing that dreaming is invariably accompanied by rapid eye movements under the lids of the sleeper. Their studies further showed that dreams keep almost as regular a schedule as do railroad trains. They are preceded by fifteen minutes of relative wakefulness, during which reveries or phantasies obtrude, and then by a deep sleep of about ninety minutes. There then occurs a dream about nine minutes long. After another ninety minutes of slightly less deep sleep, a dream nineteen minutes long obtrudes; after another ninety minutes come twenty-four minutes of dream; and ninety minutes still later comes the nearly-waking dream, which lasts some twenty-eight minutes.

Only the final dream is at all likely to be remembered unless the sleeper has been forcibly awakened during an earlier one; and it is this dream which is close enough to waking reverie to provoke, occasionally, deliberate attempts to prolong it. Self-awakening nightmares, such as those discussed by Burton, occur earlier. Subsequent studies of sleeplessness by Richard Dement show further that either the repeated interruption of dreams, or prolonged deprivation of sleep, leads to psychotic states.

Burton had foreseen this, too; he said, in fact, that sleeplessness prepares "the body, as one observes, to many perilous diseases... Waking overmuch is both a symptom and an ordinary cause" of melancholy (by which he appeared to mean pathological depression; the present evidence indicates that schizophrenic symptoms are much the more likely to occur). This much is thoroughly established experimentally, and buttressed by studies on the effects of hallucinogenic drugs such as LSD.[20]

Upon these foundations, plus considerable direct experimentation with the memory functions of computers, Christopher Evans and Edward A. Newman have evolved a theory of the function of dream which has the unique virtue of being founded upon hard information. Briefly, Dr. Evans compares sleep and dreaming with the removal from service of a computer in order that its programmes may be revised and cleared in the light of new events and experiences. According to this model, sleep is a process whose chief function is to allow us to dream, with as little interruptions as possible from the outside world, which otherwise would interfere with the clearing process, and eventually with sanity.

Dr. Evans adds:

The content of most dreams... is probably trivial, since most of our experiences are of the useless variety. At first thought, this seems to conflict with one's own subjective impressions. The apparent significance of much of our dreaming can be understood, however, when we remember that we are talking about *interrupted* dreams in this context, and it is dreams with *effect*, and provoking autonomic bodily reactions, that are most likely to wake us up. The vast bulk of undisturbed dreaming, in fact, will probably consist of very drab, routine material — the bread-and-butter experiences of the previous day being fitted into the programmes system. Occasionally we become aware of this boring rubbish when a fever brings fitful sleep. Then we see the core of dreams for what they really are: endless sessions of counting; reading nonsense; attempts to solve weird problems; driving vast distances; and so on. To slightly misquote an ac-

---

[20] It now appears that digestion has nothing to do with dreaming — but what one has previously read may be highly important.

knowledged expert on the topic, this is really 'the stuff of dreams,' and we should be very glad that we normally sleep through it all.

It must be borne in mind that the Evans theory is at present only a simile; it does not propose that the brain *is* a computer, but that in certain important respects it seems to act *like* one.

Like all such models, its validity must now be tested to destruction, and Dr. Evans himself proposes six unconfirmed consequences which, if they do not follow, will be destructive of the model.

They are, in his own words:

(1)...Many gross psychological disorders are due to a dysfunction of the *dreaming* process; confusion, loss of touch with reality, paranoid symptions and persecution complexes are symptomatic of experimentally dream-deprived subjects, and also of schizophrenic states.

(2) If the latter is true, then a crash programme of research should be instituted by the pharmacological research organizations to develop a drug which allows the maximum amount of dreaming to take place during sleep. Such a drug might have dramatic therapeutic effects on chronic schizophrenics.

(3) Barbiturate sedation might act by depressing the central nervous system so much that the dream process itself is inhibited, for at least part of the night. Thus, though apparently sleeping like logs, nightly barbiturate takers could be gradually depriving themselves into a state equivalent to that of chronic sleep deprivation.

(4) The hallucinations characteristic of schizoid conditions, and of advanced alcoholic addiction, might be waking dreams forced into action because of the dysfunction or suppression of normal dreaming at night. Grim warning for all experimental and joy-riding takers of hallucinogenic drugs, including LSD:

the long-term effect might be to permanently interfere with the dream mechanism...

(5) The more new material processed in the course of the day, the more programme revision and updating required. Therefore the younger one is, the more dreaming one will need. Old people who put down very little new material, and who have in general a very constant environment, will need substantially less dreaming and thus less sleep. Should they not be taught to accept without worry their natural tendency to sleeplessness, and learn to make use of the bonus hours they have gained?

(6) Sleep learning is *out*. It might work, but only at the risk of muddling vital programme clearance activities. Not quite, but nearly as dangerous as LSD.

Some of these ideas have obvious applicability to the recorded dreams and hallucinations of drug users such as De Quincey, Coleridge and James Thomson. Others apply less directly, as for example the relationship, more complex than it first might appear, between Idea Six and Huxley's use of hypnopaedia in *Brave New World* (and Huxley, it will be recalled, later joined the ranks of those to whom Idea Four might apply). More generally, we may understand better the annoyance of a Coleridge or a Byron — or by most of the rest of us — at being unable to finish a dream, or a dream-record, of obvious inner importance.

In the light cast by the model, moreover, it would appear that the literary dreamers for the most part have been constructing their works around the last, and longest, dream of early morning. Since virtually everyone has four dreams per night and remembers only one of them, it seems logical to suppose that the immensely consistent dreams written about by everyone from Kepler to Cabell — granting for the sake of argument that these writers were trying to write naturalistically, to a major extent, about dreaming itself—cannot encompass four different dreams experienced at four different levels of sleep.

Dr. Evans' Idea Three applies with peculiar vividness to the reports of De Quincey and Thomson. In both the *Confessions* and *The City of Dreadful Night,* the most agonising hallucinations were those experienced in nocturnal sleeplessness produced by a previous opium trance: "As I came through the desert thus it was..."

All the literary dreamers agree with the model—and with Aristotle—that most dreams, even the most fantastic, consist of reshuffling of commonplace daily concerns.

Kepler thought constantly about the problem of the planetary orbits, and his dream (which is heavily loaded with footnotes) is a fantasia upon the best knowledge—his own—of his time about actual conditions on the Moon.

Bunyan, a divine, remoulds theological matters in his literary sleep.

Walpole testified directly that *The Castle of Otranto* began with awakening "one morning, in the beginning of last June, from a dream, of which, all I could recover, was, that I had thought myself in an ancient castle (a very natural dream for a head like mine filled with Gothic story)..."

Ann Radcliffe, in a direct reversal of Burton's prescription against nightmares, ate "hard meats" before bedtime to induce them, her own head full of *The Castle of Otranto* and its successors, the results being *The Mysteries of Udolpho* and its successors.[21]

Lewis Carroll brooded over little girls and logical paradoxes awake, and these in his dreams become erected into operating principles.

---

[21] *Smirt* (New York: McBride, 1934), *Smith* (McBride, 1934), *Smire* (Doubleday, Doran, 1937). *The Works of James Branch Cabell* (McBride, 1928-1929), 18 vols.
The King Was in His Counting House (Farrar, 1938), There Were Two Pirates (Farrar, 1946), The Devil's Own Dear Son (Farrar, 1949).

Peter Ibhetson is a pre-dream or early-morning sexual fantasy of an easily recognizable sort, buttered over with conventional literary sentiment.

Joyce's dreamer dreams about his family imbroglio and, in the process, about Joyce's own family, books and critics.

All these matters are very close to the surface of the waking mind, and in the books and poems have undergone little of the process Freud called "secondary elaboration," the process of turning the basic concerns of the psyche into logical or semi-logical constructs. On the contrary, the waking material seems to be the stuff of these dreams, with not much serious transformation from what might be thought of—in the Freudian sense—as fundamental, deeply buried concerns.

Nor do the Jungian archetypes play more than a superficial, imposed, literary role, even in *Finnegans Wake,* which is most successful as a book of dream where it particularizes the ongoing dream itself and allows the archetypes to fend for themselves; *FW* fascinates most readers through its word games, which are particular to Joyce and Carroll, and moves most readers by means of the naturalistic novel which lies beneath them; the archetypes and other recurrent figures, like the numeralogy, are relatively sterile ground.

The nightmares of interrupted or fevered sleep, the dreams which occur earlier in the night when we surface from the abyss for nineteen or twenty-four minutes, are less well represented. It can be seen, however, that *Alice's Adventures in Wonderland* is a blacker—as befits an earlier—dream than is *Through the Looking-Glass;* the trial scene, with its atmosphere of fear, rising to Alice's sudden denunciation—"Who cares for you? You're nothing but a pack of cards!"—and the cards' attack upon her, contrasts rather sharply with the later, little more than petulant shaking of the Red Queen down into a kitten—"And it really was a kitten, after all."

The ninth chapter of *Finnegans Wake,* immensely long and dense and menacing, culminates in a mass attack upon the dreamer by his customers and a growing mob, from which he can escape only by turning his tavern into a houseboat and putting out to sea; it is followed at once by a short, disjunct erotic dream in which the dreamer seems to be only an observer, and then by a whole series of increasingly shallow trial scenes during the last of which the dreamer may actually have awakened for the course of several pages. Overall, furthermore, *Finnegans Wake* is divided into four sections which both in length and in content prefigure the four stages of dream which have since been observed by Kleitman, Aserinsky and their followers. Finally, the three books of Cabell's dream-cycle, as I have mentioned above, include a central one in which the personality of the dreamer is almost obliterated, only returning — as in Joyce — as sleep lightens and morning threatens.

It may be untrue to maintain, as Oscar Wilde did, that Life imitates Art; but the naturalism of the literary dreams from Kepler to Cabell is notable for its faithfulness to and prediction of current scientific fact and theory.

It will be interesting to see what subsequent artists will build upon the facts and models now in hand... or in what way they will reject them in favor of some newer model only more centuries can test. Thus far, they have been well ahead of research in the field — which may not justify Wilde's dictum, but does suggest that Ezra Pound might have been right to believe that "Artists are the antennae of the race."

8. THE LONG NIGHT OF A VIRGINIA AUTHOR

1. Two 20th Century Dreams

James Branch Cabell's trilogy *The Nightmare Has Triplets* [22] stands at the heart of his later work much as *Figures of Earth*, *The Silver Stallion*, and *Jurgen* stand at the heart of his 18-volume "Biography of the Life of Manuel" (which was never actually published under this title).[23] It was in this trilogy that Cabell defined his dream country, with the Forest of Branlon brooding in its midst—a Forest to which Poictesme was only one of a number of outlying countries, and which was to recur in three of Cabell's five subsequent novels.[24]

The work itself is a dream, and before considering it in its own terms, it is tempting to use it to push a little farther Nathan Halper's comparisons of Cabell with James Joyce.[25] Neither man, probably, would have welcomed the comparison, but it has its critical uses.

---

[22] Nathan Halper, "Joyce and James Branch Cabell," A Wake Newslitter, VI (August 1969), 49; "Cabell/Joyce and Joyce/Cabell," Kalki, IV (Spring 1970), 9.

[23] *Smirt*, p. viii.
Smirt, p. vii.

[24] Padraic Colum and Margaret Freeman Cabell, eds., *Between Friends* (Harcourt, 1962).
James Branch Cabell, *L'incubo*, intro. Fernanda Pivano, illus. Fabrizion Clerici (Milan: Mondadori).

[25] James Branch Cabell, *Quiet, Please* (University of Florida Press, 1952), p. 27.
Maurice Duke, *James Branch Cabell's Library: A Catalogue*. Unpublished thesis, Virginia Commonwealth University, 1968, items 1422, 1423.
Duke, item 1421.

Like Cabell, Joyce produced one play, *Exiles,* and one volume of poetry (for though *Chamber Music, Pomes Penyeach* and *Ecce Homo* were published separately, combining them as the *Collected Poems,* as is now customary, still results in a slim book); but, like Cabell, his reputation rests upon a multi-volume opus dealing with a recurrent cast over a fairly long period of time (in Joyce's case, roughly 1885-1904; in Cabell's 1231-1909): *Dubliners, A Portrait of the Artist as a Young Man,* and *Ulysses.* Like Cabell, he followed this huge "work of day" (even a paperback text of the Joyce trilogy fills 1,172 closely-set pages) with a somewhat shorter (628 pp.) "book of night," *Finnegans Wake.*

The *Wake* and the *Nightmare* are alike in many respects. For example:

1) *Finnegans Wake* seems to be the dream of a Dublin publican during a single night's sleep, beginning shortly after "chucking-out time" (before midnight) and ending at dawn. It begins just as the dreamer falls asleep; it is possible that he is awake for ten or twenty minutes in the penultimate chapter, but he may be dreaming this, too.

Cabell's *Nightmare* is the dream of a Virginia author during a single night's sleep, or possibly only during the last half hour of it. Like Joyce's dreamer, Cabell's is still asleep at the end of the work; though he is intermittently conscious of the ticking of the clock in his bedroom, as Joyce's dreamer hears the Dublin churchbells, this only serves to remind him that he is still dreaming.

2) Both works, despite their surface peculiarities, are naturalistic novels—the Joyce implicitly through the story it reflects, the Cabell by its direct claim to be a "full-length dream-story which obeyed the actual and well-known laws of a normal dream" of an adult male.[26] Cabell's dream, he says, "attempts to extend the naturalism of Lewis Carroll."[27]

---

[26] A contemporary reviewer of *Smirt,* however, took quite the opposite tack: "No doubt Mr. Cabell is aware that he is anticipating James Joyce's 'Work in Progress.' It may be open to question whether 'Anna Livia' or 'Smirt' does more to repair the sexlessness of 'Alice'; it cannot be

3) Both present a dreamer who is not supposed to be the author, yet both dreams contain important autobiographical elements, even going so far—in both cases—as to include quotations from unfavorable book reviews of the authors' previous works.

4) Both are concerned in part with a father-son rivalry.

5) In both, the main character becomes divided into two persons, one a poet, the other a man of affairs.

6) In both, a letter written by one of these persons is carried by the other to the father.

7) In both, the dreamer sees himself buried, and later displaced by his progeny, but returns, though with his powers somewhat diminished.

8) Both dreams range widely through history, literature, mythology and folklore.

9) Both contain both overt and covert literary criticism, some of it in the form of pastiche.

10) Both cannibalize material from newspapers and other daylight sources contemporary with the dreamer, to the point where both books must become steadily more incomprehensible on this level to readers born too late to remember the ephemerae of the period.

11) Stylistically, both works make considerable use of anagrams, catalogues, puns, tropes and verse.

12) Even the fates of these two "night" works were similar, allowing for the difference in stature and reputation between the two authors. *Finnegans Wake* is not the incomprehensible coterie novel those unfamiliar with its text and history often de-

---

doubted, however, that Mr. Joyce makes the greater contribution to the literature of the dream... there is... a paragraph which seems to be a parody of the Joycean dream, and quite a good one..."—George Stevens, "The Two Cabells," March 10, 1934. These quotations come from an apparently incomplete clipping found by William Leigh Godshalk in a second-hand copy of *Smirt* purchased in 1969. We have been unable to identify it further.

[27] *The Witch-Woman* (Farrar, Straus, 1948).
The Nightmare Has Triplets (Doubleday, Doran, 1937).

scribe it to be, but even those critics most devoted to it feel uneasily that it is not the masterpiece *Ulysses* is, and it seems wholly unlikely that Penguin Books will ever pay The Society of Authors $50,000 for the paperback rights to it. Cabell's dream trilogy has had even harder sledding: McBride optimistically put both *Smirt* and *Smith* through two printings before publication day, but evidently the books died, for two years passed before *Smire* appeared from a different publisher. (It would be interesting to know the details of this falling-out between Cabell and his major publisher from 1915. The correspondence published in *Between Friends*[28] does not reach that far.) Apparently, too, there was only one foreign edition, a deluxe Italian one[29]; in contrast, not only was there a Penguin *Jurgen* as well as an English hardback, but the novel was also translated into Yiddish, German, Dutch, Czech and Swedish. (There will almost surely never be a translation of *Finnegans Wake*, although one chapter of it, *Anna Livia Plurabelle*, was put into French under Joyce's supervision.)

These parallels are doubtless somewhat misleading, startling though they are in many ways, especially when they are added to those made by Halper. Let me now stress some differences:

1) Cabell maintained to the end of his life the stance of a non-reader of *Ulysses*[30] (although he owned two copies, one of them kept with his vacation detective stories[31]) and the last volume of the *Nightmare* was published two years before *Finnegans Wake;* although Cabell owned a 1928 version, in a presentation copy,

---

[28] Anthony Burgess, *A Shorter Finnegans Wake* (Faber and Faber, 1966), pp. 7-8.
[29] See my "Cabell as Kabbalist," *Kalki*, III (1969), 11.
[30] James Branch Cabell, *Preface to the Past* (McBride, 1936), p. 67.
  Preface to the Past, p. 44.
[31] See my "The Geography of Dream," *Kalki*, IV (1970), 90.

of *Anna Livia Plurabelle*[32] there is not the faintest evidence that he ever read it.

2) Cabell's dream is written in the cadenced, elliptical, but otherwise standard English of his mature style. Joyce's, as is notorious, is written in a vastly complex language the author called Eurish, based on English but much of it nearly impossible to read without the same kind of attention one would devote to a foreign dialect in a highly decadent state.

3) Cabell's dream works on several levels, but the most complex of these does not go much beyond allegory. Joyce's dream is symbolic, and in addition, psychoanalytic, with specific indebtedness to Jung's concept of the collective unconscious.

4) As a result of these differences in approach—from Carroll on the one hand, and Jung on the other—the ranging of Cabell's dreamer through space, time and literature never passes beyond the bounds of what the dreamer has personally experienced or read; while Joyce's dreamer is Everyman, who dreams of all times and all places and all events, in all languages.

5) There is not a word of direct explanation in *Finnegans Wake* about what kind of book it is; the dream stands alone, colossal, enigmatic, poetic and frightening. Cabell's *Nightmare* leads off with an 11-page preface which tells the reader just what the author is up to, and his dreamer drifts from wakefulness into sleep almost imperceptibly during the first three chapters of the main text.

Clearly, as Dr. Johnson said of Ossian, a man could go on like this forever if only he would abandon his mind to it. I repeat specifically, therefore, what I have implied above: There seems to be no possibility that *Finnegans Wake* influenced *The Nightmare Has Triplets*, or vice versa.[33] The parallels are interesting

---

[32] See my "Cabell as Kabbalist," *op. cit.*; "Ninzian Gets One Right," *Kalki*, II (1967), 2; "More Spells," *Kalki*, II (1968), 62.

[33] Dr. Christopher Evans, "25,000 Dreams," *The Sunday Times Magazine* (London), 30 November 1969.

only insofar as they illuminate what might be common operations of the creative process in contemporary authors of stature sharing a common culture and tackling what was fundamentally the same fiction problem: writing a novel cast throughout as a dream.

We must return, however, to the really major point of similarity: That both works involved an attempt by the author to follow up his major and successful work—successful in terms of fame as well as form—with another which was both an extension of the earlier work and a new development. In Cabell's case, there are a number of conscious allusions to details in the "Biography" (as *Finnegans Wake* also refers to earlier Joyce works) which I shall note below, but it is perhaps more interesting to note that Cabell had been edging in this general direction for many years. His first novel to be a popular success, *The Cream of the Jest*, contains a series of dreams, and furthermore, they are the dreams of an author the name of whose country home, Alcluid, conceals Cabell's own farm, Dumbarton Grange. Jurgen considers all the adventures recorded in his novel to have been a dream, and it contains a dream-within-a-dream (his meeting with Horvendile and Perion de la Foret). And the whole of *The High Place,* as is revealed on the last page, is a dream.

But though some of the dream episodes of *The Cream of the Jest* are convincing as such, both *Jurgen* and *The High Place* are too consistent and too highly structured to resemble real dreams. In these, the dream is a convention, or as Cabell himself puts it, one of the commonest of the romancer's devices. It was not until the trilogy that Cabell addressed himself to writing a work which should be truly dream-like in detail, in structure, and even in the systematic omission of the sense of taste and smell. (Joyce's dream includes both but is very low in visual emphasis.) The outcome, though seriously flawed, is unique in American literature and deserves to be better known.

2. The Structure of the Nightmare

The imaginary countries of Rorn and Ecben are important in the *Nightmare* (as is Poictesme); they also appear in one part of the "Biography," *The Way of Ecben* (1929). However, the Forest of Branlon does not so appear, even in a 1948 revision.[34] More surprisingly, it is not mentioned in *Smirt,* either. This fact is one of several pieces of internal evidence—which of course would need to be confirmed by Cabell letters—that Cabell did not originally intend his nightmare to be a trilogy. The "Author's Note" to *Smirt* makes no mention of a sequel; instead, it concludes in apparent valedictory: "Finally, I rejoice to have rectified, at least, and at howsoever long a last, my own delinquency in this matter [i.e., to write truthfully about human dreams]" (p. xvii). *Smith* has no preface, but the list of previous works facing the title page announces *Smire* to be in preparation; yet not even with *Smire* does the trilogy acquire its overall title, which appears for the first time in a later pamphlet.[35] Against this view it might be argued that *Smirt* ends rather suddenly and without any emergence from the dream, the entry to which has been gradual and carefully prepared—indeed, Cabell almost sneaks into it; but I think quite a good case could be made for *Smirt* as a novel complete in itself, all the same.

Be that as it may, the work as it now stands *is* a trilogy, tied together in the last two volumes with all the cunning that Cabell, a master of the afterthought, had developed through the experience of trying (I do not think he succeeded) to make one work of his first twenty. Told with the baldness necessary to abridgement, the course of the nightmare is this:

The hero is a successful Virginia author, living in Richmond, whose waking name we do not know, though he is very like Cabell. (Another parallel with *Finnegans Wake;* there the hero's

---

[34] Personal communication from Professor Godshalk, cf. footnote on p. 110 above.
[35] "To Rhadamanthus, Snarling," *Kalki,* II (1968), 43.

name is Humphrey Chimpden Earwicker, but Anthony Burgess has offered persuasive arguments that this is only a dream name, and that in waking life the dreamer's name may be Porter.[36]) He is dozing off one afternoon when the black wooden dog in which he keeps bits of string (Cabell owned such a dog, made for him by his son Ballard) speaks to him, which makes him aware that he is beginning to dream. Apparently, however, he resists the dream, for it does not recur until a half-hour before dawn of the succeeding night, announced by a flowing 188-word sentence of free association (which includes the phrases "stream of consciousness" and "it is a poor art that never re-Joyces nowadays"). At first his dreams are close to his waking concerns; he meets his readers and gives a newspaper interview. Then, however, he meets the legendary Arachne, whose husband-hunting he avoids by referring to his wife of waking life, Jane. Arachne, like the black dog, knows his dream name, which he reluctantly accepts.

Leaving her in her spider-lair-cum-gateway, Smirt finds himself in Heaven conversing with the All-Highest, Who greets him as a fellow-author, discusses literary matters with him—Smirt persuades Him not to write a sequel to the Bible—and bestows upon him a lucky coin. Again pursued by his admirers, Smirt encounters another girl, this time the blonde princess of his childhood dreams, who, when he rejects her, turns into the Devil, now a business partner of the All Highest, who tells him that the lucky piece confers omnipotence—within limits. The Devil too makes him a present, of a planet, suitably revised to satisfy Smirt's criticism of it; and on Smirt's acceptance of this, vanishes, leaving Smirt to contemplate his own grave and that of his wife, both graves apparently several hundred years old. Here he is again surrounded by his admirers, and encounters a new young woman, Tana, who lives in a cave furnished by,

---

[36] "Romance and the Novel," *American Mercury*, January 1936, p. 114.

among other things, the black onyx clock of his waking life. This she stops at 6:12, since at 13:00 he will become a god. *(Finnegans Wake* also has two magic times with a similar arithmetical relationship, 5:66 and 11:32.) He seduces her, but his curiosity leads him to start the clock again; whereupon she deserts him for a rabbit which lives in the moon.

The black dog comes for Smirt, and leads him out of the cave to Amit, the home of the Stewards of Heaven—the seven demiurges of the talmudic creation myths, here appearing as named and described in the *Arbatel of Magic,* a grimoire of 1575.[37] After some literary discussion, the Stewards get drunk; and when they recover, Smirt criticizes their management of the universe and as an example of better things calls up a vision of Arachne, by means of his lucky piece. The Stewards warn him against her and the vision vanishes, whereupon Smirt replaces it with a vision of the blonde princess, for whom he creates a world; but this too is dismissed, and he descends to the planet he was given, now revised to consist exclusively of "lands beyond common-sense," to search for the legend of Arachne.

Here upon a glass mountain he fathers upon Airel, a "conversation woman," a son named Elair; marries Oriana the wife of the Dwarf King, but without issue; is cursed and lives witlessly for two fortnights in the dead city of Ras Sem, where he is again visited by the black dog; and marries Rani, the South Wind's third daughter, in a paper palace erected upon a weather-vane. (Actually, he avoids marrying her in *Smirt,* but counts her among his past wives in *Smith.*) None of these women satisfies him, and hence he returns to Amit to write for Arachne a new legend.

Here he is repeatedly interrupted at this task by his public, and against them invokes first the Angel of Death and then someone named Wise Aldemis, who turns out to be a past mis-

---

[37] The price in 1964.

tress now called Mrs. Murgatroyd; but they cannot help him. The onyx clock strikes thirteen, and the Stewards of Heaven return. These, followed by the black dog, abandon Amit to Smirt. After being briefly pestered by a brash young realistic novelist, Smirt is left alone with a spider, who covers Heaven with webs and divests Smirt even of his past. The spider, of course, is the true Arachne, who persuades him to abandon Amit and godhead to become a shopkeeper; but Smirt warns her that if anything serious were to happen to him (such as being eaten by his wife), he would wake up, a condition which she reluctantly accepts. *Explicit* volume one.

All this is indeed exceedingly dreamlike, and although the fairy-tale recurrent structure somewhat recalls *Jurgen*—which also purported to be a dream—its logic is true dream logic, and quite new from Cabell. In *Smith*, however, he reverts to more familiar ground. Here we find that Arachne has indeed tried to eat Smirt, despite the warning, and that he has not in fact awakened, but now finds himself only the local deity of the Forest of Branlon, under his new name. The pocket piece has lost all its power but that of providing him with cigarettes, although he can perform some other small magics; and he makes his living selling to the inhabitants of Dreamland small leaden keys which give them temporary access to the sordid lives of the waking world—in short, slumming expeditions. The Forest he has designed, and maintains, as a refuge for dreams in the broader sense, that is, the heroic and nonsensical aspirations of mankind.

Most of this is established in a preliminary meeting with Charlemagne, whose lieutenants explore the Forest and duly report what sort of place it is. At this point, however, Smith desires to be reunited with the four sons he fathered upon Tana, Airel, Rani and Arachne. Almost all of the remainder of *Smith*, from page 49 to page 298 (of 313), consists of four novellas about the sons, Volmar, Clitandre, Elair and Little Smirt, who are summoned to Branlon by four of five magics of a magician named Urc Tabaron. The fifth magic re-unites Smith with Tana, with whom he rests content despite the ticking of the onyx clock.

This sub-structure—almost independent stories inside a frame—is that of *The Silver Stallion,* and Smith's role in it is very like that of Horvendile in the earlier novel and indeed elsewhere in the "Biography." Considered alone, *Smith* is a well-made novel of a peculiar kind (Arthur Machen's *The Three Imposters,* 1897, is a possible antecedent), but it is not in the least dream-like. In fact, were it not for the reminders of its ties with *Smirt,* it would pass for just another volume of the "Biography"; and it is perhaps not unindicative that one of its four central episodes could well sail under the title of one of the unwritten episodes of *The Witch-Woman,* "The Lean Hands of Volmar,"[38] while the Bel-Imperia of Little Smirt's story, who may have come from Kyd's *The Spanish Tragedy,* was once to have been a mistress of Dom Manuel himself.

With *Smire* we are back upon true dream ground. The newly renamed dreamer has been expelled from Branlon and is trying to find his way back, through Carthage, where he has an affair (pre-Aeneas) with Dido and again meets the Devil in the guise of a priest of Apollo named Smike; through Israel, where he meets Miriam just before the Annunciation and is sent packing by Gabriel; past his waking wife Jane, and thence to a reunion with Arachne outside the castle of Brunbelois in Poictesme. (The relationships of the dream countries and the real ones are most carefully worked out, but are not to the purpose here.) He finds that his first dream self, Smirt, is now the Count of Poictesme, and Arachne his Countess. Smirt tells him that he can recover

---

[38] Escape velocity was first attained a good deal earlier than orbital velocity, in point of fact. Several years before Sputnik I, an American group sent aloft an unmanned rocket bearing as its payload a shotgun cartridge; the pellets from that cartridge were the first human artifacts to leave the Earth forever.

Branlon only through the All-Highest, and gives him a letter of introduction to Him, which Smire, now no longer even a local god but only "a tired letter carrier," bears through an endless grey space to the ticking of the onyx clock.

After another long literary discussion with the All-Highest, and another encounter with his public, Smire passes on to the House of Moera (Gk. *moira,* fate?), "the power above all gods and the mother of all myths," whom Smire suspects of having created him, too. She sends him back to the Devil, who gives him magic spectacles by which he is able to enter a picture which is (though it is not so named) the Garden Between Dawn and Sunrise from *Jurgen.* Here he recovers the memories of which Arachne had robbed him in the first volume, and, like Jurgen, meets himself as a boy, who of course is able at once to tell him the way to Branlon.

So Smirt-Smith-Smire returns to his beloved Forest—but he finds it in the keeping of his four sons, to whom he is less than a ghost. Not entirely dissatisfied—for Branlon still seems to him to be a superb creation—he goes down to Clioth to share "in the fate common to every god," that is, to be forgotten. A part of this fate is Moera, who turns out to be also Jane (or the other way around). Then, rejoined by the black dog, and to a chorus of greetings by his public, the dreamer—now nameless—is ferried by Charon back into waking life.

Thus the *Nightmare,* structurally and in tone, is as a whole an uneven work. It is a sandwich, two volumes of authentic dream with a very good but—for Cabell—standard fantasy-saga in its middle.

3. Some Other Ticks of the Clock

Cabell would not be Cabell without cross reference and self-quotation, and the *Nightmare* contains many carry-overs and additional elucidations (especially the geographical ones) of interest to readers of the "Biography." I have already noted the relationship to *The Way of Ecben*, and the reappearances of Poictesme, Volmar, Bel-Imperia, and the Heavenly Stewards (Och and Bethor are in *The Silver Stallion*), as well as the Garden from *Jurgen*. As the two Stewards are joined in the *Nightmare* by their five fellows, so on page 170 of *Smith* Cabell finally names most of the grimoires from which he had been drawing his magic from *The Silver Stallion* on (though, as he says, not all of them). Antan reappears from *The High Place, Figures of Earth* and *Something About Eve*, and so, through an obviously accidental confusion with a town named Strathgor, does the Rathgar of *Figures of Earth*. And, at the beginning of *Smith*, Dom Manuel's sword Flamberge has at last returned to the hands of its original and greatest owner.

The creator of Ageus, Vel-Tyno, Sesphra, and the countries of *Something About Eve* may also be seen playing the anagram game in the *Nightmare,* though with his customary ambiguity. Urc Tabaron, the rustic magician and contriver of the elixir of eternal youth, is appropriately *contra urba*. Elair the Song-Maker, if one allows in Middle English (which Cabell knew very well), is "a lire," and both he and his mother Airel are anagrams of Shakespeare's Ariel; his mother, this "conversation woman" with her four winds from the four quarters, suggests a wind-harp, and Elair appropriately pipes them both away upon the west wind (*Smirt,* p. 163). Rani, or rain, the third daughter of the South Wind, is served by and rules philosophers, good companions for an Austral day. The dead city of Ras Sem, in which Smirt wanders brainless for two fortnights observing petrified citizens captured like the inhabitants of Pompeii while shopping, love-making, straining at stool, shaving and "other kindly and laborious and trivial doings," while he hears the ticking of the onyx clock and the buzzing of a blue-bottle fly, and sees only faintly beyond grey clouds the faces of his beloved dead, is the world of the naturalistic novel, which reduces to "smears"—for "these were not the instruments, Smirt reflected, with which people made urbane thoughts" (p. 175). The Wise Aldemis of the same book, whom Smirt thinks he might have invented on the spot, turns out to be simply "mislead"; while the respelled mother of all myths and the power above all gods—who is also Jane—is, not at all surprisingly, *amore*. (Nor is it surprising that Jane, like Felix Kennaston's wife in *The Cream of the Jest*, should turn out to be a female Janus.)

These minutiae are of course of little inherent interest; but as is usual with Cabell, together they offer clues to approaching the allegory.

4. A Preliminary Assessment

What does it all come to? As I have noted, *Smith* cannot be a dream; for one thing, for the most part it has no dreamer, the point of view shifting to each of the four sons in turn. We can say confidently that this never happens in real dreams; the unconscious part of the mind seems to be as determinedly egocentric as is the waking consciousness, as has been shown by an analysis of 25,000 dreams, the largest sample in psychological history. (This criticism has also been made of *Finnegans Wake*, which for a few pages seems to move out of Earwicker's mind into that of Joyce himself.) Yet it would be impossible to cut *Smith* out of the *Nightmare*. Not only is Branlon one of Cabell's finest concepts—however belatedly arrived at—but the search for it, and the bittersweet outcome of the search, is at the very center, and is the motive power, of *Smire*.

Nevertheless, the stories of the four sons could well have gone in some other place. (William Leigh Godshalk suggests that the ego, as in the *Wake*, moves into the offspring, but I can see no sign that Cabell intended us to understand this.) They are good stories, and they do have the additional virtue of containing most of the new geography, but Smith's role in them is minor to the point of superfluity and they advance the dream only insofar as they set the stage for the sons' eventual usurpation of

Branlon. This much could have been done in a quarter of the space Cabell allots it.

I could wish, too, that Cabell had devoted less space to attacking his critics and the stupidity of his public, as I have said in more detail elsewhere. Since his dreamer is an author, it is natural for him to have a consciousness in his dream of hostility and incomprehension, but the trilogy would have been the better for a more muted and less bitter handling of it. *Smirt*, after all, does bear the sub-title "An *Urbane* Nightmare" (italics mine).

For all its bitterness, though, I think that Smirt's confrontation with the young realistic novelist who is going to supplant him, the "heir presumptive," belongs in the work. This sense of having successors in one's footsteps who will inevitably replace one, and whom, far worse, one doesn't even understand, is common in male dreams, and not only the dreams of male novelists, either. Cabell handles it well, and, as it turns out, it also serves as an adumbration of the obsolescence of the dreamer by his sons.

But Cabell's thrifty habit of using up every one of his occasional pieces — on this score he has the single-mindedness of a pack-rat — also flaws the work. The long lecture on the theory of the novel, imported into Chapter 24 of *Smire* almost verbatim from his review of E. R. Eddison's *Mistress of Mistresses* is quite unnecessary, since the action of the third volume demonstrates the point so well that we do not need to be hectored about it too. (In the "Author's Note" to *Smire*, Cabell defends this as a parabasis, to replace a formal preface — perhaps one requested by his new publisher; but superfluous it remains.) No doubt most readers are as stupid as Cabell depicts them to be, but one wishes for the return of the Cabell who wrote solely for an ideal audience and to the devil with the rest of it.

In short, the *Nightmare* is weak on two of Cabell's seven auctorial virtues, urbanity and symmetry. Of course it is economical in the narrow sense to use up one's old book reviews, but it is a false economy in the end to shovel into a work of art huge patches of material—they account for a full third of the length of the *Nightmare*—which it doesn't need.

However, the lapse was temporary. *Smire* was followed immediately by *The King Was In His Counting House*, one of the best novels Cabell ever wrote; that it was not also an instant best seller completely baffles me, for it has all the ingredients.

And the two thirds of the *Nightmare* that are relevant are also brilliant, original and very moving. Perhaps only Cabell, too, could have managed to bring it to a climax not in dramatic action or emotional confrontation, but in a credo:

"Now, but this absurd out-of-date creature is telling us, yet again, that the dream is better than the reality!"

He said then: "To the contrary, I am telling you that for humankind the dream is the one true reality."

One does not have to agree to be able to see, and with admiration, that *The Nightmare Has Triplets* mounts to this point with the inevitability common to all genuine works of art.

9. MUSIC OF THE ABSURD

As he faces the audience, the artist is at the focus of a battery of eight tape recorders, with an attendant by each. At a signal, he begins to speak. So do all eight tape recorders. Each one is playing a speech in his voice—but all the speeches are different, and in addition none of them is the speech the live artist himself is delivering.

Let us pause here, dear friends and gentle hearts, and ask: What is going on here? Is the artist actually a madman addressing an audience of psychiatrists? Or is it an experiment in one-man choral poetry reading which has gotten out of sync? Or is it just a Greenwich Village "happening"?

Any of these explanations would make sense, but the truth is almost beyond belief. The truth is:

This is supposed to be music.

The man with the nine voices is a dead-serious American composer named John Cage, and his composition of the moment is far from the weirdest he has concocted in the course of a relatively short career. If there are any committable cases in this hall, they are all in the audience, which consists almost entirely of people who are so afraid of being thought Philistines by posterity that they will sit earnestly still for anything that is offered to them as serious modern music, even if—as in this and a number of other famous cases—not a single musical note can be heard.

Let us repeat, this is by no means an extreme example, nor is Cage the only offender. The new concert music of the 20th Century has finally gone off the deep end, and is now more remote from its potential audience than the worst of avant-garde poetry ever was in any danger of becoming. If this trend continues—and it is in fact accelerating—the concert music that will be offered our children will be as minor an art as flower arranging, and communicating just as little.

The essence of this change is remarkably simple, though it has a complicated history and a disastrous outcome. Until our century, the serious composer's main concern was primarily to show that he was a better master of his medium than his predecessors. Today, with few but important exceptions, his primary concern is to be different.

Nobody denies, or would want to deny, the great changes that have occurred in Western music since the Greeks made the primary harmonic discovery—that women tend to sing the "same" melody an octave higher than men do. Almost all of these changes added to the expressivity of formal composition by allowing into the art devices, procedures, instruments and forms thought inadmissible by the preceding era. And it's also true that most of the innovators were denounced by their peers—composers and critics alike—as musical anarchists; and that in general, it is the innovators to whom we still listen with pleasure.

What's often forgotten in this defense of change for its own sake, however, is that the innovation did *not* always increase the expressivity of music by expanding the resources available to the composer. For example, in Bach's time, the elaborately contrapuntal Baroque style reached the end of its resources in the work of Bach himself, and was about to slide into decadence. At the time of his death, he was engaged in writing *The Art of the Fugue,* the definitive summary of what Baroque counterpoint alone could be expected to accomplish. The succeeding homophonic style, the style galant pioneered by the Mannheim school (which included several of Bach's own sons, two of them brilliant composers), was strikingly less demanding both to write and to listen to than the fugal knots into which Baroque music customarily tied itself.

None of the historical expansions and contractions are analogous in the least to what has been happening to music lately. All the changes of the past, no matter how radical, were changes within the traditional language in which music is written. Today's serious composers—or at least those who are being taken most seriously—have abandoned that language entirely, with results as predictable as those which would follow were a poet or novelist to abandon the use of words.

This comparison is not the utterance of a fanatic musical reactionary—the sort of concertgoing John Bircher who thinks that nothing worth listening to was written after Palestrina, Bach or Mozart—but that of a man who has drawn joy and sustenance from composers of all periods for all of his listening years. Worse: It is not even a metaphor, wild-eyed or otherwise, but a literal description of the situation as it obtains now.

What are we to make, for instance, of a composition for piano in which the hammers of the instrument are forbidden to strike the strings? In this work, only two sorts of sounds are to be heard: first, the almost inaudible percussive thump of a key being depressed, gently enough so that no note results; and second, the clicking of the pianist's fingernails as he draws the backs of his fingers over the ivory surfaces of the keyboard.

This composition is relatively conservative by present-day standards; that is, it is written in something vaguely resembling standard musical notation, and the instrument to be used is specified. A more typical product of this school of scoring is a geometrical diagram, in no way resembling the standard musical staff, over which the composer shakes ink blots from an old-fashioned fountain pen. It is then up to the performer to decide what these blots may represent in terms of standard musical notation, and what instruments, time signatures, durations of performance, and other musical parameters shall be assigned to them. This is called "realizing" the music, and of course every performer's realization is different, and a complete surprise to the composer.

Any man with a normal indignation quotient will decide for himself which composition of this school he considers most outrageous. My favorite, which is also one of the funniest, is a piece in which the notes (of which there are only a few, covering almost the entire possible tonal range) are written in a highly deformed oval, like a botched Rorschach test. The composer (guess who?) "specifies" that these notes may be played backward or forward, that the piece may last any length of time, and that any number and kinds of instruments may be used. One that actually *has* been used is the kazoo. (Many readers by now probably suspect me of making all this up, and I can't say that I blame them. I refer these doubters to Avakian JC-1, a recording of a *25-Year Retrospective Concert* [1934-1958] of Cage's music, including jeers and catcalls from the audience [which the random-music purist considers properly a part of the composition]. The recording is a three-record set, will cost you $25, and goes on forever.)

One of the most recent outbursts of the random composers is a subschool called "gestural," because it gives you something to look at as well as listen to. Gestural compositions were the core of six concerts at New York's Judson Hall in the fall of 1963. Their flavor is hard to convey, but it can be vaguely suggested. One composition by Karlheinz Stockhausen required the pianist (Frederic Rzewski, himself a gestural composer) to hammer the piano so mercilessly that he had to wear cutout gloves and dust the piano keys with baby powder. As critic John Gruen of the *New York Herald Tribune* remarked, "Avant-garde piano music is decidedly something to watch—it might even get worse."

Rzewski also participated in a thing called *Teatrino*, by Giuseppe Chiari, which called for, in addition to the piano, an alarm clock, a tape recorder, a power saw, a ping-pong ball and a family of squeaking rubber dolls. Against this assemblage poor Mr. Rzewski, who has only himself to blame, was required to read poetry.

This situation must seem truly incredible to anyone who has not been following the devolution of concert music over the past three decades, but such a reader can be assured that the compositions I've described above are not freaks. The men who are writing them do not represent the only group of serious lunatics in operation in our concert halls today, but about the only good thing that can be said for the competing schools is that most of their music is at least audible.

How did we get into this cul-de-sac?

The sequence of events isn't difficult to describe, but the fundamental misconceptions involved are extraordinarily rarefied. They have their common origin in the 19th Century notion that change means progress, which in the 20th Century has changed from a notion to a form of mental disease. It is a disease that has emerged from the blatant misuse of Darwin's scholium by the economic royalists, who assumed that all change must necessarily be for the better, an assumption of which we should have been thoroughly disabused by now.

In particular, there is no such thing as progress in the arts. As Richard H. Rovere remarked in an article about Ezra Pound, poetry is not a horse race. Poets differ from one another absolutely as well as relatively; and so it is with composers. The fact that Beethoven used a larger orchestra, a wider harmonic palette and a greater range of form than Mozart did is no guarantee that he was a "greater" composer. In fact, in all of these categories a good case could be made for the contention that he was a worse one. This case — to which I enthusiastically subscribe — would consist in showing that Mozart worked within his more limited compass better than Beethoven worked in his enlarged one. (As Stokowski has remarked, "Mozart understands instruments; Beethoven never did.") The ability to make a louder and more complicated noise than one's predecessor is not a patent of excellence, but a by-product of technology.

The history of the decay of 20th Century music into either noise or silence is rather straightforward. It begins almost exactly 100 years ago, when Wagner's opera *Tristan und Isolde* crawled out on the limb of what was then common harmonic practice in Western music and sawed it off. *Tristan* is a work of magic, and there is much that is traditional in it; but the parts of the opera that most disastrously influenced later composers are the sections where no one, not even Wagner, can tell you what key it is in. Wagner leaves the listener no way of avoiding this problem—he begins with it. From its very opening notes, the prelude to the first act of the opera is harmonically a seething mass of ambiguities, a snake pit of chromatic melodies squirming around one another without ever coming to rest.

Wagner's mastery of every procedure employed by his predecessors, however, was so complete that his departures from common practice are no longer in dispute; in context, they work. He was followed immediately by Richard Strauss, a thoroughgoing traditionalist who liked to mix keys occasionally, and to vary his melodies by interval stretching. The latter practice consists simply of jumping the second note in a melodic sequence to the same note one or more octaves away. Traditionally the stretched note is considered to be harmonically equivalent to the original—but the unstretched interval can be sung, whereas the stretched one can't. (In one Strauss composition, a simple theme originally heard within the compass of a single octave is pulled out to cover nine.)

Strauss' contemporaries sneered at his Mozartean formalism, but they loved his mixing of keys and the pulled-out intervals. The chromaticism of *Tristan,* the melodic leaps and clashing chords of *Elektra* and *Salome* fell on fertile ground in the person of Arnold Schoenberg, a late-Romantic composer who, finding himself unable to compete with Strauss or Gustav Mahler on traditional grounds, erected a whole church around a music which was forbidden to have any key at all, and in which the notes of the melodies are as isolated from one another as lighted windows in a deserted skyscraper.

Early on, this idiom, called atonality, was wedded to the very large late-Romantic orchestra of Strauss, Wagner and Mahler, producing a general roar of unfocused noise interesting only occasionally for its color (Schoenberg was an expert orchestrater). In response, Schoenberg — with monomaniac German thoroughness — went all the way back to the Baroque style of composition, with its overriding emphasis on counterpoint.

This was an inevitable retreat, for a music to which harmony is impossible has no other recourse but counterpoint. Thus was created the 12-tone scale, in which no key is to be respected, but the theme of any given composition is to contain all 12 notes of the chromatic scale, and the logic of all the rest of the work is to depend upon the order in which these tones occur.

This system of composition was the first major break in common practice in the history of Western music. Schoenberg was enough of a systematist to organize the new theory from top to bottom, all by himself. He was also so arid a composer that most of the works he wrote in the new idiom have as little emotional impact — though at least as much intellectual interest — as a Double-Crostic. Men of much greater gifts, among them Alban Berg and Igor Stravinsky, have since made much better use of the 12-tone system than Schoenberg was ever able to.

It is in fact impossible to manage duodecimal composition without genius, because it is so radical a departure from the whole corpus of common practice that the listener is confronted with an all-or-nothing situation: Either the music is great, or it's nowhere. As a result, there is no such thing as a minor 12-tone composer, and the system has never established itself as a new form of common practice. Instead, it went without any transition from being radical to being old hat.

But it established a precedent of enormous importance. Once given the notion that they were free to invent whole new systems of musical practice, innumerable pip-squeaks proceeded to do so with nothing else in mind but originality. One of these was Anton Webern, who had the sensible-silly notion of compressing bloop-bleep music in the Schoenberg system to a kind of *pointillisme,* to the point where each instrument in a major Webern work has only one or two notes to play, and the total work may last no longer than it would take the listener to desert the concert hall to mail a letter.

In the meantime, Schoenberg himself was further deserting music with the invention of the *Sprechstimme,* a style of vocalization in which the performer does not sing the note written, but just bleats in its approximate vicinity. The notes are written into the score, but the singer is not required to respect them.

The moment this invention was accepted, music slid all the way back to Greek drama, in which all the lines were intoned. The reintroduction of groaning and intoning into the complexities of Western concert music suddenly made it impossible for the listener to understand not only exactly what he was hearing, but what he was being asked to hear. Music now was no longer an art of organized, specific notes—which had been explored intensively by Pythagoras—but again one of the hoarse, nonspecific intonations of the jungle and the weather.

An offshoot of duodecimal composition is a system called microtonal music, in which the ordinary 12-tone octave is subdivided into further steps—usually 64. Again there is a certain maniacal logic to this procedure: All string and wind instruments can play the quarter tones impossible to the piano, and orchestral musicians with fine ears produce them automatically, thus giving the various keys their characteristic colors. (For example, to anyone but a pianist, B-sharp is not the same note as C.)

Increased fragmentation of the steps between notes, however, generates differences so small that only a very few exceedingly acute ears even profess to be able to hear them. Furthermore, if such tiny changes are to be detected at all they must be contiguous, with the inevitable result that most microtonal compositions sound like a cross between a cat fight and a distant four-alarm fire.

Microtonal music has been around at least 50 years without getting anywhere. The American composer Harry Partch, celebrated at length by *Time,* is only the most recent of a long line — though it must be admitted that Mr. Partch's names for his instruments (the Spoils of War, the Surrogate Kithara) and his compositions *(Visions Fill the Eyes of a Defeated Basketball Team in the Shower Room)* have a certain post-Satie charm, and his 43-tone octave is engagingly independent of any sort of theory.

Some of the experimentation that went on in this period was viable, as the example of Stravinsky shows. Stravinsky, like the composers of the Mannheim school, is one of music's great simplifiers: He weeded out the lush tangles of Romantic orchestration; dropped counterpoint almost completely; adopted a harmonic style which, though frequently dissonant, was much more diatonic and foursquare than the chromaticism with which his contemporaries surrounded him. All this was done in the interests of a rhythmic style of fearsome complexity, which could be sustained only by the fact that Stravinsky was — and is — a great melodist.

Stravinsky has worked in as many styles as Picasso, and, like the painter, none of his disciples has been able to make them work nearly as well. The most respected of such disciples today, the German composer Carl Orff, has not yet succeeded in saying anything that Stravinsky did not say better and with more economy 50 years ago in *Les Noces.* The years have neither forgotten nor looked kindly upon George Antheil's *Ballet Mecanique* for player pianos and an airplane engine, nor on Edgard Varese's *Ionisation* for percussion instruments and fire siren. Yet compared to what the cringing concertgoer is often asked to sit through today, these were conservative compositions—it has even become possible, given a creative imagination, to hear a sort of tune in *Ionisation*.

Today, originality in concert music is actually dominated by three different sorts of camp followers. The first of these schools contains the composers of random music, some of whom we have already met. Random music employs procedures that make it impossible for the composer to hear the work in his head as he writes it down, and no performance of a given composition can sound even remotely like another performance. The chief architect of this heap of rubble is our friend Mr. Cage, a composer of once burgeoning gifts who is now engaged in a prolonged act of artistic suicide.

Cage first came to the attention of the listening public with several compositions for what he called a "prepared" piano. The preparation consisted in placing inside the piano various objects, such as coins, erasers, bits of sponge and wooden matches, to modify the tones of various strings. There is obvious if limited promise in this invention: It makes it possible to write a work for piano and a large group of percussion instruments all of which can be handled by a single performer. Having in effect invented a whole new set of instruments, however, the composer is then obligated to go ahead and do something with them, which is exactly what John Cage has not done. Instead, he abandoned the prepared piano for his present career of noncomposition. In one work, he raises the lid of the piano keyboard, sits for three minutes listening to the noises the *audience* makes, and then closes the lid again. There exist concertgoers who take this seriously; perhaps they even exit whistling. Among these is the composer and critic Virgil Thomson, whose own music is of the simplest and most melodic sort; he finds the work of the random composers "rather jolly."

The second school of contemporary composition is *musique concrete,* a child of the tape recorder. Here the composer uses any sound that suits him—whether it is produced by a flute or a passing politician—either as is, or distorted by altering the speed of the tape. These snippets of tape are then pasted together to make a composition.

Cage has played with this idiom, too, though his finest effort with the loudspeaker is a composition that employs a number of radios, randomly tuned to whatever local stations happen to be broadcasting on the night of the concert, thus achieving a synthesis of *musique concrete* and the laws of chance.

The third school is electronic music, in which the sounds are produced directly by oscillators, such as those that make a Hammond organ go, but without any concern for whether or not the resulting notes sound like an organ, or like anything else you have ever heard in your life. Most composers in this group use pure sounds without overtones, which have no counterparts in nature or in the notes produced by any instrument—indeed, they were not even possible to produce until the age of electronics. This style attained some popular recognition a few years ago as the idiom for the musical score to an expensive but half-baked science-fiction movie called *Forbidden Planet;* and you may hear it at will by picking up your telephone, for the little tune that automatic dialing plays back to you these days is produced in the same way. Real notes are involved here, for the most part, which is a blessing; but again, all that has happened thus far is the invention of a new kind of instrument, with which nothing noteworthy has yet been done. There is a subgroup of this school: a team of French composers and engineers engaged in turning out whole new families of nonelectronic instruments. This is a good thing in itself—almost nothing new has entered the orchestra since the 18th Century—but thus far these developments are purely technological, and have no underlying inherent musical interest.

It is of course possible that both *musique concrete* and electronic noises might become beautiful in the hands of a genius, as did the 12-tone system in the hands of Berg. They are both in their infancy, and apparently still mostly in the hands of engineers and other aesthetic know-nothings. But the possibility exists. A model for it may be heard in the works of Bela Bartok, who used the 12-tone system, polytonality, interval stretching and everything else in the repertoire of his time as it suited him, without ever becoming a victim of the strictures of any single system. The recent space-travel opera, Karl-Birger Blomdahl's *Aniara,* is largely a 12-tone work which also uses *musique concrete,* electronic sounds, traditional tonalities and even folk tunes freely as expressive devices. It is a particularly interesting work, not because of its sensational libretto, but because the electronic and nonmusical sounds are thoroughly integrated into the score, and serve a musical function; they are not just sound effects.

No such hope, however, can be held out for random music, since it is and must always be in the hands of the laws of chance—not a notable source of masterpieces. It would seem axiomatic that no listener can learn to love a composition, especially if it is strange to his experience as well as to his ears, if he can hear it only once. Yet this system is inherent in random composition, and the preserving of such performances on tape or disc bears the same relationship to the theory of this kind of music as a blurred photograph of a man sliding into third base does to the game as a whole.

In the meantime, however, these schools multiply confusion, repel the listener and dehumanize the art. One of the most curious side effects is the increasing interest in computer-composer music, such as the suite for string quartet composed by a University of Illinois machine in the styles of four different (flesh-

and-blood) composers. Such works attract even musicians, because the computer can only be programed to follow set conventions, which must be fed to it by a human operator. When you set a computer to write like Bartok, it will do so faithfully (though not the least bit inventively). The computer represents the opposite side of an apothegm attributed to Arthur Miller: "We are all creative, but we are not all artists." The computer can be made to be an artist, but it cannot be made to be creative.

Most composers today are neither. Until some semblance of a common practice—either old or new—begins to emerge among them, most listeners (even the polite and the timid) will return in their hearts to a previous century, when even the most difficult music could be counted upon, with study and devotion, to make some sense.

[The following is Mr. Blish's own contribution to the excesses of modern music.]

The Art of the Sneeze

I have often been asked to reveal some of the secrets of successful sneezing, especially in the spring; and now that my farewell concert is behind me, I feel it is only fair to offer a few suggestions for the guidance of aspirants to this high art.

The novice almost invariably feels that—given a good instrument—his range can be almost limitless, since he has all of the world's languages to choose from. But this notion contradicts one of the first principles of sneezing: *The sneeze-word should never get in the way of the sneeze.* This rules out a great deal of German almost at once. In German nouns in particular, there is often so much sheer pronunciation going on as to quite overwhelm the vehicle—a phenomenon often noted by lovers of the art-song. However, quite tasteful effects can be achieved with some of the softer German infinitives, such as "umfassen."

On the other hand, most French and Portuguese words tend in themselves to suggest that the speaker has a slight head-cold. Hence they require great mastery in their use, if the audience is not to be left in doubt that anything was said at all. Needless to say, the true artist can take advantage of this apparent drawback to produce experiences of high subtlety, but in general the beginner is well advised to *avoid onomatopoeia.*

This leads naturally to the third basic rule, which is that *the sneeze should never physically affect the audience.* Only the crudest performer resorts to such assaults as "Bang, splat!" There is of course a grey or border area here, exemplified by such words as "Petrouchka," but the inexperienced had best reserve even these for *alfresco* performances.

The strictures above may lead the reader to suppose that I am counselling the avoidance of explosive consonants, but this is far from the case. Spelling is not nearly as important as where the accent falls in the word. The difficulty with "bishopric," for example, is not the initial "B" (though it does present its own problems) but the fact that the stress falls at the beginning, the rest being pure anticlimax. Russian words with delayed stresses, no matter how consonant-sprinkled, can be overwhelming; I have seen "snegourotchka" leave an entire auditorium quite dazed.

Some virtuosi are famous for the ability to sneeze entire sentences, but I have always felt that this is misapplied mastery and had best be left for sideshows. One performer, whom I shall not name, used as an encore a sentence borrowed from a Lovecraftian short story by Charles R. Tanner, which went "'Ng topuothikl Shelomoh, m'kthoqui hnirl." Since Mr. Tanner just made this sentence up out of his head—except for "Shelomoh," which he got off the top of a bottle—the stress may be placed anywhere, and the performer in question of course delayed it to the very last word. While this sort of thing can dazzle an unsophisticated audience, it will soon be seen through for what it is — the sacrifice of content to technique.

The student had far better model himself on those masters who devote themselves to the *emotional* burden of the sneeze, which can often be conveyed through apparently simple means. No one is ever likely to improve upon the magnificent Lester del Rey, who has moved millions of radio listeners to tears with an unassuming but profound "Ah-choo, Goddamit!"

Part III

10. A SCIENCE FICTION COMING OF AGE

In *The Shape of Future Things,* Brian W. Aldiss notes that his future was largely determined by the discovery of magazine science fiction at the age of thirteen. The same thing happened to me, when I was nine, and I can even place the date: June, 1931. And it seems to me that the half of the Twentieth Century that I have seen, fifty years plucked out of about the middle of it, has been science-fictional from first to last, for non-readers as well as for me. There have been very few exterior events, even including some political ones, which cannot be found earlier in the pages of some sf story. My sense of wonder seems to lie pretty near the surface, for it is capable of being turned on by almost anything; but one of the chief marvels of my existence has been the feeling that for me, events did not so much "happen" as "come true."

Curious; I cannot suppose that I'm unique in looking at events in this way, and yet though I have met about seventy-five science-fiction writers, many of whom I know or knew well, and uncountable hundreds of its readers, nobody has ever mentioned having this sensation. It is like looking at history standing on one's head. I suppose it is easier to be put off by the enormous numbers of sf predictions which *haven't* come true — its reputation as a literature of prophecy is vastly overblown, and survives only by ignoring its misses — but it seems to me that even in the 1930's it was possible to exercise a sort of common sense about the future, and to pick out the virtually inevitable coming events from the welter of sheer romancing. Speaking about some successful forecasting of his own, Robert A. Heinlein has described it as "about as startling as for a man to look out a train window, see that another train is coming head-on toward his own on the same track—and predict a train wreck." Just so; but the trick requires an instinct for the probable that doesn't seem to be very widely distributed. It has to be regarded as a gift, since I had it at the age of nine: the ability to see, for example, that interplanetary travel was as inevitable as Mr. Heinlein's train wreck, whereas time-travel was just a romancer's game.

The pulp magazines were not strangers to me even at nine; for several years I had been avidly following those which specialised in stories about World War I aerial fighting, magazines with titles like *Battle Aces, Flying Aces,* and *War Birds*.

I knew all of the major military aircraft of 1914-1918 at sight, and still do, and built clumsy balsa-wood models of some of them. All my models were of German craft, which I suppose might be interpreted as a sign that I was already seeing myself as on the outs with the world (as in fact I was, since my parents were divorced and I was the block sissy to boot), and needed to identify myself with the enemy. However, William of Occam says we must not multiply entities without reason, and it is perhaps sufficient to note that for brilliance and variety the German airplane designs far outmatched the Allied ones; I still feel both amazed and a little awed by the Fokker D-9, which had a short, stubby body and *three* wings, and by all accounts could climb faster than anything else of its period—no mean advantage in a form of combat where getting above (and behind) one's opponent was the chief aim of every maneuver. And a major difficulty with the psychological interpretation is that in this special sphere the Germans were not the losers; had air power been as important in 1914-1918 as it was in World War II, subsequent history would have been very different.

This was made clear in the stories themselves. Impossibly romantic though most of them were, they never disguised the fact that in the air, the Germans were always ahead; nor did they look away from the additional fact that the death rate among the young, badly-trained Allied pilots was enormous— once they reached an aerodrome, they had an average life expectancy of three weeks. Yet the stories also emphasized a sort of chivalry between the opposing forces, including such ceremonies as wreath-dropping when a major opponent was finally shot down. Exaggerated, beyond doubt; but while I was reading those magazines, I had a chance to question Reed Landis, a friend of my family's who had been America's tenth-ranking ace, and he said: "I think it did happen once or twice."

The stories were moderately realistic, too, in the amount of swearing they allowed to both sides. I don't recall taking any special notice of this until the summer of 1932, when I had been reading the magazines for three years. At the time, I was visiting my great-aunt in Niles, Michigan, where I fell ill; and she read the latest issue of one of the magazines to me while I convalesced, carefully expurgating as she went. The result was rather like this:

The instruments vanished in flying glass and metal as hot Spandau lead whipped into the cockpit past his shoulders.
Castor oil seared his cheeks.
"Scissors!" he grated.

I learned, in theory, how to fly from those magazines, and my interest wasn't limited to the past. In the early 1930's, the passage of an actual aircraft overhead was an event; I can remember running out of the house to watch one go over. A feature of the 1933 World's Fair ("A Century of Progress") in Chicago was an aerial tour of the city by a Giant Ford Trimotor (the word "giant" came with the aircraft as a sort of trade-mark, automatically), on which my father took me. Even after I discovered science fiction, I continued to follow the air-war magazines right up to their demise. It can hardly be surprising, in short, that I too wanted to be a pilot.

But dreams of space travel gradually overwhelmed those of actual flight. In fact, I didn't fly again after 1933 until my first commercial flight in 1948, and didn't learn to fly in actuality until 1955. After 1948, I was flown on business all over the United States, have made transatlantic flights and flights to France and Italy, and I think it still seems as marvelous to me as it ever did; but it had stopped being a major ambition before I was in my teens.

In point of fact my major ambition in those days was to become a scientist. Astronomy attracted me most, though my arithmetic marks would have discouraged me had I really known anything about the science. What little I did know was purely descriptive—such things as the order of the planets from the sun, their sizes and satellite systems, and the range of distances involved between the stars. ("It's all too vast for me," my mother said. "I don't want to hear any more about it.") All my contact with it was through reading; it was not until I was in college that I got my first look through a telescope. At the same time, I made bookish acquaintance with natural history and woodcraft through the works of Ernest Thompson Seton, thoroughly enough to win, in my second year at a summer camp in southern Michigan, all three awards given by the camp in the subject. I bought pseudoscientific toys from Johnson Smith & Co., a mail-order house in Racine, Wisconsin specialising in an astonishing variety of cheap trash. And eventually, I know not how, I became the possessor of a small Wollensak microscope, which was also a toy, but differed from all the others in that it worked. The microscope had no turret, but I discovered that I could increase its power two- to five-fold with cheap additional clip-on objectives made by the Japanese out of the bottoms of old soda-pop bottles (or that at least was my theory after I found how dim and scratchy they were). With them I made the discovery which elementary books about microscopy always try to pound home, but that every beginner must learn by experience: low powers are generally the best, and the very high powers are virtually useless except to the professional bacteriologist. I made hay infusions and discovered the protozoa and the common rotifers, which excited me, I believe, at least as much as they ever did Anton van Leeuwenhoek; and in conjunction with a Chemcraft chemistry set which I had gotten for Christmas a year earlier, I set myself up a laboratory, offering to do tests on household staples, such as counting what I called the "fat globules" in milk. One of my Johnson Smith gadgets was a printing set with moveable rubber type from which various stamps could be constructed; I had been badly disappointed to find that one couldn't turn out a whole book with this equipment, at least not without the patience of a Gutenberg, but now I turned it to use to make cards reading

BLISH LABORATORIES
MICROSCOPIC WORK

which I distributed to relatives. My few indulgent clients lost interest on discovering in turn that I was anxious to prove my efficiency by finding *everything* adulterated in some way, though in point of fact in those days probably nearly everything was—as the publication of a best-selling book called *Thirty Million Guinea Pigs* made clear only a few years later. (*Thirty* million? Now there are a hundred and eighty million of us.) I was impossible to discourage, however, and remained the owner and constant user of some kind of microscope until I was in my second year of graduate school at age 25. During the same period, I was given my first typewriter, a secondhand Smith Corona portable, badly out of alignment. On this I produced single-copy booklets containing lurid but mercifully very short stories of fire and other disasters, featuring myself and imaginary companions. These companions are among my first post-Teddybear memories; they included the hero's stalwart and faithful side-kick, simply and nobly named Bob; a girl named Velvinor whose only function was to stand about admiringly; and a weak but not necessarily inimical patsy whose role is amply indicated by his name, which was Crawly Spindling. Some of their adventures must have involved a Graustark of sorts, for I can still remember what must have been its national anthem:

Vwopdingdorp they call it,
And if Vwopdingdorp it be,
Then Vwopdingdorp and all its riches
Belongs... to... me.

In fact, I can even remember the tune, which was even less inspired. (I did a little better in the verse line when I was nine, with a poem called "South Wind" which was published in *St. Nicholas.*) These companions, however, had been replaced by others by the time I came to writing down their adventures; the heyday of Velvinor and Crawly was during the period when my father was still home, of which I really recall very little, except being struck glancingly by a car while jumping off the back of an ice-truck, and dropping my kiddy-car down an airshaft because I had decided I'd outgrown it ("But some other little boy might have used it").

The collision between the laboratory and the typewriter, now so inevitable in retrospect, was in reality curiously muffled, and did not produce any resultant until some six years later. It was begun in 1931 by one of my temporary block friends who knew of my interest in astronomy, who offered to give me "a book that tells all about life on other planets." This turned out to be the April, 1931 issue of *Astounding Stories*.

I still have a copy, although not *the* copy. The cover, by Wesso (short for Hans Waldemar Wessolowski), shows two men in tight-fitting jodhpurs jumping with apparently suicidal intent at three much bigger crocodile men, against a nocturnal background of cone-shaped buildings whose triangular openings glow an ominous orange. In the background, too, there appear two other crocodile men who seem to be trying to catch the humans in the red rays of some kind of flashlight. Seven years later, Brian Aldiss was to encounter magazines of this sort with covers "bearing only marginal relationship to the contents"; but this Wesso cover faithfully represented a scene in the leading story, "Monsters of Mars," by Edmond Hamilton, in which the human explorers are transmitted by radio to Mars just in time to stop an invasion of Earth by the crocodile men. The issue also included two other space-travel stories, a story about a visit to another dimension, one about a descent four miles into the earth, a fantastic story with a South Polar setting, and the beginning of a serial about time-travel—a very good sample, luckily, of the range of the science fiction of the time. (Two of the authors, Edmond Hamilton and Jack Williamson, were still active producers in the field more than 40 years later.)

Thanks to previous experience with the air-war pulps, I knew these pieces to be fiction at once—though the opening instalment of the serial, Ray Cummings' "The Exiles of Time," depicted a robot invasion so realistically that I decided then and there not to be anywhere near New York City in the year 1935, which did not seem even to me to be very far in the future. I think I must have been a little disappointed, but if I was, I was also sufficiently entranced by the stories so that all memory of disappointment has vanished. I promptly drummed up 20¢ for another issue, only to find that the one now on the stands was the July issue—I had missed the two middle instalments of the serial. At the time, I looked about also for other magazines of the same sort, but *Astounding*'s competitors in 1931 were larger and more expensive, and also, somehow, stodgier; one editor, indeed, regularly broke up the stories he ran with sub-heads, like a newspaper story, and appended footnotes explaining, usually incorrectly, the scientific principles behind the various gadgets. The only magazine which seemed at all like *Astounding* to me was *Weird Tales*. The covers of these, by Margaret Brundage, featured bare-bosomed girls for whom I wasn't yet ready, and even more certainly, my family (mother and grandparents and an occasional visiting uncle or aunt) weren't ready. Somewhat later, it turned out that I didn't much like traditional horror stories anyhow, even when the publishers of *Astounding* put out such a magazine. I still don't.

My faith in *Astounding* was firm, however, and its covers were never suggestive enough to earn it parental disapproval. My mother, to be sure, was quite baffled by the contents, but decided that they were harmless; in later years, she took to characterizing them vaguely as "fairy-tales for grown-ups." I began to look for science-fiction movies, and encountered one almost at once: *Just Imagine*, a musical with a future setting, starring the Scandinavian comedian El Brendel as a man struck by lightning on a golf-course in the 1920's and awakened to a world with streams of helicopter traffic, regulated by policemen in captive balloons, and on the eve of the first trip to Mars. I was much taken with this and saw it four times (during one such Saturday afternoon, Children's Admission 10¢, I won a coffee-pot in a drawing, as I was later to win — of all things unlikely in South Chicago — a live piglet). I had worse luck with the other notable sf movie of the time, *King Kong*; my mother went along with me to that one, and upon discovering during one of the battles of dinosaurs which it showed that my heart was pounding hard, she hauled me out of the theatre incontinently. I saw the rest of it by myself the next Saturday. The only other film of that era that belongs in this context was a bitter disappointment: I had spent my 10c, half the price of an issue of *Astounding*, on something called *Reaching for the Moon* which had turned out to be a soppy love story. (Love stories were as automatically soppy as the Ford Trimotor was gigantic.)

Let it be noticed that for us in those days, 20c was a good deal larger a sum than 60c looks today. My mother was living on alimony and some additional earnings as a piano teacher; my grandfather, whose house we shared, had been a candy manufacturer whose company had been the only one ever listed up to that time on the New York Stock Exchange, and who was consequently ruined by the 1929 Crash. No, "ruined" is a cliché of the period; he just lost his company; both the apartment into which mother and I moved after the divorce—1344 East 48th Street—and the subsequent brownstone—4750 Kenwood Avenue, just around the corner—were, I now realize, quite luxurious; my first laboratory was set up in the butler's pantry of 1344, and I seriously wonder if any other American who was nine in 1931 knows what a butler's pantry is. Gramps must, however, have been living on his capital, despite the presence of both his Ampico player grand and my mother's Baldwin baby grand, for I can remember considerable outright financial anguish when I broke a glass lampshade: anguish great enough so that when I promptly brought my grandmother two dollars I had saved toward a larger chemistry set, *she took it*, which seemed to me at the time to be a gross betrayal of the spirit in which it had been offered.

Certainly none of Gramps' investments can have survived, and he dwindled into smaller and smaller households as time went on, from the butler's pantry of 1344, to the Irish housemaid of 4750, and steadily downward to his and Nana's deaths, when they were both living with us rather than we with them.

My father, a tall, handsome, blond erratic man with a fine singing voice, had early on established himself as a space salesman for magazines and never seemed to be short of money; he was the advertising manager for *True Story*, which then, *pace* Katisha in *The Mikado*, had the largest circulation in the world; and after Bernarr Macfadden's death, he became Eastern advertising manager for *Esquire*, also then in its heyday. He descended upon us every other Saturday to take me out, and we never knew whether the outcome was to be a prodigal waste of money, like the Ford Trimotor flight, or a bitter session in which he upbraided my mother for spending his money all on herself and as little as possible on me (which was quite untrue) and imprisoned me in his deserted office in the Wrigley Building until I learned how to tie my own shoes. Except for the fact that he was not, financially, a failure, he was quite remarkably like Simon Dedalus.

Barring the Trimotor flight, I was already thoroughly familiar with the World's Fair. Every Friday there was Children's Day, in which the exhibits along the Midway for which one needed tickets were reduced to 10¢; and there were acres of exhibits which cost nothing on any day. I do not believe that I missed a Friday of any week during both years the Fair was open; it was quite easy to reach, by the 47th Street stop of the Illinois Central Railroad, from where I lived, and I could spend most of my time in such buildings as the Hall of Science (would you believe I carried a notebook? Well, I did); what money I had left after paying for the train fare went to Midway shows like "Buck Rogers." One reason I disliked the memory of my father teaching me to tie my own shoes is that I was already getting about South Chicago, and the vast Fair grounds, without supervision; the fact that my mother had to tie my shoes for me before I left the house was something I never noticed, and had I noticed it, would have dismissed as of no importance, until that Inquisitional session in the Wrigley Building at which it became, abruptly, a weapon which my father could use against my mother. He was, I think, looking for handles by which he could manipulate himself out of the alimony, though he must have known that legally he hadn't a prayer of doing so; in any event, he stopped bothering later, and at the same time—having remarried in the interim—took no further interest in my shoes, or me, until I was on the verge of college. Then the nature of the interest had changed, and I learned to love him, rather too late; but he was a figure of terror when I was a boy, a predictable visitation, every other Saturday, with unpredictable results.

Two key words have slipped by during this family interlude: "Buck Rogers." We are now so far advanced into a science-fiction age, in which landings on the Moon (to choose the most obvious example) have become nearly commonplace, that there is now a whole generation of science-fiction writers who have never heard their trade dismissed as "that crazy Buck Rogers stuff." Yet a daily and Sunday comic strip called *Buck Rogers in the 25th Century* was the only form of science fiction everybody knew in my boyhood (and there was a radio show derived from it during my teens). It had begun, I found much later, with a story called "Armageddon—2419 A.D." which had been published by Philip Francis Nowlan in the August 1928 *Amazing Stories*, and its sequel, "The Airlords of Han," in the March 1929 issue. Nowlan also published three additional stories in the magazines at widely spaced intervals (one in 1934 and two in 1940, the year of his death), but he made his principal impact with the comic strip, for which he wrote the continuity, starting from his first two stories. The strip was drawn by a U.S. Army Air Corps Lieutenant named Dick Calkins, who was an acquaintance of my father's and who much later provided me with my first contact with feet-of-clay by, at a party whose aftermath I saw, covering one wall of my father's kitchen in Hastings-on-Hudson (New York) with mildly erotic drawings in unmistakable Buck Rogers style.

The strip is long dead; even its successor, *Flash Gordon*, which was both better written and better drawn, by quite a different team, expired some dozen years ago. Yet let it be said in retrospect that there was nothing so crazy about that crazy Buck Rogers stuff, except, undoubtedly, its simplistic view of astronomical distances. It foresaw television, rocket-propelled space flight, the bazooka, individual rocket-powered flying harness, and a good many other innovations now realized, as well as some that haven't come down the pike yet, but look probable (e.g., the ray-gun, which will probably emerge from the laser within my lifetime). Science fiction writers can no longer be mocked by reference to Buck Rogers, not only because the strip is forgotten, but because its ideas are now the hardware of everyday life, and everyday warfare.

For some years, I collected the strips in a scrapbook, particularly the Sunday strips which covered an entire newspaper page in colour and advanced the story substantially each week. Thanks to the magazines, I knew that Nowlan's plots were rudimentary and impossible, but Calkins had a particular gift for drawing gadgets which I enjoyed; he was particularly good at imagining outlandish spaceships; I think he was the first science-fiction producer before Wernher von Braun to realize that in the vacuum of space (which he nevertheless filled with picturesque sunset clouds) there is no reason why a spaceship has to have streamlines or fairing—a discovery not to be made by the magazine illustrators for decades to come.

The child who took all this stuff seriously, and is now purveying it as worth having been taken seriously; the child who couldn't tie his own shoes but carried a notebook to the Hall of Science; the bookish child who couldn't get along with his contemporaries, and who allowed his mother to chase away peers who sat on his doorstep and divided among themselves the syllables of "Tat . tle . tale"; that child seems now an impossible little prig, and was one. I still regard as strange those people whose memories of the 1930's are memories of social events like apple-sellers in the streets: I saw apple-sellers, but I didn't know any better than Herbert Hoover why they were there; my most vivid memory of the Depression is that of the arrival over Chicago of General Balbo's fleet of flying boats from Italy, more airplanes in the sky than I had ever seen before, flying in formation right over my house. I was so thrilled that later, when Mussolini invaded Ethiopia, I went through the streets of Kenwood hawking a secondhand newspaper, crying "War! War! War!" in a triumphant voice; it seemed to me only to be a triumph, or a coming triumph, for both of my interests, air battles and science fiction. (I had perhaps been a little put off by a more direct political experience: I had adopted my father's extreme partisanship for Al Smith and had carried a sign for him, which got me beaten up by the Hoover partisans my own age, who were in a heavy majority in suburban Chicago.) I think, now, that the Balbo Armada marked the last great event in my fascination with flying; certainly I never was as thrilled again by a comparable achievement until I heard (quite erroneously, as it turned out) in the early 1940's that a rocket-powered vehicle had attained escape velocity from the Earth.

Escape velocity is the velocity—seven miles per second—which is required to free a vehicle from Earth's gravitation and turn it into a body subject to the general ballistic laws of space as a whole. Even today, these velocities are generally given by the press in terms of miles per minute or per hour—for example, orbital velocity is usually given as 25,000 miles per hour—which makes them impossible to grasp. I knew by the time I was ten, thanks to the science-fiction magazines, that orbital velocity was five miles per second, and escape velocity, seven. I also learned, from those same magazines, a good many things that weren't true, such as that the asteroids had atmospheres and were inhabitable, or that the gravity of Jupiter was crushing; and what I learned that *was* true had about as much applicability to my daily life as the knowledge of how to bail out of an aircraft which has been shot down in flames. I have never had to jump out of an airplane—a good thing, too, for parachutes are no longer issued either to airline passengers or to private flyers; but the rest of the reading matter of my boyhood nevertheless could not have been better designed to prepare me for the wild outside world in which I now live had it been designed for me by H. G. Wells. Nothing surprises me, and almost everything delights me; it is not simply happening; it is all coming true.

And it is all terribly non-traumatic for people like my present wife and mother-in-law who have been raised to believe that every bend in the grown-up human hairpin has to have been formed before the age of three. I cannot, in fact, even manage to get through the standard maneuver of disliking my mother-in-law, who in fact charms me entirely except when she is taking the psychiatric or Oh-my-God-how-awful view of Hamlet's childhood, or my own. It is certainly true that I learned early to loathe my own mother—and what a vast amount of Oh-my-God-how-awful parlor psychiatry that has produced!—but I am quite prepared to put forward, and shall, the view that I loathed the poor woman because she was genuinely awful and deserved to be loathed, without recourse to any deep-lying Oedipal interpretations. Even the terrible primal scene, which in complete contradiction to Freudian theory I remember in detail without the slightest help upon any therapeutic couch, never played an even mildly interesting role in my development; I disliked my mother and my father equally, the one as a stupid and phenomenally selfish woman, the other as an intelligent but equally selfish man. Later, as I have said, I learned to like and admire, and even to love, my father; whereas my distaste for my mother deepened inexorably into something not very short of hatred. Now that she has declined into the usual stumblings, broken hips, and inability to manage her own bank balance which is characteristic of the senile who have never led any sort of intellectual life, I cannot even begin to pity her more than abstractly. I would give quite a lot to be shut of her, and in due course I shall show why. The reasons are completely overt, and therefore, I think, sufficient — just as people who loathe me have good and sufficient reason to do so in my own behaviour; Occam's Razor requires no further excuses or overexplanations.

I could of course be damn-all wrong about this, and the psychiatrically-oriented quite right. My mother-in-law, Muriel Lawrence, knows more about the various varieties of psychiatry than I shall ever bother to learn now, and she takes a very Oh-my-God view of what I have told her of my childhood, through which she manages to forgive me for the many bends in the current Blish hairpin. For the benefit of people like Muriel, I remember:

... being spanked for masturbating, which in my household was called "lying on your stomach," while my father still lived with us; and years later contriving an excuse for the pose while in Niles. By that time I had developed an interest of sorts in music, and was able to demonstrate to my mother that a fevered brow could as easily be the outcome of listening to a phonograph record of Respighi's "The Pines of Rome" as of self-abuse;

... a backyard exploration of the panties of a little girl, devoted chiefly to our secreting pebbles in our underwear because our mothers would be so surprised to find them there. The surprise didn't come off; we had neglected to realize that we were visible from every possible window, and were snatched home long before anything of psychiatric interest occurred;

... being given a demonstration of masturbating by a fat boy before an attic audience ("Jism, Charlie, jism!") who later tried to explore my flies while giving me a ride on a bicycle;

... participating in the persecution of both the block's rich boy (we burst his model dirigible balloon) and the block Jew ("Isadore / was a door / and always will be a door") by strewing Johnson Smith & Co. itching powder in his bedroom while he was trying to show us some small strips of 35 mm. motion picture film with a toy projector;

...and, in short, being just as beastly to others, in inverse accordance with the Rabbi Hillel's Silver Rule, as others were being beastly to me. I am sorry for some of these things, particularly the persecution of Isadore, for which I paid in kind by being the object of persecution as the block sissy. But being beastly is a standard stage in childhood, and as far as I can see, is indicative of nothing but that children necessarily behave childishly, without any knowledge of what it is that they do. I believe I learned the obvious lessons from all of these incidents, better in some cases than in others; but I do not think that any of them remains buried for some later, on-the-couch discovery which will reform my whole psyche; my subsequent encounters with psychiatrists—at the urging of wife and mother-in-law, and during my parting with my previous wife—have given me little confidence in the significance of buried memories. Most of my memories from what are called in psychiatry the formative years seem to be quite out in the open, and without meaning for the man I now am; whereas the intellectual experiences of my boyhood—terrible prig though I admit myself to have been—still seem to me to have been crucial.

Should I ever find myself back on the couch (actually, I have never been on one; one of the two psychiatrists I have consulted preferred to lie on it himself, and the other didn't own one), I think I shall have an invaluable handle to offer. Whenever a painful memory, or more specifically, a memory of having done something outright and seriously wrong, surfaces in my mind, I find that I am talking to myself. The content of the talk has nothing to do with the memory, but instead consists of the last few words of what I had previously been thinking. They come out *sotto voce,* and since like most American males I don't move my lips much when I speak, this crotchet has never won me any puzzled stares; but it gives me an invaluable guide to what knots in my psyche still remain to be untied.

I have never heard of anybody else who had such a compulsion; I must ask Muriel if she has. It certainly seems characteristic that the aberration should be a wordy one. In my boyhood, I had another: a mild case of dyslexia, or scrambling of the parts of words in reading. My mother dined out for decades on the story of how I, after having seen Constance Moore's doll house, a showpiece of the 1930's, on exhibition, reported that some part of it was "all made of gold and oinks." I still so stumble now and then over new words which I have never heard pronounced, and I don't spell very well, either.

What interests me most about the crotchet, however, is that nine out of ten of the memories that trigger it are not childhood memories at all, but moral lapses committed well into an age when I not only should have known better, but did know better at the time.

In addition, neither of the psychiatrists I mentioned took any especial notice of anything they, or I, might have called the formative experiences of childhood, and now that this divertissement for the psychiatrically-oriented is over, I shall follow their lead. Talking to one's self may serve some obscure symptomatic purpose, but a book presupposes an outside audience.

I did not see Chicago and my childhood home again until a business trip in 1948, when I took time out to visit the Kenwood area. I commemorated the visit in a poem called "Caesura" which appeared in *Accent* in 1950:

I paid fare on the ice to the woods, where the stones bled me;
   there where I fell from the stoop, I was run down
   with the sliver of ice in my palm; and the alley
   yard house has grown large where I was stung.

By the mansards I watched the sound of a typewriter wink-
ing,
　swam away from the red crash. The palings were gone
　that contained randy memory's collie, the
　locust tree had almost devoured the house.

In the dark I thought to be stone like the city
that so unchanged changed me, not to stay in the knowing
woods but only in mind, mirror and stone. There,
too, every flag lidded spiders, corners
　turned themselves, old windows mouthed names, four
blocks
　of still darkbound summer a petrified funhouse,
　closed, for the night. I would buy no more candy,
　stone I would stand to confute, wanting nothing.

Thought had paid for that life with my I, for the black-blood
tree.
　Poor city of ice, I said, to stand mute for nineteen stunned
years
　waiting for nothing but me and the heat of the summer
　bitch memory! What good to be stone there,
　better to grow like a turnip, if both must bleed!

Most of the private allusions in this verse, which is the only one I ever wrote that my mother understood at sight, must now be fairly obvious to the reader. The ice is the Illinois Central railroad, of which it was said that Chicago was so cold in winter because the wind, ho ho, blew over the icy tracks. "The Mansards" was the name of the apartment building at 1344; "the red crash" was the day I broke my Corona typewriter; the collie was an over-amorous dog belonging to neighbors; the tree, actually a catalpa, was a producer of seed pods called Indian cigars which we all tried, but could never persuade to draw. As pseudo-Sandburg goes, the poem stands well enough as a farewell to the city he too commemorated, to the affliction of high school classes in poetry ever since.

II

After I had finished seventh grade, and had had a letter published in *Astounding*—the second memory is far more vivid than the first—we moved to East Orange, N.J., where my mother and father had been living when I was born. I have no idea why the change was made, except that it had something to do with my grandfather's financial situation, and perhaps also that my father was now working in New York. In addition, mother had friends in the vicinity, which was the New Jersey equivalent of Scarsdale—technically a suburb of Newark, but in actuality an exurb of New York. I didn't like it—I was homesick for Kenwood—and of my last year in grammar school I remember almost nothing. I do recall, however, that the letter in *Astounding* (which concluded archly, "Yours till spaceships drink milk") brought me a reply. The New York World's Fair was then well along into its building stage, and the letter was from a young lady who wanted to see it and hoped that I, who lived so near it (I had given my new address in the letter) would squire her around. I had to write to her and confess that I wouldn't be suitable for the purpose at the age of 13, and in fact I was so unsuitable that I wasn't even humiliated by the admission. All through my adolescence I fitfully hoped for another such letter, but none ever arrived; though I did develop a growing correspondence with other science-fiction fans, to this day a remarkably clubby group.

East Orange High School turned out to be something of a factory, but when I was there it offered three curricula: Classical, Scientific and Technical. The Classical was for students who expected to go to college but didn't yet know what they would study when they got there; the Scientific was for those who did;

and the Technical was essentially a congeries of trade schools. I took the Scientific without a moment's doubt, and in view of my later interests I think what I made of it is an interesting piece of foreshadowing. One year of a shop course was required, and I elected woodworking over metalworking as sounding less intractable; but I never got farther in woodworking than generating upon a lathe a mahogany peanut bowl so misshapen as to suggest that nothing but mahogany peanuts would go in it. (Anyone who has ever worked at a lathe will appreciate that it takes exceptional talent to turn out an irregular piece.) After one semester I discovered it was possible to substitute printing, for which the school had a complete shop; I liked this so much that I stayed with it for the entire remainder of the four years; I also very much liked the instructor, a tall stringy man by turns dour and folk-comic who seemed to come straight out of Mark Twain. A modern language was also required for two years, and not unexpectedly, I chose German, sticking with that, too, for four years. Two years of Latin: I barely passed the first, and flunked the second—I liked Caesar but found Cicero an intolerable bore. My four years of math declined from middling good in algebra to flat failure in trigonometry; this record was a fairly common one, and I think I shall be able to show in due course that it was for the most part due to unnecessarily formidable teaching methods. As for the sciences themselves, I stood a high first in biology, approximately in the middle in chemistry, and only inside the safety margin in physics—in short, in opposite order to the degree of maths required. I had told my mentor in biology that I was shooting for the Bausch and Lomb Science Award, one of which was handed out in each graduating class; I got it, but he told me later that there had been considerable doubt among the committee that I deserved it. As for Art and Mechanical Drawing, the less said about them, the better. I spent most of my time in both drawing spaceships.

This decidedly mixed record—whose consistencies I did not recognize until the very end of my academic career—would not even have allowed me to graduate, had it not been for an unbroken A+ record in all of my English courses. Here too I spent a certain amount of time drawing spaceships: for a class in writing I produced as a culminating effort a science-fiction story. It was pretty bad, but the instructor was outright staggered by it; I seriously wonder, now, if he had ever read anything like it, though certainly he must have been familiar with Wells at least at second hand. I in my turn was discovering strange realms: *Julius Caesar, The Tempest* (which, inevitably, was produced as a school play with roars of applause for Trinculo), "The Cask of Amontillado," *Great Expectations, Henry Esmond,* and (here my voice falls) the publicity-saint of American education, Carl Sandburg. I was not put off by any of this, which makes me believe that the teaching must have been quite good; I developed an enduring passion for most of Shakespeare, a qualified one for Poe, Dickens and Thackeray, and the conviction that Sandburg was ninety per cent Whitman and ten per cent charlatan, a rank order which still strikes me as fair and judicious. The highest tribute I can give my high school English instructors is that they taught me how to love poetry; if there is a Heaven, surely they will be admitted for that gift alone.

My reading at the time, however, continued to be mostly science fiction. After the March 1933 issue, *Astounding* (which had gone bi-monthly the previous year) had been sold to Street and Smith, who brought it out again in October as a mixture of adventure stories, weird tales, and a few left-over science-fiction stories from the Clayton inventory; the new editor, F. Orlin Tremaine, took only two subsequent issues, however, before converting the magazine back to science fiction only. In the interim, I finally began to read *Astounding*'s two older competitors, *Amazing Stories* and *Wonder Stories*; I still found them pretty stodgy, but they were a lot better than nothing. During this period, *Wonder Stories* launched a promotional club called the Science Fiction League which offered the equivalent of degrees for passing a test on knowledge of what had been published previously; the test also asked for an essay on one's favorite science-fiction character, to which I responded in all innocence with a paean to Hawk Carse, a series character who had appeared in the Clayton (pre-Street and Smith) *Astounding*. It got printed, although in pretty small type. It wasn't my first attempt to write for publication—by that time I had appeared several times in the letter columns of *Astounding*, and as early as 1931 I had taken enough notice of *Wonder Stories* to enter a cover-story contest they ran—but I think its appearance was the first nudge I had toward trying to become a publishable writer.

The rest of the course was equally indirect. Through my published letters, I had gotten into correspondence with another youngster named Nils Frome, of Frazer's Mills, Canada, who did very skillful fine-line drawings with the back of an ordinary fountain pen, and who also wrote gloomily Lovecraftian stories with the front side of the same pen. He was extraordinarily sure of himself from the outset, offering to teach me both to draw and to write, and sent me thousands of words of closely handwritten strictures on both subjects. His advice about drawing probably was good, had I been able to take it, but I have no eye whatsoever; my organ is the ear. His advice about writing was bad, I now recognize, but I was equally impressed by it, and by the samples of his own stories which he sent me, incomplete though they all were. Since I already knew that Nils' lack of a typewriter was a major drawback to publication, I offered to type one of these beginnings for him, and, if he would permit it, to append an ending; to this he gave rather grudging consent. Since neither of us really knew what we were doing, the story didn't sell. To the best of my knowledge, Nils Frome never did break into print.

The growingly manifest holes in his teaching, however, had succeeded in derailing me from trying to break into print via a collaboration with another dub. Instead, I founded a science fiction fan magazine called *The Planeteer*, featuring the adventures of a Hawk Carse-like interplanetary adventurer and various sidekicks who were the newest incarnations of Bob, Velvinor and Crawly Spindling. In the course of six issues, this turned from a sticky purple affair run off on hektograph jelly, to a fairly sizable mimeographed magazine, to a never-completed issue done on a hand Kelsey press part of which was hand-set and part linotyped, with the aid of what I had learned in my printing course. What I did not know was that sf fan magazines did not need to be this pretentious; and in fact, a fan magazine was not what I had started out to produce, but instead, a sort of infant *Astounding*. I even bought two stories from professionals — Edmond Hamilton and Laurence Manning — at a penny a word. They were not very good stories (fan magazine fiction by professionals necessarily consists of rejects) but the cheques were not at fault; the going professional rate at the time, as a contemporary writer, Horace Gold, later put it, was microscopic fractions of a cent payable upon lawsuit; and I was paying my rate out of my allowance of perhaps 25c a week.

In this period, I did submit one of my collaborations with Nils Frome to *Astounding*. At the time I thought highly of it, particularly of the highly literary parts of it that Nils had written, so I was utterly astonished when it was rejected. The printed refusal arrived while my mother and I were back on a visit to Chicago, and in the middle of a summer when I was having many happy successes at elementary laboratory projects like germinating seeds, growing chemical gardens in sodium silicate, contriving a methane lamp out of the propellant supplied with a toy Bangsite cannon, and drawing the frustules of diatoms. I was baffled by the rejection slip and could only conclude that *Astounding* didn't like unhappy ends; I wrote Tremaine to ask if this was the case, but never got an answer. Gradually, I began to conclude instead that if there was a secret to breaking into print with a science-fiction story, Nils didn't know it. Our correspondence dwindled and died. I wonder what happened to him; out of my absolute ignorance of the graphic arts, I still have the feeling that he drew very well, gluey though his prose undeniably was, but as far as the record shows, he never sold a drawing, either.

During this same period I had made friends with a contemporary named William Miller Jr., who illustrated issues four through six of *The Planeteer*, who was my companion in my first face-to-face meetings with live science-fiction fans, and with whom I had the only fist-fight of my life over a girl—though at 15 my interest in that girl, or girls in general, can only be characterised as retarded. I also had a less intense, and hence firmer, friendship with a budding chemist who had made himself a far grander basement laboratory than mine (though mine now included the noblest microscope I ever did own, a brass-and-glass medical model complete with substage condenser, oil-immersion objective, and mechanical stage, all of which I knew how to use with fair expertise), and who converted me from my mother's wobbly Christian Science—which must be at once the silliest and the least exciting religion the West has ever contrived—to an atheism around which I have been wobbling uneasily ever since. He was also very good at contriving original experiments, one of which was the construction of small paper rockets which we fired off the windowsill of my apartment (he lived in a basement of another one); the grand climax of this was a Buck Rogers rocket pistol made of a bored dowel-rod, fed with home-made gunpowder from a hopper on its top. When this was lit at its muzzle, it produced a satisfyingly long tongue of flame, but the hopper also ignited. It was sheer dumb luck that my face was not over it; I got away with a badly burned hand, which Andy had the good sense to wind up in butter and linen, so expertly that the doctor I was taken to thereafter decided not to disturb it. When the windings finally fell off, the back of that hand was a little freckled, as though it had become much older than the other; and I notice that it is still gathering age spots at a considerably faster rate; but it was otherwise quite unharmed.

I have lost track of Andy, and of Miller, but I do not now miss either of them. On the other hand, I do much wonder what happened to Erwin Lane, to whose passion for Italian opera I owe the awakening of my subsequent love for the whole art of music.

III

I didn't actually sell a story until I was a sophomore in college (1940), and of the first ten I had published, only one had any merit whatsoever. The eleventh, however, "Sunken Universe" (1942), contained the germ of, and eventually was incorporated into, "Surface Tension" (1952), by far the most popular single story I have ever written. Together, they reflect the most directly of all my works my continuing interest in microbiology, which I pursued formally in university; but I think it is fair to add that the biological sciences play important roles in more of my output than in that of any other living sf writer known to me.

I was drafted soon after I graduated, in 1942, and during my two years in the Army, spent entirely Stateside as a medical laboratory technician, I wrote nothing. Once out, however, I went back into production with a vengeance, not only of sf but of almost every other kind of thing for which a market existed, including Westerns, detectives, sports stories, popular science articles, and even poetry and criticism for the literary quarterlies (these last two still make up an important part of my output, although, of course, not of my income). It was during this period (1945-6) that I wrote my first sf novel, *The Duplicated Man*, in collaboration with Robert W. Lowndes, with whom I was sharing a New York City apartment while I did graduate work at Columbia University; but it didn't see publication until 1953, and then in a magazine Bob himself edited. By 1948 I was selling so much—though to be sure at pretty tiny rates—that I was emboldened to try becoming a full-time free-lance author.

My timing couldn't have been worse. I had by that time also acquired a wife, an infant and a mortgage; furthermore, that was the year most of my non-sf markets chose to collapse. Defeated, I got a job as a trade newspaper sub-editor, continuing to write nights and weekends. I was also forced to sell the house.

Nevertheless, 1948 was an important year for me in another way besides teaching me some bitter economic lessons; it was then that I wrote the first of my stories about space-flying cities. John Campbell of *Astounding* rejected this but with an enormously detailed commentary, the gist of which was that what I had submitted couldn't be an independent story but a rather late stage of a series, made possible (the series) by the fact that I'd failed to consider almost all the implications of the central idea. The series was written, and bought, and the rejected story did appear in its proper order. (That story, "Earthman, Come Home," is to be in Volume II of *Science Fiction Hall of Fame,* as "Surface Tension" is in Volume I.) By 1962, the original 15,000 words had grown into four novels, now published collectively under the title *Cities in Flight,* and I hope to add a coda for the forthcoming Campbell memorial volume. In addition, the motion picture rights have been sold and I have myself written the shooting script for the first of the films.

These books, despite some novelties *en passant,* are rather old-fashioned, essentially slam-bang interstellar adventure in the direct line of descent from E. E. Smith (and, for that matter, early Campbell). Yet despite their actual age—the most recent of them is now a decade old—and their more fundamental mustiness, they're still bringing in substantial royalties and subsidiary sales; and the popularity of Larry Niven's *Known Space* series more recently would seem additional evidence that the mode of the interstellar epic is still viable. (*What are you guys going to write about now they've actually landed on the Moon?*)

I think, however, that I have done much more original work, which will in the end also prove to be more lasting. In order to keep this essay down to manageable length (and in part, I suspect, because I seldom enjoy reading autobiography and actively loathe writing it), I have barely managed to mention literary interests of mine quite outside sf, and among these is philosophy. A number of them surfaced at the same time in *A Case of Conscience,* which began its quite astonishing publishing history — at the time I was writing it, I was convinced that it was unsaleable — as a 23,000-word magazine story in 1953. Later, against stern resistance from me, Frederik Pohl and Betty Ballantine persuaded me to make a novel of it, which appeared, under the same title, in 1958, and won me my only Hugo. It has stayed in print ever since and has been translated in many unlikely places, including Japan — I very much wonder how an Asiatic audience, even as thoroughly modern a one as the Japanese, could make much sense of a novel the central problem of which is presented in terms of Christian theology, and sectarian Christian to boot.

I do not claim that I invented the theological sf story, in fact, I took pains to point out my ancestors in one of my two books of critical essays on sf, *The Issue at Hand* (1964) — but mine seems to have been the first to have captured and held the attention of what seems to be a majority of the modern sf audience. One reason why this happened may be that I took what had been for me, up to that time, quite exceptional pains to make it full, well rounded and rich *as a novel,* so that it might hold the reader to whom its decidedly Scholastic theological involutions might prove dull or even outright repugnant. I have since discovered what I think may be an even more important reason, which I shall have to approach roundabout by way of a long anecdote, for which I ask forgiveness; I can see no other way to clarify it. As follows:

With some exceptions, I do not like fantasy, but I have had a lifelong affection and admiration for E. R. Eddison's *The Worm Ouroboros,* and had often thought of trying to write a novel in which the rituals of ceremonial magic as it was actually practiced would play a similarly important part. In 1957, the same year in which I wrote what is now the final novel of *Cities in Flight* and the novel version of *A Case of Conscience* — as well as a sort of novelised monster movie called *VOR* — I decided to try this, and for my central figure settled upon Roger Bacon, of whom I knew very little except the rather Faust-like legend best exemplified in Robert Greene's Elizabethan play *Friar Bacon and Friar Bungay.* When I began to investigate the historical Bacon, however, I found first of all that he had been an *opponent* of magic all his life, and second that his actual life as a pioneer of scientific method — perhaps its inventor — and his complex career and prickly personality made him far more interesting to me than he would have been as a magician. The outcome, years later, was a straight historical novel, *Doctor Mirabilis* (Faber & Faber, 1965; Dodd, Mead, revised, 1971).

Doctor Mirabilis is my choice as the best book I have ever written, but it left unscratched the original itch to write a novel about magic. I finally (as I thought) satisfied this with a book called *Black Easter* (1969, after a magazine appearance), which generated more reviews than anything I had ever written before, most of them in newspapers which previously had been quite unaware of my existence. This was gratifying, but for me *Black Easter* had a much more important outcome: when I had just finished it, I realised that I had now written three novels, widely separated in times of composition and even more in ostensible subject-matter, each one of which was a dramatisation in its own terms of one of the oldest problems of philosophy: *Is the desire for secular knowledge, let alone the acquisition of it, a misuse of the mind, and perhaps even actively evil?*

I would not suggest for an instant that any of the three novels proposes an answer to this ancient question, let alone that I have one now or indeed ever expect to find one. I report only that it struck me that in each of the three books the question had been raised, from different angles and without my being aware of it while I was writing them. I therefore noted, in the third one to be written, that in their peculiar way they constituted a trilogy, to which I gave the over-all title *After Such Knowledge*, and subsequently explained my reasons (including acknowledging that the concept of making them a trilogy had been hindsight) in a fan magazine article. Thereafter, and this time in full awareness of what my theme was, I wrote a fourth novel for the group, but since this was a direct sequel to *Black Easter*, I still regard it as a trilogy and hope that some day it will be republished as such, although at present it includes four titles: in the order in which they are best read, not in order of composition, *Doctor Mirabilis*, *Black Easter*, *The Day After Judgment* and *A Case of Conscience*.

I don't like propaganda disguised as fiction and have never written any—though one recent story of mine, "We All Die Naked," has been widely mistaken to be such a hybrid; though sf has been extensively exploited as a vehicle for social criticism, from Swift on, my own credo is that I am a sort of artist (a severely crippled one, as nobody can know as well as I do) and that whatever the artist's positive function in society may be, he has the negative obligation to avoid carrying placards and to stay off barricades. I think this may apply with special force to the science fiction writer, part of whose stock in trade it is to imagine many different kinds of futures most of which will contradict each other and in none of which he can invest more than a temporary acceptance for the sake of the story and the people in it, which is where his primary allegiance must remain. I have never seen a Utopia or any other kind of fictional future, including many of my own, that on inspection did not turn into something I would hate to live in, or want anybody I cared for to have to live in; and much more pragmatically, I've observed that every example of what is now being called relevant sf (in the social political sense) that I have ever read has been turned into unreadable nonsense by subsequent history unless it also contained and indeed depended upon some essentially timeless riddle of the human condition, one still capable of invoking wonder, joy or sorrow as no amount of technological ingenuity or future shock can ever do.

And this, I flatter myself, is what explains why *A Case of Conscience* and its three successors had so extraordinary and unexpected an impact on the SF audience and widely beyond it, despite the fact that they belong to different genres and are all packed with esoteric details about subjects—Thirteenth Century politics and theological disputes, modern black magic, and far future technology—which seems to have nothing in common and should have split the readers into utterly disparate groups which might like one of the books but have no use at all for the others. But that's not what happened, and I now think I know why: the problem of the misuse of secular knowledge, and the intense distrust of it, runs through all four novels... and without any such intention on my part, it turned out to be relevant as well as timeless.

I'm through with that problem now, since I'm not a philosopher and have nothing more to contribute to it. But I've got another one of that kind on the fire, and though I've no idea what fictional form it will take, I know now that this has become my metier—though I'll continue to write sf novels which are only games, because I like to and I still seem to be good at it—and I think I've found, at long last, why I wanted to be a writer in the first place, and why I continue to be one.

11. IN CONVERSATION: JAMES BLISH TALKS TO BRIAN ALDISS

Aldiss: James Blish, first of all I think I should congratulate you on surviving four years in England! May I say on behalf of myself, if of no one else, that it's a great pleasure to have you here; I personally count it as one of the major pleasures of my life that you are over here, and have managed to stay for four years without getting kicked out. The first question stems directly from these four years, and, like all the questions, it's going to be impossible to answer. Can you give us some sort of feeling of whether and how you feel the stay in England — or to put it another way — the exile from the States, has affected you and your writing?

Blish: I think I can answer that quite clearly. In the first place I am not an exile, I am an immigrant. I came here because I loved England on my first few acquaintances with it, and Judy did too. I was actually headed for Italy when I stopped off here, and I felt no reason to go any further. I am not an exile, political or otherwise, from the U.S.A.; I am here because I like England better in general than I do the States. It has benefited me because it has made it financially possible for me to live on my income from writing, which I could not do, under the terms I demand, in the U.S.A. Here everything seems to be made for me. It's not ideal. Every earthly paradise has a snake in it, and I've met a few. On the whole, I feel more at home here, and find more things I love here, than I do in my own country; and to this I should add that I have lived in, worked in, or vacationed in twenty-eight of the American states, and that's not counting any I have simply passed through or passed over. Of course, there are still vast sections of my own country that I have never seen at all; this includes the Pacific Northwest, which everyone tells me is very beautiful, and the desert states—but I feel no attraction to the desert states. I would like to see Oregon, I've seen San Francisco, which I loved, and Los Angeles, which I hated. I have in fact, pretty much, for my own purposes, exhausted America. I didn't come to this decision lightly. Every day here I find more and more things that I love, that are personal to me, that enrich me, whereas in the States I was finding fewer and fewer.

Aldiss: I remember the first time you walked around All Souls, Oxford, the sense of homecoming you had then.

Blish: I still feel that many years after, it was in 1965, was it not? After the London Worldcon. I still feel that; I turn around every corner in England and find things that are part of my heritage. My bank in London has a blue circle on it saying that Charles Dickens once lived there; about three blocks away, near my publishers, is a little tiny church which is called "The Church of Chimney Sweeps," it was one of the first churches built in London after the great fire. It's called "The Church of Chimney Sweeps" because, every Christmas, Lord somebody or other gathered together all the chimney sweeps in London and threw them a big blast on Christmas Eve. I am not, as a matter of fact, anything like a recent Englishman, my wife is much more so, one of her grandparents was Scottish, the other was English. The most remote ancestor that I can trace is one Abraham Blish, who, by God, came over on the *Mayflower*. And I consider that makes me just as English as Judy.

Aldiss: I feel that part of the attraction of England is the academic associations, which obviously have a great appeal for you. I can see you fitting in very well with All Souls, which we both know, at least tangentially. We could talk about this very pleasantly for a long time, but, I think, we should move on to a leading question that I have lined up. When I first came across your writing, and noted your name, was with "Bridge" in Campbell's *Astounding* in 1952. It was an early bit of the *Cities in Flight* series. One of the things that made me take notice of the "Okies," as we then knew them, was that there was a certain academic strain in them. This is something that I think I detected very early, but which is now more apparent in your writing. I would like to ask you now specifically about the strictly contemporary interpretation of *Cities in Flight*. It's very easy to be wise now, but you were writing those stories in the fifties when the emphasis in *Astounding* was on power politics and power fantasy, and your stories showed the Okies going out into the galaxy—that old van Vogtian and Asimovian galaxy—not for conquest, but for work. You're on record in *The Issue at Hand* as saying that the whole of the *Cities in Flight* series derived from a four-page letter from John W. Campbell; and that, for the next few years, you hacked your way through it sentence by sentence. This to me is one of the agreeable ways in which you underestimate yourself. The question I finally get around to delivering is this: were you conscious at the time that you were departing from what I would regard as the Campbellian norm, or did you feel yourself fitting in very happily there?

Blish: I was conscious that I was departing from the Campbellian norm, but only semi-conscious. The first Okie story to be written was called "Earthman, Come Home"; I came at this by an entirely roundabout way in 1948. There was a cover on an issue of *Astounding* for that period, for a van Vogt story I cannot identify, showing a van Vogtian superman standing in what looked like a spaceship yard filled with towering phallic shapes; this, at first glance, I took to be a city and not a spaceship yard. It occurred to me, suddenly, that if you have anti-gravity, there's no reason why there should be any limitation on the size or shape of the objects you lift. It was at that point that it also occurred to me: why should you want to do that? It was then that the concept of migrant workers came to me. Campbell contributed many, many ideas in that famous four-page letter that I hadn't thought up. He rejected the story with this four-page letter. The main thing that he did contribute, the central idea, was that the most valuable thing that these migrant workers could transfer in a situation involving fast interstellar travel was not gold, uranium, diamonds, the ability to drill for oil or whatever, but information. These are the pollinating bees of the galaxy. That was Campbell's idea, not mine, and it became the central idea of the whole series, it absolutely ruled out power politics in the old E. E. Smith or intergalactic epic sense. I did use a certain amount of power politics, however, because the cities are competing with each other. I used political figures of varying degrees of intelligence maneuvering against each other, and a social situation on Earth, with Earth both protecting the cities and policing them at the same time. Here I went back to an American analogy. There are two kinds of hobos in America; the ordinary migrant worker who goes from door to door saying "Can I chop wood, or do any other job you have around, for which you will give me a lard sandwich and a glass of water?"; he carries all his worldly possessions bound up in a bandana on a stick over his shoulder—this is known as a bindle. The other kind of tramp we have in America exists by robbing the others, and he's known as a bindlestiff; he does no work, but exists by robbing his fellows. I set up that situation between the cities, and this, to me, seemed to be much more interesting than interstellar wheeler-dealer politics. As a matter of fact, by and large, I don't like wheeler-dealer characters. All the characters you find in conventional interstellar intrigue turn out to be generals, or dictators of the galaxy; my people were to be work horses involved in intrigue with each other, and never mind the wheeler-dealer, they were wheeler-dealers within their own small compass. I was, without realizing it, quite tired of the kind of sf story in which the leading character rises from lieutenant-general to ruler of the galaxy, I just got fed up to the teeth with it. Therefore my migrants, carrying their information and operating their small intrigues, seemed to me to be much more interesting as humans, and more fun to work with. I didn't realize I was departing from the Campbellian norm, but in the long run I did.

Aldiss: One sees these things, of course, by hindsight. Looking back for *Billion Year Spree* I came across this departure that sf had evolved in the pulps, where the hooker was always part-fantasy, and that the supreme power fantasies—greater than Doc Savage, The Shadow and all the rest—were sf because there you had the extra powers you couldn't conjure in any other way. This was the secret of Campbell's success, and although you seemed to fit in there well because you had the highly developed technology, and all the other integrals of Campbell's *Astounding,* you were, nevertheless, departing slowly by doing away with the conquests of the galaxy, which, after all, were the ultimate in power fantasy, and this became more noticeable as the series went on.

Blish: I did some of the Okie stories before I did "Bridge." It was only later on that I came to realize that before I got my cities into the sky we needed two fundamental discoveries. One of these was the faster-than-light drive involved, and the other was a way of achieving longevity—often mistakenly referred to as immortality, my people were not immortal, they simply lived very long lives. So I wrote two stories to show how these discoveries were made. "Bridge" is the story of the discovery of the interstellar drive, and it's all done in terms of the little technicians who have to work on the bridge on Jupiter, who don't know why they are there, or why they should be plunged into this hell. The other one took place mostly on Earth, in a pharmaceutical company where they were working on the problem of longevity. There again you have minor characters being involved who don't know what's going on. I then tied these stories together with an Alaskan senator, who knows what both projects are about, and is doomed to death if anyone discovers what he's up to, and I do kill him off at the end. That made a third story. I made a triple sandwich of this to make a novel, which is a prequel to *Earthman, Come Home*. By that time I was working on a smaller scale than I was when I conceived the Okie society as a whole, because I wanted to show how it all started. So, in what I originally called *They Shall Have Stars*, which is still titled that in England, I was going down smaller than before. I think the signal quality of "Bridge," apart from the fact that it is faithful to what I know about Jupiter, or knew about Jupiter at the time, was that nobody who was actually working on the bridge knew what they were doing, and they were, in several ways, in revolt against it, they couldn't see any sense in it; it was just another multi-billion dollar project in which they were cogs, and their emotions were not considered. I think perhaps that's why you remember that story. It did not, however, come first, it was a conscious narrowing of focus.

Aldiss: The last of the *Cities in Flight* series was *A Clash of Cymbals*. I suppose that marked one of the points in your evolution; because for the first time we see the emergence of what I think is one of your major preoccupations, which is with—and I don't know the grand title for it—something like "the end of things." You have returned to "the end of things" over and over again, and have shown it in various ways. There's a beautiful novel which Faber published as a juvenile, which is about the end of the universe and has angels in it!

Blish: There are two such books, one a sequel to the other, but I don't feel they deal with the end of things. The two books with the angels in them deal with the possible incorporation of the Earth into a galactic system which is some one hundred thousand years in the future. By our own actions and abilities we have set back that date by about twenty-five thousand years, but still the incorporation is far ahead. In an independent story, which is in neither of these books, I raise the question of whether we really *want* to be in this galactic organization. It appears to be very ugly the more we look at it. The first book is called *The Star Dwellers* and the second *Mission to the Heart Stars*.

Aldiss: The end of things crops up again at the end of your other phase of writing with those two magnificent books *Black Easter* and *The Day After Judgment*.

Blish: Well now, Brian, I want to make another differentiation here. I seldom really like to deal with the end of things; I like to leave the end of things up to the reader, as I did in *A Case of Conscience*. I never tell anybody what I think the actual ending is. In the same way, in *Black Easter* and *The Day After Judgment*. *Black Easter* apparently ends with Armageddon and the triumph of the Devil. *The Day After Judgment* is a demonstration of something that was said, I think by Voltaire, that if the Devil ever did triumph it would be incumbent upon him to take upon himself the attributes of God. My further point on this was that it would be impossible for the Devil to do, and therefore it would fall upon us to do it. This is not the end of something, it is the beginning of something else. Again, this happens hundreds of thousands of years in the future, or at the end of eternity. We may or may not manage the job. This all started with the ending of the *Cities in Flight* series, which was essentially, to my view, a novel of how people, including very young people, might react in their very different ways if they knew the exact day of their deaths. That *is* a novel of finality, and you will remember that at the end of the novel we revert to Amalfi, who has always been my central figure, and some slight hope is given that even this apparent ultimate disaster might be survived in some way, with some fragments of one's personality left. Amalfi says no, he's lived so long and seen so much, and been in charge of so much of his universe, that he knows all the nuts and bolts are coming out of it, and he's dead tired.

Aldiss: I will be repentant to this degree: let's do away with this phrase "the end of things" and use your word—"finality." I always regard you as a novelist of finality. This is the essence that I get most powerfully from your novels, and that I like very much. We're going to have to skate over the whole indulgent thing I wanted you to do, discussing some of my favorite stories, but I at least insist on listing them. You'll be happy to know that "Surface Tension" is not among them. I doted on "Bridge" and I doted on "Beep," which I think is marvelous, and I doted on "Common Time," which, again, is absolutely splendid; it is exactly the right length for the content, and this is rare in sf, as I think you'll agree. I would like you, for posterity, to recite your anecdote on what happened at Heath House when I was entertaining you and Harry Harrison, and you revealed to us that you were going to write a sequel to *Black Easter*.

Blish: When I finished *Black Easter* I thought I had finished it. It turned out to be the most commercially successful novel I have ever written; it eventually got 78 reviews in general newspapers in the States, newspapers which almost never notice sf at all, or fantasy; most of the reviews were highly favorable, and the book sold like mad. There could be no more final and black an ending for a novel than *Black Easter*, so my editor at Doubleday said "how about a sequel?" At Heath House, with you and Margaret and Judy and Harry, I mentioned this mad project, and tried to see how I could undertake it. Harry, who is a master of the over-reaction, threw up his hands, staggered backwards across the room, brought up against the wall with his hands thrown up against it, clasped his brow, then he stopped and thought about it for a moment, and said "Well, meanwhile in another universe very similar to ours...," which I thought was a great opening sentence. It would, of course, have been out of the terms of any possible sequel to *Black Easter*.

Aldiss: One of the beautiful and silencing things about the sequel, which I refuse to accept as a sequel, is that the join is seamless; you actually take up from the very next sentence, and that extraordinary Brughelesque ending just goes on into the next book.

Blish: I'm glad to hear this because I no longer regard them as two books. I hope that when the New York edition of *After Such Knowledge* appears this will be a trilogy, not a tetralogy, in which *Black Easter* and *The Day After Judgment* will be put together as one book without the synopsis that I opened *The Day After Judgment* with, then, I think perhaps it will be smooth and seamless.

Aldiss: I wish you would forget that title, but I know you are very addicted to it.

Blish: I'm wedded to it. This is because all four of my characters are allegorical characters; at the end of *The Day After Judgment* all four turn out to be epitomies of deadly sins, that's why they find themselves in this position at the end.

Aldiss: So that I don't appear entirely as a claque in this discussion let me offer you a quotation from the worthy Philip Strick who talks about Blish's "glacial surfaces." I know what he means by that; I wonder if you do?

Blish: This has often puzzled me. So many people have said that my writing is cold, in one way or another, that I must assume it to be true. Now, when I hear it from Harlan Ellison, who lives at the top of his voice, I discount it, but Harlan is not the only one to have said it by any means, I've recently seen it in fanzines. I'm supposed to be an intellectual writer with virtually no emotional content, and I do not understand this. It seems to me, that at least in my best work, there is a great deal of emotional content, and I could tell you of scenes in some of my work that I have wept over because I did not want them to happen, but I saw from the logic of the stories they had to happen that way. Perhaps "glacial surface" is simply a way of saying that while I am writing a story which I think has emotional content, I am, at the same time, trying to get things right. I also like to present characters arguing at their best, so as to make issues clear, so that I can get on to the emotional involvements and outcomes which come from apparently abstract questions. This is my whole principle in writing a science-fiction story that I take seriously, particularly if I start with the background. The next question I ask myself after I've looked at this background and worked it out is "who does this hurt?"—and the person that background hurts most becomes my central character.

Aldiss: I think you've approached very close to the heart of the matter, but the answer to this must be that you place the emphasis on the "hurt" all the time—not on the warmth but the chill of hurt. You know how I admire *Black Easter* and *The Day After Judgment*; precisely what I like about them is what I like in what is for me the best of your writing, which is the hurt and the glacial surfaces. There are plenty of people around spewing raw emotion; your virtue is that you are one of the intellectuals of the field, and I would hate to think that you were ever on the defensive about it.

Blish: I am not defensive about it, it is one of the qualities of my writing that I value. In *Foundation 3*, Poul Anderson says that Heinlein has been insufficiently credited for realizing that love is tragic; this does not prevent him from valuing love, and showing that he values it. I think, whether this is actually true of Heinlein or not, it's much more true of Poul, it is an insight that I value enormously. It becomes more valuable, and more complicated, and more to be valued, when you realize that you do have, and are constantly driving, Plato's two horses, Reason and Passion. Which one is on top depends not on the horses but on the driver. What I want to do is to produce work which contains passion controlled by reason, in as an exact a balance as I, as a driver, can achieve.

Aldiss: Let's move on to a more personal theme, if you don't mind. We have both lived through the wrenching experiences of failed first marriages, so can we, from that viewpoint, approach that beautiful, though not unflawed book of yours, *Fallen Star*?

Blish: Indeed. It's almost totally autobiographical, on the surface as well as at the bottom. These events actually happened to me, I just pushed them a little further than they actually went.

Aldiss: I liked that novel when I read it. In fact, I think I was a reader for Faber when it came in, and I said yes to it. I was, nevertheless, mystified by it, and my reservation was that towards the end you had to bring an alien in, a Martian trekking across the wastes of the Antarctic, in what was otherwise an assured and complete novel. Did you feel that perhaps you were being too personal and that it had better be sf?

Blish: This is one of my signal failures. I had three intentions in succession on that one. The events in which I had been involved were, on the surface, so comic that I thought I would make it a pure comic novel. It couldn't possibly be funnier. As a matter of fact I left out some incidents which would have reduced it to farce as a novel. As I went into it, however, the business of the failing marriage and the emotional relationships began to sneak in under the comic elements. I have a madman in that novel; it seemed to me to be likely that in the days of flying saucer mania, which had by then been running on fifteen or twenty years, a paranoid's delusions might very well take on a science-fictional coloration. So I gave you a madman who might or might not be a Martian, and left it to you to decide whether he was or not. The novel fails in its last line when I weighted the damned thing on the science-fictional side. That was a failure of nerve on my part, and I'm sorry for it. The central mistake was in introducing all the science-fictional elements in the middle, because I was wrong about my assumption that a mainstream audience would accept that a madman's delusions might take a science-fictional form. Then I made the final, crucial mistake of weighting the thing a little bit on the sf side, that he was more likely a Martian than not. I should not have done that.

Aldiss: Most sf is about madness, or what is currently ruled to be madness; this is part of its attraction—it's always playing with how much the human mind can encompass. You were being so beautifully subtle in that novel, and things work so well until the end. I think if you'd left it as an open question it would have been better.

Blish: It's the way I prefer to work when I have my full mind on a job; I like to leave some questions at the end open, for the reader to decide for himself, which I think will tell him something about himself.

Aldiss: One question I would like to get in—it's a question I think always rides along in sf, and is part of the two strains of sf, not the old wave or the new wave, or anything like that, but the question of thinking vs. feeling in sf. I suppose you'd agree that sf has a large didactic element—your books have, even my books have—the wish to teach people something, to make them learn. Don't you think that one of the main divisions is whether you want to make them think or whether you want to make them feel? Don't you feel that your novels have changed, and that to begin with you wanted to make people think and now you want to make them feel?

Blish: Yes, I do. A simple three word answer. I have myself changed in this direction and I hope my work has. The old business of "write what you know" is, I think, totally false after all. I have never been on Mars or Jupiter, and there are elements in all my work of many situations in which I have not been. "Write what you know" is a prison, so write what you feel, it opens up the world, and it depends on the type of man you are gradually becoming. I hope that I am becoming more open in feeling and what Philip Strick calls my "glacial surface" is simply my attempt to keep reason and passion in aesthetic balance. So far as my intent is concerned, writing what I feel is what I am doing now.

Aldiss: My own cast of mind has always inclined me to believe that your scenes on Jupiter in "Bridge," and your scenes in interstellar space in "Common Time," represent feelings as much as places. After all, if you set anything on the moon, you're writing about a feeling as well as a place, you're writing about the feeling of being alienated from Earth. Presumably that means the feeling of being alienated from your family or whatever — so there isn't a great dichotomy.

Blish: "Common Time" is, I think, the most perfect example of the transitional point in my writing. This is the story with all the "glacial surface" and trappings of a first interstellar crossing, but the story is about lost love.

Aldiss: One of the objections I have against Campbell's *Astounding* was that there was too little love in it. It was a very loveless magazine. They never took enough account of the *feeling* that is always in sf. You said, somewhere in *The Issue at Hand*, that if you wanted to be a writer you could always write sf and your mother could read it. I remember that, it chimed with me personally, and this is something that's hard to grow out of, isn't it?

Blish: Some of us never grow out of it. I think what I actually said was that when you begin writing anything, and verge upon taboo areas such as sex, the question is "what if mom should read this and discover that I know things I'm not supposed to know?" For sf it's perfectly possible to do this, and mom will say "it's utterly incomprehensible and I wish you'd write something else," and never reveal that you know things that mom would disapprove of. I think we've been out of that for some time now.

Aldiss: One wonders what Mrs. Philip José Farmer senior thinks! Now, as I've run out of questions, ask yourself one.

Blish: What would you like me to ask?

Aldiss: Well, what I would like to hear is—no, I think it's always a bad thing to ask a writer what he's going to do next, because it tempts him to issue a platform, a futurist manifesto...

Blish: But I think I can answer it. I am attempting to open out and become more receptive as best I can. Become, in particular, more conscious of the tragic consequences of our most immediate concerns, and still keep as tight a rein upon the surface control of the thing as a work of art as I ever did before. I started out as a pure technician with a little bag of tricks. I am now attempting more and more to write what I feel, and attempting to feel more and more and still retain conscious control. Into what subjects that is going to lead me I don't know. I know where I am at the moment—in an area I've never been before. I have high hopes for this in my own personal terms, although whether anyone will buy it or not is another matter. I have a strong suspicion my agent will groan audibly across three thousand miles when he sees it. It is something I'm very much bound up in, and is something I feel is widening me in mind in the direction I want to go. That's not a platform, just an ambition. I won't consider it a finished work of art unless it not only has the wider feeling that I'm hoping for, but that it still has the control I feel an artist absolutely must have in order to say what he means.

Aldiss: We differ there very strongly, because I'm trying to lose control, not all the time, but on occasions, especially in the short stories I'm writing now. I want to lose control and see what happens.

Blish: I did that in "Common Time" and it worked very nicely, and I may try it again, but having spent most of my life being a typewriter with a "glacial surface" I'm going to carry on being a typewriter with a "glacial surface" for a while yet, and still try to widen my emotional range and talk about what really matters to me. I don't dare lose control because I don't know who I'm becoming yet.

Aldiss: That's a good line—"I don't know who I'm becoming yet."

Blish: I know who I hope I'm becoming, but that's another matter, and I may hope for something else later on. I'm approaching my 51st birthday, and my time is short to become a wider and more open person than I was before.

Aldiss: Isn't it extraordinary how we all have such fame, how we're household words—in a limited number of households! I wonder what the future will make of us? I suppose it won't bother at all; the important thing is that we should bother.

Blish: That's where you have to start. If you can't love yourself, there's no point in doing anything. It's impossible to love anyone else if you don't love yourself, but one can try.

BIBLIOGRAPHY

Compiled by Judith Lawrence Blish
(The bibliogrpahy is included as page images from the hardback edition because of the complex formatting of the tables.)

bibliography

of the works of

James Blish

compiled by
Judith Lawrence Blish

Contents

Novels	201
Short Stories	212
Anthologies	235
Short Story Collections	236
Science Fiction Criticism	
"The Issue at Hand" Column	240
Books	241
Literary Criticism	243
Book Reviews	249
Articles and Interviews	256
Introductions	265
Poetry	267
Star Trek Books	273
Title Index	278
Name Index	288

NOVELS

Title	Publisher	Country	Date

AFTER SUCH KNOWLEDGE See *Doctor Mirabilis; Black Easter; The Day After Judgment; A Case of Conscience*

AND ALL THE STARS A STAGE (author's working title: *Crab Nebula*)

	Publisher	Country	Date
	Serialized in *Amazing Stories*, Vol. 34, Nos. 6, 7. Ziff-Davis Pub. Co.	U.S.A.	6,7-60
	Doubleday (revised, new copyright)	U.S.A.	1971
	Avon Books	U.S.A.	1974
	Faber & Faber	U.K.	1971
	Corgi/Transworld Pubs.	U.K.	1975
As *L'Armade Des Étoiles*	Bibliotheque Marabout, Verviers	Belgium	1974
As *Die Supernova*	Wilhelm Goldmann Verlag	Germany	1975
As *Le Mappe Del Cielo*	Dall'Oglio	Italy	1974
	Mondadori, Gli Oscar Edition	Italy	1978
As *Zolong Het Duurt*	Born	Netherlands	1975

THE TALE THAT WAGS THE GOD

Title	Publisher	Country	Date
BLACK EASTER [Vol. 2 of *AFTER SUCH KNOWLEDGE*]			
As *Faust Aleph-Null*	*If*, Vol 17, Nos. 8, 9, 10. Galaxy Pub. Corp.	U.S.A.	8,9, 10-67
As *Black Easter*	Doubleday (revised, new copyright)	U.S.A.	1968
Same	Dell	U.S.A.	1969
Same	Equinox	U.S.A.	1977
Same	Gregg Press (with *The Day After Judgment*)	U.S.A.	1980
Same	Avon	U.S.A.	1982
Same	Faber & Faber	U.K.	1968
Same	Penguin	U.K.	1972
Same	Faber (with *The Day After Judgment*)	U.K.	1981
As *Pâques Noires*	*Galaxie*, Editions Opta	France	2,3-69
Same	Editions Planete (with *The Day After Judgment*)	France	1969
Same	Bibliotheque Marabout, Verviers	Belgium	1975
Same	Nouvelles Editions Oswald	France	1983
As *Der Hexenmeister*	Wilhelm Heyne Verlag	Germany	1974 1983
As *Pasqua Nera*	Editrice Nord, Arcano	Italy	1972
As ?	Hayakawa Shobo	Japan	1972
As *Het Helse Paasvur*	Born	Netherlands	1971
As *Sort Påske*	Stig Vendelkaers Forlag	Sweden	1974
A CASE OF CONSCIENCE (Vol. 4 of *AFTER SUCH KNOWLEDGE*)			
	Novelette version: *If*, Vol. 2, No. 4, Quinn Pub. Co.	U.S.A.	9-53
	Ballantine Books (revised, new copyright)	U.S.A.	1958 1966 1972 1975+
	Walker & Co.	U.S.A.	1969
	Ballantine (Book Club edition, cloth)	U.S.A.	1983

[continued]

BIBLIOGRAPHY   203

Title	Publisher	Country	Date
A CASE OF CONSCIENCE [continued]			
	Faber & Faber	U.K.	1959
	Science Fiction Book Club	U.K.	1960
	Penguin	U.K.	1961
			1963
	Arrow	U.K.	1972
			1975
			1979
As *Un Caso de Conscienza*	Editions Grd.	Brazil	1962
As *Paradis Planeten*	Hasselbalchs	Denmark	1969
Same	Stig Vendelkars Forlag	Denmark	1973
As *Un Cas de Conscience*	Editions Denoël	France	1959
As *Der Gewissensfall*	Wilhelm Heyne	Germany	1973
			1983
As *Guerra Al Grande Nulla*	Mondadori	Italy	1960
			1966
	Mondadori, Gli Oscar Ed.	Italy	1976
	Editrice Nord	Italy	1973
As *Akuma No Hoshi*	Tokyo Sogensha	Japan	1967
As ?	Westpress, Vaduz (with Westprint, AG Kriens, Switzerland)	Lichtenstein	1968
As *De Goddeloze Tuin Van Eden*			
	Born	Netherlands	1969
As *Un Caso de Consciencia*	Ediciones Martinez-Roca	Spain	1977
As ?	Askild & Karnekull Forlag	Sweden	1975

CITIES IN FLIGHT (Contents: *They Shall Have Stars; A Life for the Stars; Earthman, Come Home; The Triumph of Time* [*A Clash of Cymbals*]; afterword by R. D. Mullen; table of historical chronology)

	Avon Books	U.S.A.	1970+
	Science Fiction Book Club	U.S.A.	1972
	Arrow	U.K.	1974
			1981
	Bastei Verlag	Germany	1981
	Mondadori	Italy	1979
	Hayakawa Shobo	Japan	1979
	Meulenhoff	Netherlands	1979

204 THE TALE THAT WAGS THE GOD

Title	Publisher	Country	Date

A CLASH OF CYMBALS See *THE TRIUMPH OF TIME*

CRAB NEBULA See *AND ALL THE STARS A STAGE*

THE DAY AFTER JUDGMENT (Vol. 3 of *AFTER SUCH KNOWLEDGE*)

	In *Galaxy*: Vol. 30, No. 5. U.P.D.	U.S.A.	8/9-70
	Doubleday (revised, new copyright)	U.S.	1970
	Gregg Press (with *Black Easter*)	U.S.A.	1980
	Avon	U.S.A.	1982
	Faber & Faber	U.K.	1972
	Penguin	U.K.	1974
As *Le Lendemain de Jugement Dernier*			
	Presses Pocket	France	1977
As *Der Tag nach dem Jüngsten Gericht*			
	Wilhelm Heyne	Germany	1974
			1983
As ?	Longanesi	Italy	1979

DOCTOR MIRABILIS (Vol. 1 of *AFTER SUCH KNOWLEDGE*)

	James Blish, mimeo edition	U.S.A.	1966
	Dodd, Mead (revised, new copyright)	U.S.A.	1971
	Avon	U.S.A.	1982
	Faber & Faber	U.K.	1964
			1974
	Granada (Panther)	U.K.	1976

THE DUPLICATED MAN [with Robert Lowndes]

	In *Dynamic S.F.*, Vol. 1, No. 4, Columbia Pubs.	U.S.A.	8-53
	Avalon Books	U.S.A.	1959
	Airmont	U.S.A.	1964

BIBLIOGRAPHY 205

Title	Publisher	Country	Date
EARTHMAN, COME HOME (novelization of "Okie"; "Bindlestiff"; "Sargasso of Lost Cities"; "Earthman, Come Home"; Vol. 3 of *CITIES IN FLIGHT*)	G. P. Putnam's Sons (new copyright)	U.S.A.	1955
	Science Fiction Book Club	U.S.A.	1956
	Avon Pubs.	U.S.A.	1956
			1958
			1966
			1968
	Faber & Faber	U.K.	1956
			1966
	Science Fiction Book Club	U.K.	1958
	Arrow	U.K.	1974
	Allen	Canada	1955
As *La Terre Est Une Idée*	Editions Denoël	France	1967
As *Stadt Zwischen Den Planeten*	Wilhelm Goldmann	Germany	1960
As *Il Ritorno Dall'Infinito*	Mondadori	Italy	1955
As *Chikyujin Yo Kokyo Ni Kaere*	Hayakawa Shobo	Japan	1965
			1971

ESPER See *JACK OF EAGLES*

FALLEN STAR
As *The Frozen Year*	Ballantine	U.S.A.	1957
As *Fallen Star*	Signet/New American Library	U.S.A.	1977
Same	Avon	U.S.A.	1983
Same	Faber & Faber	U.K.	1957
Same	Four Square/NEL	U.K.	1961
Same	Arrow	U.K.	1977

FAUST ALEPH-NULL See *BLACK EASTER*

THE FROZEN YEAR See *FALLEN STAR*

THE HOUR BEFORE EARTHRISE See *WELCOME TO MARS*

206   THE TALE THAT WAGS THE GOD

Title	Publisher	Country	Date
JACK OF EAGLES	As "Let the Finder Beware!": *Thrilling Wonder Stories*, Vol. 35, No. 2. Standard Magazines	U.S.A.	12-49
	Corwin, Greenberg (revised, new copyright)	U.S.A.	1952
	Galaxy Science Fiction Novel, No. 19. Galaxy Pub. Corp. (abridged)	U.S.A.	1953
As *Esper*	Avon Pubs.	U.S.A.	1958
As *Jack of Eagles*	Avon Books	U.S.A.	1968
			1982
Same	Nova Novel No. 4. Nova Pubs.	U.K.	1955
Same	Faber & Faber	U.K.	1973
Same	Arrow	U.K.	1975
As ?	Editions Guenaud	France	1977
As *Terras Letzte Chance*	Widekind: Balue	Germany	1961
	Transgalaxis Verlag	Germany	1962
As *Der Psi-Man*	Wilhelm Heyne Verlag	Germany	1969
	Bastei Verlag	Germany	1981
As *Mondi Invisible*	Urania, No. 47, Mondadori	Italy	6-54
As *L'Asso Di Coppe*	Galassia, No. 8	Italy	8-61

A LIFE FOR THE STARS (Vol. 2 of *CITIES IN FLIGHT*)

	Publisher	Country	Date
	Serialized in *Analog*, Vol. 70, Nos. 1, 2. Condé Nast.	U.S.A.	9,10-62
	G. P. Putnam's Sons	U.S.A.	1962
	Avon	U.S.A.	1963
			1966
	Faber & Faber	U.K.	1964
	Arrow	U.K.	1974
As *St. Jernebyerne*	Forlaget Notabene	Denmark	1974
As *Villes Nomades*	Editions Denoël	France	1967
As ?	Hayakawa Shobo	Japan	1974
As *Rymdstaden*	Delta Forlags	Sweden	1975

BIBLIOGRAPHY 207

Title	Publisher	Country	Date
MIDSUMMER CENTURY	In *Mag. of Fantasy & Science Fiction*, Vol. 42, No. 4. Mercury Press. (See Short Story list.)	U.S.A.	4-72
	Doubleday (revised, new copyright)	U.S.A.	1972
	DAW Books	U.S.A.	1974
	Faber & Faber	U.K.	1973
	Arrow	U.K.	1975
Portuguese language ed.	Hemus-Livraria Editora	Brazil	1975
As ?	Editions Albin Michel	France	1973
As *Zeit der Vogel*	Wilhelm Heyne	Germany	1974 1983
As ?	Sanrio	Japan	1978
As *Midzomereeuw in Gevecht met de Vogels*	Born	Netherlands	1973
As ?	Delta Forlag	Sweden	1977
MISSION TO THE HEART STARS (see also *THE STAR DWELLERS*)			
	G. P. Putnam's Sons	U.S.A.	1965
	Avon	U.S.A.	1982
	Faber & Faber	U.K.	1965
	Granada (Panther)	U.K.	1977 1980
THE NIGHT SHAPES	Ballantine Books	U.S.A.	1962
	Avon	U.S.A.	1983
	Four Square/NEL	U.K.	1963
	Arrow	U.K.	1978
	Severn House	U.K.	1979
	Tokyo Sogensha	Japan	1975
(Screenplay)	Motion Picture Corp.	U.S.A.	1963
THE QUINCUNX OF TIME	As "Beep," *Galaxy*, Vol. 7, No. 5-A. Galaxy Publ. (See Short Story list.)	U.S.A.	2-54
	Dell Books (revised, new copyright)	U.S.A.	1973

[continued]

208   THE TALE THAT WAGS THE GOD

Title	Publisher	Country	Date
THE QUINCUNX OF TIME [continued]			
	Avon	U.S.A.	1983
	Faber & Faber	U.K.	1975
	Arrow	U.K.	1976
	Forlaget Irlov-Regulus	Denmark	1977
	Editions Denoël	France	1976
	Goldmann Verlag (with *The Warriors of Day*)	Germany	1981
THE SEEDLING STARS (contents: "A Time to Survive"; "The Thing in the Attic"; "Sunken Universe"; "Surface Tension"; "Watershed"; see Short Story list)	Gnome Press	U.S.A.	1957
	Signet (New American Library)	U.S.A.	1959
	Signet/NAL (with *Galactic Cluster*)	U.S.A.	1983
	Faber & Faber	U.K.	1957
	Arrow	U.K.	1972
			1975
As ?	Überreuter Verlag (Tosa imprint)	Austria	1981
As *Semailles Humaines*	Editions Opta, *Galaxie Bis*, No. 46	France	1967
Same	J'ai Lu	France	1977
As *Auch Sie Sind Menschen*	Goldmann Verlag	Germany	1960
As *Il Seme Tra le Stelle*	Mondadori, Urania Ed.	Italy	1970
Same	Mondadori, Gli Oscar Ed.	Italy	1976
As ?	Hayakawa Shobo	Japan	1967
As ?	Ediciones Roca	Spain	1983
As *Zvezdane Spore*	Izdavački Zavod	Yugoslavia	1967
THE STAR DWELLERS (sequel to *MISSION TO THE HEART STARS*)	Serialized in *Boys' Life*, Vol. ?, Nos. 6, 7	U.S.A.	6,7-61
	G. P. Putnam's Sons	U.S.A.	1961
	Searchlight (New York Assn. for the Blind)	U.S.A.	1961

[continued]

BIBLIOGRAPHY 209

Title	Publisher	Country	Date
THE STAR DWELLERS [continued]			
	Avon	U.S.A.	1962
			1965
			1982
	Berkley	U.S.A.	1970
	Faber & Faber	U.K.	1961
	Sphere	U.K.	1977
As *Das Zeichen des Blitzes*	Goldmann Verlag	Germany	1963
			1965
As ?	Hayakawa Shobo	Japan	1969
As *St. Jernetid*	Forlagt-Irlov-Regulus	Sweden	1974
THEY SHALL HAVE STARS (Vol. 1 of *CITIES IN FLIGHT*)			
	Expansion of "Bridge" and "At Death's End," *Astounding Science Fiction* (see Short Story list).	U.S.A.	1952, 1954
As *Year 2018!*	Avon (revised, new copyright)	U.S.A.	1957+
As *They Shall Have Stars*	Faber & Faber	U.K.	1956
			1964
	New English Library	U.K.	1968
	Arrow	U.K.	1974
As *2018; Rumo Ao Infinito*	Coleçao Galaxia O Cruzeiro	Brazil	1969
As *De Vil Fa Stjerner*	Forlaget Notabene	Denmark	1969
As *Aux Hommes, Les Étoiles*	Gallimard	France	1960
	Editions Denoël	France	1965
As *Brücke Zur Ewigkeit*	Wilhelm Heyne Verlag	Germany	1973
As *Uchu Reinen*	Hayakawa Shobo	Japan	1966
TITANS' DAUGHTER			
	As "Beanstalk," *Future Tense*, Greenberg (see Short Story list).	U.S.A.	1952
	Berkley (revised, new copyright)	U.S.A.	1961
	Berkley, Medallion Edition	U.S.A.	1966
	Avon	U.S.A.	1981
			[continued]

210 *THE TALE THAT WAGS THE GOD*

Title	Publisher	Country	Date
TITANS' DAUGHTER [continued]			
	Four Square/NEL	U.K.	1963+
	White Lion	U.K.	1975
As *I Tetraploidi*	Galassia Romanzi di Fantascienza, No. 27	Italy	1963
As *Die Tochter des Giganten*	Utopia Zukunftsroman, No. 384	Germany	1964
As *Auf Titan*	Fischer Orbit	Germany	1972
As *Gigantes en la Tierra*	Organisacion Edit. Novaro	Mexico	1976

A TORRENT OF FACES [with Norman L. Knight] Novelization of "The Shipwrecked Hotel"; "The Piper of Dis"; "To Love Another" (see Short Story list).

	Doubleday (revised, new copyright)	U.S.A.	1967
	Ace	U.S.A.	1967
			1968
			1978
	Faber & Faber	U.K.	1968
	Arrow	U.K.	1968
As *Tausend Milliarden Glückliche Menschen*			
	Marion Von Schroder (Claasen Verlag?)	Germany	1969
Same	Wilhelm Heyne Verlag	Germany	1972

THE TRIUMPH OF TIME (Vol. 4 of *CITIES IN FLIGHT*)

	Avon	U.S.A.	1958+
As *A Clash of Cymbals*	Faber & Faber	U.K.	1959
			1965
			1972
Same	Arrow	U.K.	1974
As *Un Coup de Cymbales*	Editions Denoël	France	1968
As *Triumph der Zeit*	Wilhelm Heyne Verlag	Germany	1973
As *Il Trionfo del Tempo*	I Romanzi di Cosmo Fantascienza, No. 87	Italy	1961
Same	Ponzoni	Italy	1962

THE VANISHED JET	Weybright & Talley	U.S.A.	1968

BIBLIOGRAPHY

Title	Publisher	Country	Date
VOR	As "The Weakness of RVOG" [with Damon Knight], *Thrilling Wonder Stories*, Vol. 33, No. 3 (see also Short Story list)	U.S.A.	2-49
	Avon (revised, new copyright)	U.S.A.	1958 1967
	Corgi/Transworld	U.K.	1959
	Arrow	U.K.	1978
	Severn House	U.K.	1979
As *Flammande Fara*	Wahlstroms	Sweden	1973
THE WARRIORS OF DAY	As "Sword of Xota," *Two Complete Science Adventure Books*, Vol. 1, No. 3. Wings Pub. Co.	U.S.A.	Sum 51
	Galaxy Novel, No. 16	U.S.A.	1953
	Lancer	U.S.A.	1967
	Severn House	U.K.	1978
	Arrow	U.K.	1979
As *Les Guerriers de Day*	Presses de la Cité	France	1975
As *Das Ratsel von Xota*	Wilhelm Goldmann (with *The Quincunx of Time*)	Germany	1981
As *I Guerrieri del Planeta Giorno*	Galassia, No. 4	Italy	4,5-61
WELCOME TO MARS	Serialized as "The Hour Before Earthrise," *If*, Vol. 16, Nos. 7, 8, 9. Galaxy Publ.	U.S.A.	7,8,9-66
	G. P. Putnam's Sons (revised, new copyright)	U.S.A.	1968
	Avon	U.S.A.	1983
	Faber & Faber	U.K.	1967
	Sphere	U.K.	1977

YEAR 2018! See *THEY SHALL HAVE STARS*

SHORT STORIES

Title Publication	Publisher	Country	Date
"The Abattoir Effect"			
So Close to Home	Ballantine	U.S.A.	1961
"Against the Stone Beasts" (10,000 words)			
Planet Stories, Vol. 3 No. 12	Love Romances	U.S.A.	Fall 48
"The Airwhale" (3,000 words)			
Future Fiction, Vol. 2 No. 6	Columbia	U.S.A.	8-42
"And Some Were Savages" (9,300 words)			
Amazing Stories, Vol. 34 No. 11	Ziff-Davis	U.S.A.	11-60
The Most Thrilling Science Fiction Ever Told, No. 6	Ultimate	U.S.A.	Fall 67
Anywhen	Doubleday	U.S.A.	1970
(See *Anywhen*, Collections list, for further reprintings)			
"The Art of the Sneeze" (700 words)			
Mag. of F.&S.F., Vol. 63 No. 5	Mercury Press	U.S.A.	11-82
The Tale That Wags the God	Advent:Publishers	U.S.A.	1987

BIBLIOGRAPHY *213*

Title Publication	Publisher	Country	Date

"Art Work" See "A Work of Art"

"At Death's End" (15,000 words) (see also *They Shall Have Stars*, Novels list) *Astounding Science Fiction*, Vol. 53 No. 3 — Street & Smith — U.S.A. — 5-54
Galaxie — Editions Opta — France — 1977

"Back Seat Hoopster" (5,900 words)
Ace Sports, Vol. 16 No. 2 — Periodical House — U.S.A. — 1-48

"Backfield Business" (5,700 words)
All Football Stories, Vol. 1 No. 1 — Interstate — U.S.A. — 12-47

"Barb-Wire Law" (5,000 words) [as Luke Torley]
Blue Ribbon Western, Vol. 7 No. 5 — Columbia — U.S.A. — 5-47

"Bats for Brains" (6,000 words)
Sports Fiction, Vol. 5 No. 5 — Columbia — U.S.A. — 12-47

"Battle of the Unborn" (2,800 words) ("Struggle in the Womb")
Future Fiction, Vol. 1 No. 1 — Columbia — U.S.A. — 5/6-50
As "Struggle in the Womb"
So Close to Home (collection) — Ballantine — U.S.A. — 1961
Science Fiction Adventures in Mutation (Ed. Groff Conklin) — Vanguard — U.S.A. — 1955
— Berkley — U.S.A. — 1965

"Beanstalk" (25,000 words) (see also *Titans' Daughter*, Novels list)
Future Tense (Ed. K. F. Crossen) — Greenberg — U.S.A. — 1952
Original Science Fiction Stories, Vol. 6 No. 4 (as "Giants in the Earth") — Columbia — U.S.A. — 1-56
Galactic Cluster — Faber & Faber — U.K. — 1960
(see *Galactic Cluster*, Collections list, for futher reprintings)
A Pair From Space — Belmont — U.S.A. — 1965

Title	Publication	Publisher	Country	Date
"Beep" (17,000 words) (see also *The Quincunx of Time*, Novels list)				
	Galaxy, Vol. 7 No. 5-A	Galaxy	U.S.A.	2-54
	Stories for Tomorrow (Ed. William Sloane)	Funk & Wagnalls	U.S.A.	1954
		Eyre Spottiswoode	U.K.	1955
	Space Police (Ed. Andre Norton)	World	U.S.A.	1956
	Galactic Cluster	Signet/NAL	U.S.A.	1959
	(see *Galactic Cluster*, Collections list, for further reprintings)			
	The Best of James Blish (Ed. R. A. W. Lowndes)	Del Rey/Ballantine	U.S.A.	1979
	Galactic Empires (Ed. B. Aldiss)	Futura	U.K.	1977
		Avon	U.S.A.	1979
As ?				
	Het Testament van Andros	A. W. Bruna	Netherlands	1972
"Bequest of the Angel" (6,000 words)				
	Super Science Stories, Vol. 1 No. 2	Fictioneers	U.S.A.	5-40

"The Billion Year Binge" See "With Malice to Come"

Title	Publication	Publisher	Country	Date
"Bindlestiff" (16,000 words) (see *Earthman, Come Home*, in Novels list)				
	Astounding Science Fiction, Vol. 46 No. 4	Street & Smith	U.S.A.	12-50
"Blackout in Cygni"				
	Planet Stories, Vol. 5 No. 1	Love Romances	U.S.A.	7-51
"Bonanza in Lead" (7,600 words)				
	Famous Westerns, Vol. 9 No. 2	Columbia	U.S.A.	4-48
"The Book of Your Life" (4,500 words)				
	Mag. of F.&S.F., Vol. 8 No. 3	Fantasy House	U.S.A.	3-55
As "Le Livre de Vie"				
	13 Histoires D'Objets Malefiques	Bibliotheque Marabout Verviers	Belgium	1975
	Fiction, No. 28	Editions Opta	France	3-56

BIBLIOGRAPHY *215*

Title Publication	Publisher	Country	Date
"The Bore" (3,600 words)			
Fantastic Story Quarterly, Vol. 1 No. 2	Best Books	U.S.A.	Sum 50
"The Bounding Crown" (7,750 words)			
Super Science & Fantastic Stories, Vol. 1 No. 15	Popular Pubs.	Canada	12-44
Super Science Stories Vol. 5 No. 1	Fictioneers	U.S.A.	1-49
"The Box" (7,700 words)			
Thrilling Wonder Stories, Vol. 34 No. 1	Standard Mags.	U.S.A.	4-49
Omnibus of Science Fiction (Ed. Groff Conklin)	Crown	U.S.A.	1953
[television version]	Du Mont	U.S.A.	9 Sep 53
So Close to Home (collection)	Ballantine	U.S.A.	1961
The Shape of Things (Ed. Damon Knight)	Popular Library	U.S.A.	1965
Beyond Control (Ed. Robert Silverberg)	Thomas Nelson	U.S.A.	1972
The Best of James Blish, (Ed. R. A. W. Lowndes)	Del Rey/Ballantine	U.S.A.	1979
Strange Adventures in Science Fiction (Ed. Groff Conklin)	Grayson & Grayson	U.K.	1955
Roboter (Ed. Peter Naujack)	Diogenes Verlag	Switz.	1962
"Bridge" (12,000 words) (see also *They Shall Have Stars*, Novels list)			
Astounding Science Fiction, Vol. 48 No. 6	Street & Smith	U.S.A.	2-52
Spectrum II (Eds. K. Amis & R. Conquest)	Harcourt, Brace & World	U.S.A.	1962
	Berkley	U.S.A.	1964
	Gollancz	U.K.	1962
The Astounding-Analog Reader, Vol. 12 (Eds. B. Aldiss & H. Harrison)	Doubleday	U.S.A.	1973
Jupiter (Eds. C. & F. Pohl)	Ballantine	U.S.A.	1973
Science Fictional Solar System (Ed. M. H. Greenberg)	Harper & Row	U.S.A.	1979

Title Publication	Publisher	Country	Date

"Buckshot Legacy" (3,800 words) [as Luke Torley]
   Western Action, Vol. 2 No. 4   Columbia   U.S.A.   4-47

"Callistan Cabal" (6,000 words)
   Stirring Science Stories,   Albing   U.S.A.   4-41
   Vol. 1 No. 2

Captain Video and the Sub-Space Corsair
   Du Mont T.V., 15 half-hour scripts   U.S.A.   8-31 to 9-18-53

"A Case of Conscience" (23,000 words) (see also Novels list)
   If, Vol. 2 No. 4   Quinn   U.S.A.   9-53
   Best Science Fiction   Faber & Faber   U.K.   1955
   (Ed. E. Crispin)
   The Arbor House Treasury of   Arbor House   U.S.A.   1980
   Great Science Fiction Short
   Novels (Eds. R. Silverberg &
   M. H. Greenberg)
   As "Et Samvittighetsspørsmål,"   Gyldendal Norsk   Norway   1974
   Himmelstorm (?)

"Casey and the Second String" (5,000 words)
   Super Sports, Vol. 8 No. 3   Columbia   U.S.A.   9-50

"Chaos, Co-ordinated" (13,000 words) [as John MacDougal, joint pseud.
with R. W. Lowndes]
   Astounding Science Fiction,   Street & Smith   U.S.A.   10-46
   Vol. 38 No. 2

"Chinook Bill and the Shooting Woman" (2,000 words)
   Complete Cowboy, Vol. 8 No. 2 Columbia   U.S.A.   11-48

"Cinder Saint" (7,300 words)
   Sports Fiction, Vol. 6 No. 3   Columbia   U.S.A.   3-49

"Citadel of Thought" (6,000 words)
   Stirring Science Stories,   Albing   U.S.A.   2-41
   Vol. 1 No. 1
   The Best of James Blish   Del Rey/Ballan-   U.S.A.   1979
   (Ed. R. A. W. Lowndes)   tine

BIBLIOGRAPHY 217

Title	Publication	Publisher	Country	Date

"The City That Was the World" (11,000 words)
    Galaxy, Vol. 28 No. 5   Universal P. & D.   U.S.A.   7-69

"Claw of the Kidnapped Idol" (3,000 words) [as Marcus Lyons]
    Crack Detective Stories,   Columbia   U.S.A.   8-53
    Vol. 8 No. 6

"Common Time" (8,000 words)
    Science Fiction Quarterly,   Columbia   U.S.A.   8-53
    Vol. 2 No. 4
    Shadow of Tomorrow   Permabooks/   U.S.A.   1953
    (Ed. F. Pohl)   Doubleday
    Galactic Cluster   Signet/NAL   U.S.A.   1959
    (see *Galactic Cluster*, Collections list, for further reprintings)
    The Mirror of Infinity   Canfield Press and U.S.A.   1970
    (Ed. R. Silverberg)   Harper & Row
    To the Stars (Ed. R. Silverberg) Hawthorn Books   U.S.A.   1971
    Survival Printout   Vintage (Random U.S.A.   1973
                                    House)
    Arbor House Treasury of   Arbor House   U.S.A.   1979
    Modern Science Fiction
    (Ed. M. Greenberg)
    The Best of James Blish   Del Rey/Ballan- U.S.A.   1979
    (Ed. R. A. W. Lowndes)   tine
    Yet More Penguin Science   Penguin   U.K.   1964
    Fiction (Ed. B. Aldiss)
    Second Orbit (Ed. G. D.   John Murray   U.K.   1965
    Doherty)
    Best Science Fiction Stories Faber & Faber   U.K.   1965
    of James Blish
    (see *Best Science Fiction Stories of James Blish*, Collections list,
        for further reprintings)
    American Science Fiction   Malian Press   Australia 1971
    Magazine
As ?
    Het Testament van Andros   A. W. Bruna   Nether-   1972
                                                 lands

THE TALE THAT WAGS THE GOD

Title Publication	Publisher	Country	Date
"Darkside Crossing"			
Galaxy Science Fiction, Vol. 31 No. 1	Universal P. & D.	U.S.A.	12-70
The Best From Galaxy Vol. 1	Award Books	U.S.A.	1972
"Death off the Record" (2,180 words) [as Marcus Lyons]			
Crack Detective Stories, Vol. 6, No. 6	Columbia	U.S.A.	11-45
"Death's Photo Finish" (3,600 words) [as Marcus Lyons]			
Crack Detective Stories, Vol. 6, No. 6	Columbia	U.S.A.	2-48
"Detour to the Stars" (7,000 words) (author's working title: "The Long Way Home")			
Infinity Science Fiction, Vol. 1 No. 6	Royal Pub.	U.S.A.	12-56
"Double-Clutch Danger" (10,500 words)			
Sports Fiction, Vol. 6 No. 1	Columbia	U.S.A.	10-48
"Dribble Trouble" (6,000 words)			
All Basketball Stories, Vol. 1 No. 1	Atlas News	U.S.A.	Winter 1947-48
"A Dusk of Idols" (8,900 words)			
Amazing Stories, Vol. 35 No. 3	Ziff-Davis	U.S.A.	3-61
Great Science Fiction From Amazing, No. 1	Ultimate	U.S.A.	1965
Anywhen	Doubleday	U.S.A.	1970
(see *Anywhen*, Collections list, for further reprintings)			
Alpha 8 (Ed. R. Silverberg)	Berkley	U.S.A.	1977
"Earthman, Come Home" (17,000 words) (see Novels list)			
Astounding Science Fiction, Vol. 52 No. 3	Street & Smith	U.S.A.	11-53
Science Fiction Hall of Fame (Ed. Ben Bova)	Doubleday	U.S.A.	1973

BIBLIOGRAPHY

Title / Publication	Publisher	Country	Date
"Elixir" (5,700 words)			
Future Fiction (Combined With Science Fiction Stories), Vol. 2 No. 3	Columbia	U.S.A.	9-51
"Emergency Refueling" (1,800 words)			
Super Science Stories, Vol. 1 No. 1	Fictioneers	U.S.A.	3-40
These Were My Best (Ed. Frederik Pohl)	Putnam's/Berkley	U.S.A.	1981
"A Feast of Reason" See "With Malice to Come"			
"Ferry to a Funeral" (2,500 words)			
Crack Detective Stories, Vol. 10 No. 3	Columbia	U.S.A.	7-49
"First Strike" (6,000 words)			
Mag. of F.&S.F., Vol. 4 No. 6	Fantasy House	U.S.A.	6-53
"Freedom Lode" (10,000 words)			
Six Gun Western, Vol. 2 No. 1	Trojan Mag.	U.S.A.	9-48
"Fullback Frankenstein" (7,200 words)			
Sports Leaders, Vol. 1 No. 1	Stadium	U.S.A.	4-48
"FYI" (3,000 words)			
Star Science Fiction, No. 2 (Ed. F. Pohl)	Ballantine	U.S.A.	1953
So Close to Home	Ballantine	U.S.A.	1961
The Mathematical Magpie (Ed. Clifton Fadiman)	Simon & Schuster	U.S.A.	1962
Beyond This Horizon (Ed. C. Carrell)	Ceolfrith Arts Council, Sunderland	U.K.	1973
"The Genius Heap" (5,600 words)			
Galaxy Science Fiction, Vol. 12 No. 4	Galaxy Pub.	U.S.A.	8-56
The Sixth Galaxy Reader (Ed. H. L. Gold)	Doubleday	U.S.A.	1962

Title   Publication | *Publisher* | *Country Date*

"Get Out of My Sky" (28,500 words)
   Astounding Science Fiction, Street & Smith   U.S.A.   1,2-57
    Vol. 58, Nos. 5 & 6
   Get Out of My Sky (selected   Crest/Fawcett   U.S.A.   1960
    by Leo Margulies)
   (with "There Shall Be No   Granada   U.K.   1978
    Darkness")

"Getting Along" (11,100 words) [with J. A. Lawrence]
   Again, Dangerous Visions   Doubleday   U.S.A.   1972
    (Ed. Harlan Ellison)
      Signet/NAL   U.S.A.   1973

"Giants in the Earth" See "Beanstalk"; also *Titans' Daughter,* Novels list

"The Glitch" (3,000 words) [with L. Jerome Stanton]
   Galaxy, Vol.35 No. 6   Universal Pub.   U.S.A.   6-74
   Antigrav (Ed. Philip Strick)   Hutchinson/   U.K.   1975
      Arrow
      Taplinger   U.S.A.   1976
   The Best From Galaxy, Vol. III   Award Books   U.S.A.   1976
    (Ed. James Baen)
   Anthology of Classic Science   Editions Aubier   France   1977
   Fiction Texts   Montaigne

"Gridiron Workhorse" (11,000 words)
   Sports Fiction, Vol. 6 No. 2   Columbia   U.S.A.   1-49

"A Hero's Life" (10,000 words) (see also "A Style in Treason")
   Impulse, Vol. 1 No. 1   Roberts & Vinter   U.K.   3-66

"Homesteader" (4,200 words)
   Thrilling Wonder Stories,   Standard Mags   U.S.A.   6-49
    Vol. 34 No. 2

"Hot Horn—Cold Heart" (3,000 words) [as Marcus Lyons]
   Crack Detective Stories,   Columbia   U.S.A.   5-46
    Vol. 7 No. 3

BIBLIOGRAPHY 221

Title Publication	Publisher	Country	Date
"The Hound of Hades" (3,000 words)			
Blue Ribbon Western, Vol. 13 No. 6	Columbia	U.S.A.	8-49
"How Beautiful With Banners" (4,200 words)			
Orbit No. 1 (Ed. D. Knight)	Putnam's/Berkley	U.S.A.	1966
	Ronald Whiting & Wheaton	U.K.	1966
	Fischer Taschenbuch Verlag	Germany	1-72
Anywhen	Doubleday	U.S.A.	1970
(see *Anywhen*, Collections list, for further reprintings)			
The Science Fiction Roll of Honor (Ed. F. Pohl)	Random House	U.S.A.	1975
The Best of James Blish (Ed. R. A. W. Lowndes)	Del Rey/Ballantine	U.S.A.	1979
Best Science Fiction Stories of James Blish	Faber & Faber	U.K.	1973
(see *Best Science Fiction Stories of James Blish*, Collections list, for further reprintings)			
"The Hustler" (3,000 words)			
Super Sports, Vol. 7 No. 1	Columbia	U.S.A.	10-48
"I Remember Murder" (2,200 words)			
Crack Detective Stories, Vol. 9 No. 6	Columbia	U.S.A.	1-49
"Invisible Armada" (1,000 words)			
Air World, Vol. 5 No. 6	Columbia	U.S.A.	9-46
"Killer Come Back to Me!" (12,000 words)			
Famous Detective Stories, Vol. 11 No. 2	Columbia	U.S.A.	6-50
"Killer of Fire" (5,800 words) [as Marcus Lyons]			
Crack Detective Stories, Vol. 8 No. 2	Columbia	U.S.A.	4-47

222 THE TALE THAT WAGS THE GOD

Title Publication	Publisher	Country	Date

"King of the Hill" (4,500 words)
    Infinity Science Fiction,   Royal Pub.   U.S.A.   11-55
    Vol. 1 No. 1
    Galactic Cluster   Signet/NAL   U.S.A.   1959
    (see *Galactic Cluster*, Collections list, for further reprintings)

"Let the Finder Beware!" (30,000 words) (see also *Jack of Eagles*, Novels list) *Thrilling Wonder Stories*,   Standard Mags.   U.S.A.   12-49
    Vol. 35 No. 2

"A Light To Fight By"
    Penthouse Magazine   U.S.A.   6-72

"The Long Way Home" See "Detour to the Stars"

"Man Without a Planet" (6,000 words) [Krantz Films; TV treatment—paid for, but not published]

"The Masks" (1,750 words)
    Teke Life   TKE Fraternity   U.S.A.   3-59
    Mag. of F.&S.F., Vol. 17 No. 5   Mercury Press   U.S.A.   11-59
    So Close to Home   Ballantine   U.S.A.   1961
As "Les Ongles"
    F.&S.F. (French edition)   Editions Opta   France   3-60

"A Matter of Energy" See "With Malice to Come"

"Mercy Death" (10,000 words) See "The Weakness of RVOG" (see also *VOR*, Novels list)

"Midsummer Century" (37,000 words) (see also Novels list)
    Mag. of F.&S.F., Vol. 42 No. 4   Mercury Press   U.S.A.   4-72
    The Best From Fantasy and   Doubleday   U.S.A.   1974
    Science Fiction [25th Anniversary anthology]
    (Ed. Edward Ferman)

BIBLIOGRAPHY 223

Title   Publication   Publisher   Country Date

"Mistake Inside" (8,500 words)
   Startling Stories, Vol. 17 No. 1   Better Pubs.   U.S.A.   3-48
   World of Wonder (Ed. F. Pratt)   Twayne   U.S.A.   1951
   The Dark Side (Ed. D. Knight)   Doubleday   U.S.A.   1965
                                     Dobson   U.K.   1966
                                     Corgi   U.K.   1967

"More Light" (11,000 words)
   Alchemy and Academe   Doubleday   U.S.A.   1970
   (Ed. Anne McCaffrey)
                                     Del Rey   U.S.A.   1980

"Murder Wears a Mourning Cloak" (3,000 words) [as Marcus Lyons]
   Crack Detective Stories,   Columbia   U.S.A.   1-46
   Vol. 8 No. 1

"Nightride and Sunrise" (11,000 words) [with Jerome Bixby; by-lined Bixby only] *Other Worlds*, Vol. 4 No. 4   Clark Pub. Co.   U.S.A.   6-62

"No Jokes on Mars" (3,000 words)
   Mag. of F.&S.F., Vol. 29 No. 4   Mercury Press   U.S.A.   10-65
   Anywhen   Doubleday   U.S.A.   1970
   (see *Anywhen*, Collections list, for further reprintings)

"No Winter, No Summer" (4,500 words) [as Donald Laverty (joint pseud. with Damon Knight)]
   Thrilling Wonder Stories,   Standard Mags   U.S.A.   10-48
   Vol. 33 No. 1

"None So Blind" (2,000 words) (see also "Who's in Charge Here?")
   Mag. of F.&S.F., Vol. 22 No. 5   Mercury Press   U.S.A.   5-62
   The Best From Fantasy and   Doubleday   U.S.A.   1963
   Science Fiction, 12th Series
                                     Ace   U.S.A.   1966
   Anywhen   Doubleday   U.S.A.   1970
   (see *Anywhen*, Collections list, for further reprintings)
   Mag. of F.&S.F., No. 10   Atlas Distr. Co.   U.K.   9-62
As "L'Ordre de Choses"
   Fiction, No. 166   ?   France   1962

THE TALE THAT WAGS THE GOD

Title	Publication	Publisher	Country	Date
"Nor Iron Bars" (4,800 words)				
	Infinity Science Fiction, Vol. 3 No. 1	Royal Pubs.	U.S.A.	11-57
	Galactic Cluster	Signet/NAL	U.S.A.	1959
	(see *Galactic Cluster*, Collections list, for futher reprintings)			
As ?				
	Het Testament van Andros	A. W. Bruna	Netherlands	1979
"Now That Man Has Gone" (3,000 words)				
	If, Vol. 18 No. 11	Galaxy Pub.	U.S.A.	11-68
"The Oath" (8,700 words)				
	Mag. of F.&S.F., Vol. 19 No. 4	Mercury Press	U.S.A.	10-60
	So Close to Home	Ballantine	U.S.A.	1961
	The Best of James Blish (Ed. R. A. W. Lowndes)	Del Rey/Ballantine	U.S.A.	1979
	Best Science Fiction Stories of James Blish	Faber & Faber	U.K.	1965 / 1973
	(see *Best Science Fiction Stories of James Blish*, Collections list, for further reprintings)			
	Beyond Tomorrow (Ed. L. Harding)	Wren	Australia	?
As "Le Serment"				
	Mag. of F.&S.F., (French edition) No. 85	Editions Opta	France	12-60
As ?				
	Het Testament van Andros	A. W. Bruna	Netherlands	1972
"Okie" (15,000 words) (see *Earthman, Come Home*, Novels list)				
	Astounding Science Fiction, Vol. 45 No. 2	Street & Smith	U.S.A.	4-50
	Stories for Tomorrow (Ed. W. M. Sloane)	Funk & Wagnalls	U.S.A.	1954
	Cities of Wonder (Ed. D. Knight)	Doubleday	U.S.A.	1966
As ?				
	Het Testament van Andros	A. W. Bruna	Netherlands	1972

BIBLIOGRAPHY 225

Title Publication	Publisher	Country	Date

"On the Wall of the Lodge" (9,000 words) [with Virginia Blish]
    Galaxy Science Fiction,   Galaxy Pub.   U.S.A.   6-62
    Vol. 20 No. 5
    Dark Stars (Ed. R. Silverberg)   Ballantine   U.S.A.   1969
As "Le Clown et le Chasseur"
    Galaxie, No. 60   Editions Opta   France   5-69
As "An der Wand der Jagdheitte"
    Die Ratte im Labyrinth   Insel Verlag   Germany 1971

"One-Shot" (5,000 words)
    Astounding Science Fiction,   Street & Smith   U.S.A.   8-55
    Vol. 55 No. 6

"Our Binary Brothers" (7,000 words)
    Galaxy, Vol. 28 No. 1   Galaxy Pub.   U.S.A.   2-69

"Peace Declared!" (2,500 words)
    Man's World, Vol. 1 No. 1   U.S.A.   1-51

"Phantom Blades" (5,600 words)
    Complete Sports, Vol. 5 No. 6   Skyline Pubs.   U.S.A.   12-47

"Phoenix Planet" (10,000 words)
    Cosmic Stories, Vol. 1 No. 2   Albing Pubs.   U.S.A.   5-41

"Pigskin Payoff" See "Touchdown Destiny"

"The Piper of Dis" (13,500 words) [with Norman L. Knight] (see *A Torrent of Faces*, Novels list)
    Galaxy Science Fiction,   Galaxy Pub.   U.S.A.   8-66
    Vol. 24 No. 6

"Puck Poison" (6,300 words)
    Best Sports, Vol. 2 No. 3   Columbia   U.S.A.   5-48

"The Real Thrill" (3,500 words)
    Cosmic Stories, Vol. 1 No. 3   Albing Pubs.   U.S.A.   7-41

Title Publication	Publisher	Country	Date

"Red Chip for Blackmail" (2,100 words) [as Marcus Lyons]
    Crack Detective Stories, Vol. 7 No. 4 — Columbia — U.S.A. — 7-46

"Sabers Are for Saps" (3,500 words) [as Luke Torley]
    Sports Fiction, Vol. 5 No. 3 — Columbia — U.S.A. — 6-47

"Sargasso of Lost Cities" (38,000 words) (see *Earthman, Come Home,* Novels list)
    Two Complete Science Adventure Novels, Vol. 1 No. 8 — Wings Pub. — U.S.A. — Spr 53

"Scrapple at the Crease" (2,900 words)
    Sports Fiction, Vol. 5 No. 6 — Columbia — U.S.A. — 7-48

"The Secret People" (10,000 words) [with Damon Knight]
    Future Fiction, Vol. 1 No. 4 — Columbia — U.S.A. — 11-50

"Serpent's Fetish" (7,000 words)
    Jungle Stories, Vol. 4 No. 3 — Glen-Kel Pub. — U.S.A. — Win 48-49

"The Shipwrecked Hotel" [with Norman L. Knight] (see *A Torrent of Faces,* Novels list)
    Galaxy Science Fiction, Vol. 23 No. 6 — Galaxy Pub. — U.S.A. — 8-65

"Skysign" (17,500 words)
    Analog Science Fiction, Vol. 81 No. 3 — Condé Nast — U.S.A. — 5-68
    Four for the Future (Ed. Harry Harrison) — Macdonald — U.K. — 1969
    — Quartet — U.K. — 1974
    Anywhen — Doubleday — U.S.A. — 1970
    (see *Anywhen,* Collections list, for further reprintings)

"Slide, Sucker, Slide" (9,500 words)
    Big Baseball Stories, Vol. 1 No. 2 — Interstate Pub. — U.S.A. — 8-48

BIBLIOGRAPHY 227

Title Publication	Publisher	Country	Date
"The Snake-Headed Spectre" [as V. K. Emden]			
Jungle Stories, Vol. 4 No. 5	Glen-Kel Pub.	U.S.A.	Sum 49
"The Solar Comedy" (8,500 words)			
Future Fiction, Vol. 2 No. 5	Columbia	U.S.A.	6-42
"Solar Plexus" (3,000 words)			
Astonishing Stories, Vol. 3 No. 1	Fictioneers	U.S.A.	9-41
Beyond Human Ken (Ed. Judith Merrill)	Random House	U.S.A.	1952
	Grayson & Grayson	U.K.	1953
Selections From Beyond Human Ken	Pennant	U.S.A.	1954
Men and Machines (Ed. Robert Silverberg)	Meredith	U.S.A.	1968
	Award Books	U.S.A.	1968
As *Des Hommes et des Machines*	Bibliotheque Marabout, Verviers	Belgium	1973
Great Science Fiction Stories Vol. III (Ed. M. H. Greenberg)	DAW Books	U.S.A.	1979
"The Spirit Is Killing" (2,500 words) [as Marcus Lyons]			
Crack Detective Stories, Vol. 7 No. 6	Columbia	U.S.A.	11-46
"Sponge Dive" (5,000 words)			
Infinity Science Fiction, Vol. 1 No. 3	Royal Pubs.	U.S.A.	6-56
"Statistician's Day" (4,100 words)			
Science Against Man (Ed. Anthony Cheetham)	Avon	U.S.A.	1970
	Sphere	U.K.	1972
Best SF: 1971 No. 5 (Eds. H. Harrison & B. Aldiss)	G. P. Putnam's Sons	U.S.A.	1972
	Sphere	U.K.	1972
	Světov á literatura, Odeon	Czechoslovakia	1977

228   THE TALE THAT WAGS THE GOD

Title Publication	Publisher	Country	Date
"A Style in Treason" (12,000 words) (see also "A Hero's Life")			
Four for the Future	Macdonald	U.K.	1969
(Ed. H. Harrison)			
	Quartet	U.K.	1974
Galaxy Science Fiction,	Universal Pub.	U.S.A.	5-70
Vol. 30 No. 2			
Anywhen	Doubleday	U.S.A.	1970
(see *Anywhen*, Collections list, for further reprintings)			
The Best of James Blish,	Del Rey/Ballan-	U.S.A.	1979
(Ed. R. A. W. Lowndes)	tine		
As "La Style dans la Trahison"			
Galaxie, No. 84	Editions Opta	France	5-71
"Sunken Universe" (6,700 words) [as Arthur Merlyn] (see also *The Seedling Stars*, Novels list)			
Super Science Stories,	Fictioneers	U.S.A.	5-42
Vol. 3 No. 4			
Super Science Stories,	Fictioneers	U.S.A.	11-50
Vol. 7 No. 3			
Worlds to Come (Ed. Damon	Harper & Row	U.S.A.	1967
Knight)			
	Gollancz	U.K.	1967
As "Onderwaterwereld"			
Kleine Science Fiction Omnibus 3	A. W. Bruna-Zoon	Belgium	1972
"Surface Tension" (17,000 words) (see also *The Seedling Stars*, Novels list)			
(first sold to *Worlds Beyond*, summer 1951, but returned unpublished)			
Galaxy Science Fiction,	Universal Pub.	U.S.A.	8-52
Vol. 4 No. 5			
The Second Galaxy Reader	Crown	U.S.A.	1954
(Ed. H. L. Gold)			
6 Great Short Novels of Science Fiction (Ed. G. Conklin)	Dell	U.S.A.	1954
Year's Best Science Fiction Novels 1953 (Eds. E. F. Bleiler & T. E. Dikty)	Frederick Fell	U.S.A.	1953
X Minus One (radio show)	NBC	U.S.A.	1956

[continued]

BIBLIOGRAPHY 229

Title Publication	Publisher	Country	Date
"Surface Tension" [continued]			
Science Fiction Hall of Fame, Vol. I (Ed. R. Silverberg)	Doubleday	U.S.A.	1970
	Gollancz	U.K.	1971
Where Do We Go From Here? (Ed. Isaac Asimov)	Doubleday	U.S.A.	1971
Wonder Makers (Ed. Robert Hoskins)	Fawcett Premier	U.S.A.	1972
Science Fiction Reader (Ed. Harry Harrison)	Scribner's	U.S.A.	1973
The Great Science Fiction Series (Eds. F. Pohl, M. H. Greenberg, & J. Olander)	Harper & Row	U.S.A.	1980
The Best of James Blish (Ed. R. A. W. Lowndes)	Del Rey/Ballantine	U.S.A.	1979
Category Phoenix (Eds. E. F. Bleiler & T. E. Dikty)	John Lane	U.K.	1955
Best Science Fiction Stories of James Blish	Faber & Faber	U.K.	1965
(see *Best Science Fiction Stories of James Blish*, Collections list, for further reprintings)			
As "Alfa Vier"			
Oppervlaktespanning	Meulenhoff	Netherlands	1976
As "Ytspanning"			
Galaxy, No. 17	?	Sweden	2-60
"Ten Yards to Glory" (5,400 words)			
Big Sports, Vol. 1 No. 1	Exclusive Detective Stories	U.S.A.	5-48
"Testament of Andros" (8,000 words)			
Future Fiction, Vol. 3 No. 5	Columbia	U.S.A.	1-53
Portals of Tomorrow (Ed. August Derleth)	Rinehart	U.S.A.	1954
	?	U.K.	1955
So Close to Home	Ballantine	U.S.A.	1961
			[continued]

230   THE TALE THAT WAGS THE GOD

Title Publication	Publisher	Country	Date
"Testament of Andros" [continued]			
Novelets of Science Fiction (Ed. Ivan Howard)	Belmont	U.S.A.	1963
Alpha 1 (Ed. R. Silverberg)	Ballantine	U.S.A.	1970
Best Science Fiction Stories of James Blish	Faber & Faber	U.K.	1965
(see *Best Science Fiction Stories of James Blish*, Collection list, for further reprintings)			
The Best of James Blish (Ed. R. A. W. Lowndes)	Del Rey/Ballantine	U.S.A.	1972
Het Testament van Andros	A. W. Bruna	Netherlands	1972
"There Shall Be No Darkness" (15,000 words)			
Thrilling Wonder Stories, Vol. 36 No. 1	Standard Mags	U.S.A.	4-50
Witches Three (3 novellas by Leiber, Blish, Pratt)	Twayne	U.S.A.	1952
Zacherley's Vulture Stew (Ed. Zacherley)	Ballantine	U.S.A.	1960
The Magazine of Horror, No. 25 (Vol. 5 No. 1)	Health Knowledge	U.S.A.	1-69
Treasury of Modern Fantasy (Ed. M. H. Greenberg)	Avon	U.S.A.	1980
Best Science Fiction Stories of James Blish	Faber & Faber	U.K.	1965
(see *Best Science Fiction Stories of James Blish*, Collections list, for further reprintings)			
The Best of James Blish (Ed. R. A. W. Lowndes)	Del Rey/Ballantine	U.S.A.	1979
Tales of a Monster Hunter (Ed. Peter Cushing)	Arthur Barker	U.K.	1977
With "Get Out of My Sky"	Granada	U.K.	1978
Filmed as *The Beast Must Die*		U.K.	197?
Max J. Rosenberg & Milt Subotsky			
"The Thing in the Attic" (12,000 words) (see *The Seedling Stars*, Novels list) *If*, Vol. 3 No. 5	Quinn	U.S.A.	7-54
The Second World of If (Eds. J. L. Quinn & E. Wulff)	Quinn	U.S.A.	1958

BIBLIOGRAPHY 231

Title Publication	Publisher	Country	Date
"This Earth of Hours" (9,000 words)			
Mag. of F.&S.F., Vol. 16 No. 6	Mercury Press	U.S.A.	6-59
Galactic Cluster	Signet/NAL	U.S.A.	1959
(see *Galactic Cluster*, Collections list, for further reprintings)			
The Best of James Blish	Del Rey/Ballan-	U.S.A.	1979
(Ed. R. A. W. Lowndes)	tine		
Blood and Iron (Ed. J. Pournelle)	TOR	U.S.A.	1984
As "Cette Terre Dont Les Heures Sont Comptees"			
Fiction, No. 70	Editions Opta	France	9-59
As ?			
Het Testament van Andros	A. W. Bruna	Netherlands	1972
"Tiger Ride" (5,000 words) [with Damon Knight]			
Astounding Science Fiction, Vol. 42 No. 2	Street & Smith	U.S.A.	10-48
SF: Authors' Choice	Berkley	U.S.A.	1968
(Ed. Harry Harrison)			
Backdrop of Stars (Ed. Harry Harrison)	Dobson	U.K.	1968
The Old Masters (Ed. B. Davis)	New English Lib.	U.K.	1970
Analog: The Best of Science Fiction	Galahad Books	U.S.A.	1982
"A Time to Survive" (20,000 words) (see *The Seedling Stars*, Novels list)			
Mag. of F.&S.F., Vol. 10 No. 2	Fantasy House	U.S.A.	2-56
As "Survivance"			
F.&S.F., No. 45	Editions Opta	France	8-57
As "Una Oportunidad de Vivir"			
Ciencia y Fantasia	Editorial Novaro	Mexico	1957
"To Love Another" (18,000 words) [with Norman Knight] (see *A Torrent of Faces*, Novels list)			
Analog Science Fiction, Vol. 79 No. 2	Condé Nast	U.S.A.	4-67
"To Pay the Piper" (6,500 words)			
If, Vol. 6 No. 2	Quinn Pub.	U.S.A.	2-56
Galactic Cluster	Signet/NAL	U.S.A.	1959
(see *Galactic Cluster*, Collections list, for further reprintings)			

232　　　THE TALE THAT WAGS THE GOD

Title	Publication	Publisher	Country	Date

"Tomb Tapper" (8,500 words)
    Astounding Science Fiction,　　Street & Smith　　U.S.A.　　7-56
    Vol. 57 No. 5
    Galactic Cluster　　　　　　　Signet/NAL　　　U.S.A.　　1959
    (see *Galactic Cluster*, Collections list, for further reprintings)
    Best Science Fiction Stories　Faber & Faber　　U.K.　　　1965
    of James Blish
    (see *Best Science Fiction Stories of James Blish*, Collections list,
        for further reprintings)
  As?
    Het Testament van Andros　　A. W. Bruna　　　Nether-　　1972
    　　　　　　　　　　　　　　　　　　　　　　　　lands

"The Topaz Gate" (7,000 words)
    Future Fiction, Vol. 1 No. 6　Columbia　　　　U.S.A.　　8-41

"The Torrid Type" (1,500 words)
    The Link, Vol. 7 No. 7　　　　　　　　　　　　U.S.A.　　7-49

"Touchdown Destiny" (5,000 words) (author's working title: "Pigskin
  Payoff")
    Real Sports, Vol. 1 No. 9　　Columbia　　　　U.S.A.　　4-48

"Touchdown Tenderfoot" (5,800 words)
    Super Sports, Vol. 7 No. 2　Columbia　　　　U.S.A.　　1-49

"Translation" (2,200 words)
    Fantastic Universe, Vol. 3 No. 2　King-Size Pubs.　U.S.A.　3-55

"Turn of a Century" (1,200 words)
    Dynamic Science Fiction,　　Columbia　　　　U.S.A.　　3-53
    Vol. 1 No. 2
    Things (Ed. Ivan Howard)　　Belmont　　　　　U.S.A.　　1964

"Two Worlds in Peril" (12,000 words) [with Phil Barnhart]
    Science Fiction Adventures,　Royal Pubs.　　　U.S.A.　　2-57
    Vol. 1 No. 2

BIBLIOGRAPHY 233

Title Publication *Publisher* *Country Date*

"The Void Is My Coffin" (4,200 words)
    Imagination, Vol. 2 No. 3 Greenleaf Pub. U.S.A. 6-51

"Watershed" (3,600 words) (see *The Seedling Stars*, Novels list)
    If, Vol. 5 No. 3 Quinn Pub. U.S.A. 5-55
    The First World of If Quinn Pub. U.S.A. 1957
    (Eds. J. L. Quinn & E. Wulff)
    Mutants (Ed. R. Silverberg) Thomas Nelson U.S.A. 1974
    Bio-Futures (Ed. P. Sargent) Vintage Books, U.S.A. 1974
        Random House

"We All Die Naked" (18,000 words)
    Three for Tomorrow Meredith Press U.S.A. 1969
    (Ed. R. Silverberg)
      Dell U.S.A. 1970
      Gollancz U.K. 1970
    As *La Fabrica Dei Flagelli* Mondadori Italy 1970
    Alpha 4 (Ed. R. Silverberg) Ballantine U.S.A. 1973
    Best Science Fiction Stories Faber & Faber U.K. 1973
      of James Blish
    (see *Best Science Fiction Stories of James Blish*, Collections list,
      for further reprintings)
    Best Science Fiction Stories Hamlyn U.K. 1977

"The Weakness of RVOG" (9,000 words) [with Damon Knight] (see *VOR*,
  Novels list)
    Thrilling Wonder Stories, Standard Mags U.S.A. 2-49
    Vol. 33 No. 3

"Weapon out of Time" (2,000 words)
    Science Fiction Quarterly, No. 3 Columbia U.S.A. Spr 41

"When Anteros Came" (1,000 words)
    Science Fiction Quarterly, No. 5 Columbia U.S.A. Winter 41-42

"Who's in Charge Here?" (2,000 words) See "None So Blind"

Title Publication	Publisher	Country	Date

"With Malice to Come" (1,900 words) (3 vignettes: I. "A Feast of Reason"; II. "The Billion-Year Binge"; III. "A Matter of Energy")

Mag. of F.&S.F., Vol. 8 No. 5	Fantasy House	U.S.A.	5-55
"A Matter of Energy" only, *The Best From F.&S.F., Fifth Series* (Ed. A. Boucher)	Doubleday	U.S.A.	1956
	S.F. Book Club	U.S.A.	1957

"A Work of Art" (6,300 words) ("Art Work")

Original Science Fiction Stories, Vol. 7 No. 1	Columbia	U.S.A.	7-56
Science Fiction Showcase (Ed. Mary Kornbluth)	Doubleday	U.S.A.	1959
Galactic Cluster	Signet/NAL	U.S.A	1959
(see *Galactic Cluster*, Collections list, for further reprintings)			
Worlds of Science Fiction (Ed. Robert P. Mills)	Dial	U.S.A.	1963
	Paperback Library	U.S.A.	1965
The Stars Around Us	Signet/NAL	U.S.A.	1970
The Best of James Blish (Ed. R. A. W. Lowndes)	Del Rey/Ballantine	U.S.A.	1979
Best Science Fiction Stories of James Blish	Faber & Faber	U.K.	1965
(see *Best Science Fiction Stories of James Blish*, Collections list, for further reprintings)			

As "Et Kunstvoerk"

Den Electriste Myre	Borgens Forlag	Netherlands	1972

"Writing of the Rat" (4,900 words)

Galaxy, Vol. 12 No. 3	Galaxy	U.S.A.	7-56
Anywhen	Doubleday	U.S.A.	1970
(see *Anywhen*, Collections list, for further reprintings)			

ANTHOLOGIES EDITED BY JAMES BLISH

Title	Publisher	Country	Date
NEBULA AWARD STORIES 5, edited by James Blish. Introduction pp. 6-10.	Doubleday	U.S.A.	1970
Same	Gollancz	U.K.	1970
Same	Pocket Books	U.S.A.	1972
NEW DREAMS THIS MORNING. Introduction by James Blish (3000 words).	Ballantine Books	U.S.A.	1966
THIRTEEN O'CLOCK (and Other Zero Hours). Stories by C. M. Kornbluth writing as Cecil Corwin. Ed. by James Blish. Preface pp. 7-10.	Dell	U.S.A.	1970
Same	Robert Hale	U.K.	1972

SHORT STORY COLLECTIONS

Title and Contents	Publisher	Country	Date
ANYWHEN Contents: "Preface"; "A Style in Treason"; "The Writing of the Rat"; "And Some Were Savages"; "A Dusk of Idols"; "None So Blind"; "No Jokes on Mars"; "How Beautiful With Banners."	Doubleday	U.S.A.	1970
Same Contents: Same as Doubleday edition, plus "Skysign."	Faber & Faber	U.K.	1971
Same As *L'Oeil de Saturn*. Contents: "The Writing of the Rat"; "And Some Were Savages"; "A Dusk of Idols"; "None So Blind"; "How Beautiful With Banners."	Editions Denoël	France	1973
Same As *Irgendwann*	Wilhelm Goldmann Verlag	Germany	1973

BIBLIOGRAPHY 237

Title and Contents	Publisher	Country	Date
THE BEST OF JAMES BLISH (Ed. R. A. W. Lowndes) Contents: "Citadel of Thought"; "The Box"; "There Shall Be No Darkness"; "Surface Tension"; "Testament of Andros"; "Common Time"; "Beep"; "A Work of Art"; "This Earth of Hours"; "The Oath"; "How Beautiful With Banners"; "A Style in Treason"; "A Probapossible Prolegomena to Ideareal History."	Del Rey/Ballantine	U.S.A.	1979
BEST SCIENCE FICTION STORIES OF JAMES BLISH Contents: "Preface to Tomorrow"; "Surface Tension"; "There Shall Be No Darkness"; "Testament of Andros"; "Common Time"; "A Work of Art"; "Tomb Tapper"; "The Oath."	Faber & Faber	U.K.	1965
BEST SCIENCE FICTION STORIES OF JAMES BLISH Contents: "Preface to Tomorrow"; "Surface Tension"; "There Shall Be No Darkness"; "Testament of Andros"; "Common Time"; "A Work of Art"; "Tomb Tapper"; "The Oath"; "How Beautiful With Banners"; "We All Die Naked."	Faber & Faber	U.K.	1973
Same As *Testament of Andros*	Arrow	U.K.	1977
Same As *Flykt Mot Framtiden*	Delta Forlag	Sweden	1975

FLYKT MOT FRAMTIDEN See BEST SCIENCE FICTION STORIES OF JAMES BLISH

Title and Contents	Publisher	Country	Date
GALACTIC CLUSTER Contents: "Tomb Tapper"; "King of the Hill"; "Common Time"; "A Work of Art"; "To Pay the Piper"; "Nor Iron Bars"; "Beep"; "This Earth of Hours."	Signet/NAL	U.S.A.	1959+
Same 　As *Terre, Il Faut Mourir*	Editions Denoël	France	1961
GALACTIC CLUSTER Contents: "Common Time"; "A Work of Art"; "To Pay the Piper"; "Nor Iron Bars"; "Beep"; "Beanstalk."	Faber & Faber	U.K.	1960
Same	S.F. Book Club	U.K.	1961
Same	Four Square/NEL	U.K.	1963 1968
Same 　As *Rigione Senza Sbarre*	Futuro Biblioteca di Fantascienza Fanucci	Italy	1977

IRGENDWANN See *ANYWHEN*

L'OEIL DE SATURN See *ANYWHEN*

RIGIONE SENZA SBARRE See *GALACTIC CLUSTER*

| SO CLOSE TO HOME
Contents: "Struggle in the Womb"; "Sponge Dive"; "One-Shot"; "The Box"; "First Strike"; "The Abattoir Effect"; "The Oath"; "FYI"; "The Masks"; "Testament of Andros." | Ballantine Books | U.S.A. | 1961 |

TERRE, IL FAUT MOURIR See *GALACTIC CLUSTER*

TESTAMENT OF ANDROS See *BEST SCIENCE FICTION STORIES OF JAMES BLISH*

BIBLIOGRAPHY 239

Title and Contents   *Publisher*   *Country*   *Date*

HET TESTAMENT VAN ANDROS   A. W. Bruna   Nether-   1972
     Contents: "Tomb Tapper"; "Beep";   lands
     "This Earth of Hours"; "Common
     Time"; "Testament of Andros";
     "Nor Iron Bars"; "Okie"; "The Oath."

SCIENCE FICTION CRITICISM

"THE ISSUE AT HAND" COLUMN
[Reprinted in *The Issue at Hand*]

Title	Publication	Publisher [Editor]	Date
"The Okies and Others"	*Skyhook*, No. 15	Gafia Press, Minneapolis [Redd Boggs]	Aut 52
"Pro-Phile" [as William Atheling, Jr.]	*Skyhook*, No. 16	(Same)	Win 52-53
"The Issue at Hand" [As William Atheling, Jr.]			
(Same)	*Skyhook*, No. 17	(Same)	Spr 53
(Same)	*Skyhook*, No. 17	(Same)	Sum 53
(Same)	*Skyhook*, No. 18	(Same)	Sum 53
(Same)	*Skyhook*, No. 19	(Same)	Aut 53
(Same)	*Skyhook*, No. 20	(Same)	Win 53-54
(Same)	*Skyhook*, No. 21	(Same)	Spr 54
(Same)	*Skyhook*, No. 23	(Same)	Win 54-55

SCIENCE FICTION CRITICISM

BOOKS

Title	Publisher	Date
THE ISSUE AT HAND [as William Atheling, Jr.] Contents: "Introduction" [by James Blish]; "Some Propositions"; "Some Missing Rebuttals"; "Rebuttals, Token Punches and Violence"; "A Sprig of Editors"; "Cathedrals in Space"; "Negative Judgments: Swashbungling, Series and Second-Guessing"; "One Completely Lousy Story, With Feetnote"; "Scattershot"; "One Way Trip"; "The Short Novel: Three Ranging Shots and Two Duds"; "The Fens Revisited: 'Said' Books and Incest"; "An Answer of Sorts"; "A Question of Content"; Index.	Advent:Publishers, Chicago. Cloth. Paperback.	1964 1970 1974 1967 1970 1973 1974

242   THE TALE THAT WAGS THE GOD

Title	Publisher	Date
MORE ISSUES AT HAND [as William Atheling, Jr.] Contents: "Introduction: Criticism—Who Needs It?" [by James Blish]; "Science Fiction as a Movement: A Tattoo for Needles"; "New Maps and Old Saws: The Critical Literature"; "Things Still To Come: Gadgetry and Prediction"; "First Person Singular: Heinlein, Son of Heinlein"; "Death and the Beloved: Algis Budrys and the Great Theme"; "Caviar and Kisses: The Many Loves of Theodore Sturgeon"; "Exit Euphues: The Monstrosities of Merritt"; "Scattershot: Practice Makes Perfect—But It Can Also Cut Your Throat"; "Science-Fantasy and Translations: Two More Cans of Worms"; "Making Waves: The Good, the Bad, the Indifferent." Index.	Advent:Publishers, Chicago. Cloth. Paperback.	1970 1971 1974 1972 1974
THE TALE THAT WAGS THE GOD [edited by Cy Chauvin] Contents: "Preface" [by Cy Chauvin]; "Introduction—William Atheling, Jr.: A Critic of Science Fiction" [by John Foyster]; "The Function of Science Fiction"; "The Science in Science Fiction"; "The Arts in Science Fiction"; "A New Totemism?"; "Probapossible Prolegomena to Ideareal History"; "Poul Anderson: The Enduring Explosion"; "The Literary Dreamers"; "The Long Night of a Virginia Author"; "Music of the Absurd" [with "The Art of the Sneeze"]; "A Science Fiction Coming of Age"; "In Conversation: James Blish Talks to Brian Aldiss." Index. Bibliography [by Judith Lawrence Blish].	Advent:Publishers, Chicago. Cloth.	1987

See also Articles list.

LITERARY CRITICISM

Title / Publication	Publisher [Editor]	Date
"American Fantasy Boom"		
Books and Bookmen, Vol. 15 No. 1	Hansom Books, London	10-69
"Announcement—A Wake Appendix"		
A Wake Newslitter (New Series), Vol. 8 No. 6	English Dept., Univ. of Dundee [Fritz Senn & Clive Hart]	10-71
"Another Book at the Wake"		
A Wake Newslitter (New Series), Vol. 8 No. 6	English Dept., Univ. of Dundee [Fritz Senn & Clive Hart]	10-71
"At the Altar of Sesphra: An Approach to the Allegory"		
Kalki, Vol. 2 No. 1, Whole No. 5	James Blish	1967

244   *THE TALE THAT WAGS THE GOD*

Title Publication	Publisher [Editor]	Date
"Book Review" *A Wake Newslitter*, Vol. 3 No. 7		8-66
"Book Review" [of the Swedish translation of Cabell's *Figures of Earth*] *Kalki*, Vol. 6 No. 2, Whole No. 22 James Blish		1974
"A Bough to Cabell" *Kalki*, Vol. 5 No. 3, Whole No. 19 James Blish		19??
"Cabell as Historical Actor" [with James N. Hall] *Kalki*, Vol. 3 No. 2, Whole No. 10 James Blish		1969
"Cabell as Kabbalist" *Kalki*, Vol. 3 No. 1, Whole No. 9 James Blish		1969
"Cabell as Playwright" *Kalki*, Vol. 5 No. 2, Whole No. 18 James Blish		19??
"Cabell as Voluntarist" *Kalki*, Vol. 3 No. 4, Whole No. 12 James Blish		1969
"The Climate of Insult" *The Sewanee Review*, Vol. 80 No. 2	Univ. of the South, Sewanee, Tenn. [Andrew Lytle]	Spr 72
"Eclectic Occultism" [Review of *The Occult*, by Colin Wilson] *The Spectator*, Vol. 227, No. 7380	The Spectator, London	6 Nov 71

"The Economist" [Reviews and discussions]
   Kalki, Vol. 2 No. 2, Whole No. 6   James Blish
   Kalki, Vol. 3 No. 1, Whole No. 9   James Blish
   Kalki, Vol. 3 No. 2, Whole No. 10   James Blish
		19??
		1969
		1969

"Figure of Earth" etc. *Shadow*, Vol. 2 No. 6	David Sutton, Birmingham, U.K.	3-72

BIBLIOGRAPHY 245

Title Publication	Publisher [Editor]	Date
"Formal Music at the Wake" (Part I)		
A Wake Newslitter (New Series), Vol. 7 No. 2	English Dept., Univ. of Newcastle, N.S.W., Australia [Fritz Senn & Clive Hart]	4-70
"Formal Music at the Wake" (Part II)		
A Wake Newslitter (New Series), Vol. 7 No. 3	English Dept., Univ. of Dundee [Fritz Senn & Clive Hart]	4-70
"Formal Music at the Wake" (Part III)		
A Wake Newslitter (New Series), Vol. 7 No. 4	English Dept., Univ. of Dundee [Fritz Senn & Clive Hart]	8-70
"From the Third Window" [Editorials, with no further subtitle]		
Kalki, Vol. 2 No. 1, Whole No. 5	James Blish	1967
Kalki, Vol. 2 No. 2, Whole No. 6	James Blish	19??
Kalki, Vol. 2 No. 3, Whole No. 7	James Blish	1968
Kalki, Vol. 2 No. 4a, Whole No. 8a	James Blish	19??
Kalki, Vol. 3 No. 4, Whole No. 12	James Blish	1969
Kalki, Vol. 4 No. 2, Whole No. 14	James Blish	19??
Kalki, Vol. 4 No. 3, Whole No. 15	James Blish	19??
Kalki, Vol. 4 No. 4, Whole No. 16	James Blish	19??
Kalki, Vol. 5 No. 1, Whole No. 17 [with Paul Spencer]	James Blish	19??
Kalki, Vol. 5 No. 2, Whole No. 18	James Blish	19??
Kalki, Vol. 5 No. 3, Whole No. 19	James Blish	19??
Kalki, Vol. 6 No. 1, Whole No. 21	James Blish	19??
Kalki, Vol. 6 No. 2, Whole No. 22	James Blish	1974
"From the Third Window: An Attitude Toward Gallantry"		
Kalki, Vol. 4 No. 1, Whole No. 13	James Blish	1969
"From the Third Window: Cabell in Paperback"		
Kalki, Vol. 3 No. 1, Whole No. 9	James Blish	1969
"From the Third Window: On Secondary Universes"		
Kalki, Vol. 3 No. 3, Whole No. 11	James Blish	1969

THE TALE THAT WAGS THE GOD

Title / Publication	Publisher [Editor]	Date
"From the Third Window: Seminar and Aftermath" *Kalki*, Vol. 3 No. 2, Whole No. 10	James Blish	1969
"The Geography of Dream" *Kalki*, Vol. 4 No. 3, Whole No. 15	James Blish	19??
"Kram Revisited" *A Wake Newslitter (New Series)*, Vol. 4 No. 4	English Dept., Univ. of Newcastle, N.S.W., Australia [Fritz Senn & Clive Hart]	8-67
"The Literary Dreamers" [reprinted in *The Tale That Wags the God*] *The Alien Critic*, Vol. 2 No. 5	Richard E. Geis Portland, Ore.	5-73
"The Long Night of a Virginia Author" [reprinted in *The Tale That Wags the God*] *Journal of Modern Literature*, Vol. 2 No. 3	Temple University [Maurice Beebe]	6-70
"Manuel's Second Coming" *Cypher*, No. 3	Goddard/Sandow, Milford-on-Sea, U.K.	12-70
"Movie Review" *A Wake Newslitter*, Vol. 11 No. 6		12-65
"New Myth for Ulysses" [Review of *Ulysses on the Liffey*, by Ellman] *The Spectator*, Vol. 228, No. 7496	The Spectator, London	26 Feb 72
"The Pound Scandal" [Book Review] *The Sewanee Review*, Vol. 67 No. 4	Univ. of the South, Sewanee, Tenn. [Monroe K. Spears]	Aut 59
"Primitive Cabell—and Cabellians" *Kalki*, Vol. 5 No. 1, Whole No. 17	James Blish	19??

BIBLIOGRAPHY 247

Title / Publication	Publisher [Editor]	Date
"The Problem of Scoteia" *Kalki*, Vol. 2 No. 3, Whole No. 7	James Blish	1968
"Review: Mary Ellen Bute: *Passages From Finnegans Wake*" *A Wake Newslitter (New Series)*, Vol. 11 No. 6	English Dept., Univ. of Newcastle, N.S.W., Australia [Fritz Senn & Clive Hart]	12-65
"Rituals on Ezra Pound" *The Sewanee Review*, Vol. 58 No. 2	Univ. of the South, Sewanee, Tenn. [J. E. Palmer]	Spr 50
"Some Cabellian Tropes" *Kalki*, Vol. 2 No. 3, Whole No. 7	James Blish	1968
"Some Fictional Descendants of Carroll" *Jabberwocky*, No. 3	The Lewis Carroll Society, London [Mrs. Anne Clark]	3-70
"Source Notes: A Horrible Quiet Noise" *Kalki*, Vol. 2 No. 2, Whole No. 6	James Blish	19??
"Source Notes: Birdsong" *Kalki*, Vol. 2 No. 1, Whole No. 5	James Blish	1967
"Source Notes: Cabell Gets One Wrong" *Kalki*, Vol. 2 No. 2, Whole No. 6	James Blish	19??
"Source Notes: More Spells" *Kalki*, Vol. 2 No. 3, Whole No. 7	James Blish	1968
"Source Notes: Ninzian Gets One Right" *Kalki*, Vol. 2 No. 1, Whole No. 5	James Blish	1967
"Source Notes: The Mirror and Pigeons Resolved" *Kalki*, Vol. 2 No. 4a, Whole No. 8a	James Blish	19??

Title Publication	Publisher [Editor]	Date
"Source Notes: Witches, Demons and Spells" *Kalki*, Vol. 5 No. 1, Whole No. 17	James Blish	19??
"Special Announcement—A 'Wake' Appendix" *James Joyce Quarterly—Finnegans Wake Issue*, Vol. 9 No. 2	Univ. of Tulsa, Oklahoma [Thomas F. Staley]	Win 71
"The Stallion's Other Members" *Kalki*, Vol. 4 No. 2, Whole No. 14	James Blish	19??
"The Tale That Wags the God" [same as "The Function of Science Fiction"] [reprinted in *The Tale That Wags the God*] *American Libraries*		12-70
"To Rhadamanthus, Snarling: Cabell Against His Critics" *Kalki*, Vol. 2 No. 3, Whole No. 7	James Blish	1968
"The Tolkien of the Twenties Returns" *Book World*		6 July 69
"The View From Mispec Moor" *Kalki*, Vol. 5 No. 3[4], Whole No. 20	James Blish	19??
"The View From Mispec Moor: Footnotes to The Long Night" *Kalki*, Vol. 6 No. 1, Whole No. 21	James Blish	19??
"Why Do Poets Bother?" *Books and Bookmen*, Vol. 15 No. 5		2-70
"Die Wiederentdeckung James Branch Cabell" *Quarber Merkur*, No. 2	Franz Rottensteiner	2-71
"A Wildean Echo?" [with Paul Spencer] *Kalki*, Vol. 3 No. 3, Whole No. 11	James Blish	1969
"Wine and Water" *Prairie Schooner*, Vol. 34 No. 2	Univ. of Nebraska Press [Karl Shapiro]	Sum 60

BOOK REVIEWS

By-lined Blish unless noted as William Atheling, Jr. [W.A.Jr.]

Title	Publisher	Date
Amazing Stories, Vol. 42 No. 1: "The Future in Books": *Seekers of Tomorrow*, by Sam Moskowitz [W.A.Jr.]; *Dangerous Visions*, by Harlan Ellison [W.A.Jr.]	Ultimate Pub. Co., Flushing, N.Y.	6-68
Amazing Stories, Vol. 42 No. 3: "The Future in Books": *Cryptozoic!*, by Brian W. Aldiss [W.A.Jr.]; *Best SF: 1967*, ed. by Harry Harrison & Brian W. Aldiss	Ultimate Pub. Co., Flushing, N.Y.	9-68
Amazing Stories, Vol. 42 No. 4: "The Future in Books": *Neutron Star*, by Larry Niven [W.A.Jr.]	Ultimate Pub. Co., Flushing, N.Y.	11-68

Title	Publisher	Date
Amazing Stories, Vol. 42 No. 5: "The Future in Books": *2001—A Space Odyssey*, by Arthur C. Clarke [W.A.Jr.]; *Synthajoy*, by D. G. Compton [W.A.Jr.]	Ultimate Pub. Co., Flushing, N.Y.	1-69
Amazing Stories, Vol. 42 No. 6: "The Future in Books": *The Demon Breed*, by James H. Schmitz [W.A.Jr.]; *The Making of Star Trek*, by Stephen E. Whitfield (with Gene Roddenberry); *Picnic on Paradise*, by Joanna Russ [W.A.Jr.]	Ultimate Pub. Co., Flushing, N.Y.	3-69
Amazing Stories, Vol. 43 No. 2: "The Future in Books": *A Voyage to Arcturus*, by David Lindsay [W.A.Jr.]; *The Ring of Ritornel*, by Charles L. Harness [W.A.Jr.]	Ultimate Pub. Co., Flushing, N.Y.	7-69
Amazing Stories, Vol. 43 No. 3: "The Future in Books": *The Jagged Orbit*, by John Brunner; *Brother Assassin*, by Fred Saberhagen [W.A.Jr.]	Ultimate Pub. Co., Flushing, N.Y.	9-69
Astounding Science Fiction, Vol. 47 No. 2: "Book Reviews": *Time, Knowledge, and the Nebulae*, by Martin Johnson	Street & Smith Pubs., N.Y.	4-51
Foundation, No. 6: "A Surfeit of Lem, Please?" [review of *The Invincible*, by Stanislaw Lem]	Science Fiction Foundation	5-74
Future Science Fiction, Vol. 3 No. 3: "Readin' and Writhin'": *The Evolution of Scientific Thought From Newton to Einstein*, by A. d'Abro	Columbia Pub., Holyoke, Mass., & N.Y.	9-52
Magazine of Fantasy & Science Fiction, Vol. 20 No. 6: "Books": *Rogue Moon*, by Algis Budrys	Mercury Press, Concord, N.H. & N.Y.	6-61

BIBLIOGRAPHY 251

Title	Publisher	Date
Magazine of Fantasy & Science Fiction, Vol. 38 No. 2: "Books": *Figures of Earth,* by James Branch Cabell; *The Silver Stallion,* by James Branch Cabell; *The King of Elfland's Daughter,* by Lord Dunsany; *The Wood Beyond the World,* by William Morris; *The Blue Star,* by Fletcher Pratt	Mercury Press, Concord, N.H. & N.Y.	2-70
Magazine of Fantasy & Science Fiction, Vol. 38 No. 4: "Books": *Holding Your Eight Hands; An Anthology of Science-Fiction Verse,* ed. by Edward Lucie-Smith; *Creatures of Light and Darkness,* by Roger Zelazny; *Lilith,* by George MacDonald; *Eight Fantasms and Magics,* by Jack Vance; *The New Minds,* by Dan Morgan; *The Several Minds,* by Dan Morgan	Mercury Press, Concord, N.H. & N.Y.	4-70
Magazine of Fantasy & Science Fiction, Vol. 39 No. 2: "Books": *Ten Million Years to Friday,* by John Lymington; *The League of Grey-Eyed Women,* by Julius Fast; *The Steel Crocodile,* by D. G. Compton; *The Phoenix and the Mirror,* by Avram Davidson	Mercury Press, Concord, N.H. & N.Y.	8-70
Magazine of Fantasy & Science Fiction, Vol. 39 No. 3: "Books": *The High Place,* by James Branch Cabell; *Crime Prevention in the 30th Century,* ed. by Hans Stefan Santesson; *The General Zapped an Angel,* by Howard Fast; *Nova 1,* ed. by Harry Harrison	Mercury Press, Concord, N.H. & N.Y.	9-70

252 THE TALE THAT WAGS THE GOD

Title	Publisher	Date
Magazine of Fantasy & Science Fiction, Vol. 39 No. 6: "Books": *And Chaos Died*, by Joanna Russ; *The Rakehells of Heaven*, by John Boyd; *Barefoot in the Head*, by Brian W. Aldiss; *The Daleth Effect*, by Harry Harrison	Mercury Press, Concord, N.H. & N.Y.	12-70
Magazine of Fantasy & Science Fiction, Vol. 40 No. 1: "Books": *Other Worlds, Other Seas*, ed. by Darko Suvin; *Something About Eve*, by James Branch Cabell; *Under the Moons of Mars*, ed. by Sam Moskowitz; *The Thinking Seat*, by Peter Tate	Mercury Press, Concord, N.H. & N.Y.	1-71
Magazine of Fantasy & Science Fiction, Vol. 40 No. 3: "Books": *Tau Zero*, Poul Anderson; *The Troika Incident*, by James Cooke Brown; *Genesis Two*, by L. P. Davies; *Warlocks and Warriors*, ed. by L. Sprague de Camp; *I Will Fear No Evil*, by Robert A. Heinlein	Mercury Press, Cornwall, Conn. & N.Y.	3-71
Magazine of Fantasy & Science Fiction, Vol. 40 No. 5: "Books": *Binary Divine*, by Jon Hartridge; *Nine Princes in Amber*, by Roger Zelazny; *Whipping Star*, by Frank Herbert; *Fourth Mansions*, by R. A. Lafferty; *Solaris*, by Stanislaw Lem	Mercury Press, Cornwall, Conn. & N.Y.	5-71
Magazine of Fantasy & Science Fiction, Vol. 41 No. 2: "Books": *Atlas of the Universe*, by Patrick Moore; *The Stainless Steel Rat's Revenge*, by Harry Harrison; *The Shattered Ring*, by Lois and Stephen Rose; *A Few Last Words*, by James Sallis	Mercury Press, Cornwall, Conn. & N.Y.	8-71

BIBLIOGRAPHY 253

Title	Publisher	Date
Magazine of Fantasy & Science Fiction, Vol. 41 No. 3: "Books": *Ringworld*, by Larry Niven; *Chronocules*, by D. G. Compton; *Tomorrow Is Too Far*, by James White	Mercury Press, Cornwall, Conn. & N.Y.	9-71
Magazine of Fantasy & Science Fiction, Vol. 41 No. 6: "Books": *Sturgeon Is Alive and Well . . .*, by Theodore Sturgeon; *Strange Seas and Shores*, by Avram Davidson; *The Alien*, by L. P. Davies; *Operation Chaos*, by Poul Anderson; *Alone Against Tomorrow*, by Harlan Ellison	Mercury Press, Cornwall, Conn. & N.Y.	12-71
Magazine of Fantasy & Science Fiction, Vol. 42 No. 1: "Books": *Arrive at Easterwine*, by R. A. Lafferty; *Vector for Seven*, by Josephine Saxton; *The Shape of Further Things*, by Brian W. Aldiss; *Planet of the Voles*, by Charles Platt; *Exiled From Earth*, by Ben Bova	Mercury Press, Cornwall, Conn. & N.Y.	1-72
Magazine of Fantasy & Science Fiction, Vol. 42 No. 2: "Books": *Science Fiction: The Future*, ed. by Dick Allen; *Tactics of Mistake*, by Gordon R. Dickson; *The Flame Is Green*, by R. A. Lafferty; *The Lost Face*, by Josef Nesvadba	Mercury Press, Cornwall, Conn. & N.Y.	2-72
Magazine of Fantasy & Science Fiction, Vol. 42 No. 4: "Books": *The Cream of the Jest*, James Branch Cabell; *Gardens 1 to 5*, by Peter Tate; *Jack of Shadows*, by Roger Zelazny; *Fun With Your New Head*, Thomas M. Disch; *Chapayeca*, by G. C. Edmondson	Mercury Press, Cornwall, Conn. & N.Y.	4-72

Title	Publisher	Date
Magazine of Fantasy & Science Fiction, Vol. 42 No. 6: "Books": *No One Goes There Now*, by William H. Walling; *Absolute Zero*, by Ernest Tidyman; *The Eclipse of Dawn*, by Gordon Eklund; *The Flying Sorcerers*, by David Gerrold and Larry Niven; *Universe Day*, by K. M. O'Donnell; *Sleepwalker's World*, by Gordon R. Dickson	Mercury Press, Cornwall, Conn. & N.Y.	6-72
Magazine of Fantasy & Science Fiction, Vol. 43 No. 1: "Books": *Pstalemate*, by Lester del Rey; *The Third Ear*, by Curt Siodmak; *Hell House*, by Richard Matheson; *The Lathe of Heaven*, by Ursula K. Le Guin; *Peregrine: Primus*, by Avram Davidson; *Group Feast*, by Josephine Saxton	Mercury Press, Cornwall, Conn. & N.Y.	7-72
Magazine of Fantasy & Science Fiction, Vol. 43 No. 5: "Books": *The Moment of Eclipse*, by Brian W. Aldiss; *The Edge of Forever*, by Chad Oliver; *Four Futures*, ed. by Robert Silverberg; *New Dimensions I*, ed. by Robert Silverberg	Mercury Press, Cornwall, Conn. & N.Y.	11-72
Magazine of Fantasy & Science Fiction, Vol. 44 No. 1: "Books": *The Wrong End of Time*, by John Brunner; *Ultimate World*, by Hugo Gernsback; *Hawkshaw*, by Ron Goulart; *Strange Doings*, by R. A. Lafferty; *The Book of Skulls*, by Robert Silverberg	Mercury Press, Cornwall, Conn. & N.Y.	1-73
Planet Stories, Vol. 4 No. 9: "Dianetics: A Door to the Future": *Dianetics*, by L. Ron Hubbard	Love Romances Pub. Co., N.Y.	11-50

BIBLIOGRAPHY 255

Title	Publisher	Date
Science Fiction Review, No. 33: *The Silver Stallion*, by James Branch Cabell	Richard E. Geis, Santa Monica, Cal.	10-69
Speculation, Vol. 3 No. 1: *Barefoot in the Head*, by Brian Aldiss	Peter Weston, Birmingham, U.K.	1/2-70
Startling Stories, Vol. 27 No. 2: "Science Fiction Bookshelf": *A Doctor's Report on Dianetics*, by J. A. Winter, M.D.	Better Pubs., Kokomo, Ind., & N.Y.	9-52
[Not known] Book Reviews: 22 March 1953 and 17 May 1953	Classic Features (no other information)	(1953)

ARTICLES AND INTERVIEWS

Title Publication	Publisher [Editor]	Date
"All in a Knight's Work"		
Speculation, No. 29	Peter Weston, Birmingham, U.K.	10-71
"The Arts in Science Fiction" [reprinted in *The Tale That Wags the God*]		
Vector, No. 61	British S. F. Assn. Ltd., Harrow, U.K. [M. Edwards]	9/10-72
A Multitude of Visions	T-K Graphics, Baltimore, Md [Cy Chauvin]	1975
"Bloody Pulp Stories" ["Pulp Magazines Satire"]		
Mad, Vol. 1 No. 30	E.C. Pubs, N.Y.	12-56
"The Critical Literature" [reprinted in *More Issues at Hand*]		
S F Horizons, No. 2	S F Horizons, Sunningdale, Berks, U.K. [Brian Aldiss & H. Harrison]	Win 68

BIBLIOGRAPHY 257

Title Publication	Publisher [Editor]	Date

"The Decline of the Supernatural" See "James Blish on the Decline of the Supernatural"

"The Development of a Science Fiction Writer: II" [reprinted in *The Tale That Wags the God*, as part of "A Science Fiction Coming of Age"]
    Foundation, No. 2   Science Fiction Foundation [Peter Nicholls]   1972

"E La Logica, Scusino?" See "Is This Thinking?"

"Eine Kleine Okie-Musik"
    Australian Science Fiction Review, No. 12   John Bangsund, Northcote, Vic., Australia   10-67

"ESP and Science Fiction" See "James Blish on ESP and Science Fiction"

"Five Answers"
    Third Programme. New Comment   British Broadcasting Corp.   17 Oct 62

"The Function of Science Fiction" [reprinted in *The Tale That Wags the God*]
    The Light Fantastic   Scribners   1970

"Future Recall"
    The Disappearing Future (Ed. George Hays)   Panther Books, London   1970

"The Good, the Bad, the Indifferent" [The Speculation Conference—Comments and Panel] [reprinted in *More Issues at Hand*]
    Speculation, No. 27 (Vol. 3 No. 3)   Peter Weston, Birmingham, U.K.   9/10-70

The Grolier Encyclopedia: Articles on "Science Fiction"; "Ray Bradbury"; "Arthur C. Clarke"; "Robert A. Heinlein"; "Fantasy."
     Grolier   1959

Title Publication	Publisher [Editor]	Date
"High Fantasy—And Lots of It" *Vector*, No. 56	British S. F. Assn. Ltd., Coventry, U.K. [Bob Parkinson]	Sum 70
"If You Don't Like It Here, Why Don't You Go Back Where You Came From?" *Punch*		11 Dec 74
"In Conversation—James Blish Talks to Brian Aldiss" [reprinted in *The Tale That Wags the God*] *Cypher*, No. 10	James Goddard, Nomansland, Salisbury	10-73
"In Tomorrow's Little Black Bag" *7th Annual Year's Best Science Fiction* (Ed. Judith Merrill)	Simon & Schuster, N.Y.	1962
"Inchieste: Fantascienza e Cinema—Le Riposte" *Cinema Domani*, Vol. 2 No. 7	Milan	1/2-63
"The Invention of Science" [expansion of "The Shadowy Figure of Roger Bacon"] *Adventures in Discovery*	Doubleday	1969
"Invisible Armada" *Air World*, Vol. 5 No. 6	Columbia Pub., N.Y.	9-46
"Is This Thinking?" *S F Horizons*, No. 1	S F Horizons, Sunningdale, Berks, U.K. [H. Harrison & Brian Aldiss]	Spr 64
As "E La Logica, Scusino?" *Gamma*, Vol. 2 No. 3	Edizione Dello Scorpione, Milan	1966

BIBLIOGRAPHY 259

Title / Publication	Publisher [Editor]	Date
"The Issue at Hand"		
Axe, No. 34	Larry & Noreen Shaw, Evanston, Ill.	2-63
"James Blish"		
The Double: Bill Symposium	D : B Press, Akron, Ohio [Bill Mallardi & Bill Bowers]	1969
"James Blish Interviewed" [by Paul Walker]		
Moebius Trip, No. 13	Connor, Peoria, Ill. [Edward C. Connor]	5-72
"James Blish on ESP and Science Fiction"		
The Sunday Times Mag.	Times Newspapers, London	22 Nov 70
"James Blish on the Decline of the Supernatural"		
The Spectator, Vol. 229 No. 7521	The Spectator, London	19 Aug 72
"Let Joy Be Unconfined"		
Playboy, Vol. 13 No. 10	HMH Pub. Co., Chicago	10-66
The Pursuit of Pleasure Anthology	Playboy Press, Chicago	1972
The Sensuous Society	Playboy Press, Chicago	1973
"Let Them Say It!"		
Writer's Digest	Writer's Digest, Cincinnati, Ohio	1-48
"Letter"		
Skyhook, No. 22	Gafia Press, Minneapolis, Minn. [Red Boggs]	Sum 54
"A Letter From James Blish"		
Children's Magazine—Harris Public Library Preston, Vol. 23 No. 1	Harris Public Library, Preston, U.K.	Spr 73

Title Publication	Publisher [Editor]	Date
"Lewis Padgett's Private Eye" *The Mirror of Infinity*	[R. Silverberg]	1969
"The Little Mag" *Kirgo's*, No. 1		4-51
"Maxipen—Unique New Penicillin"	Chas. Pfizer Co.	1960
"Medical News Stories" *Factor*, Vol. 1 No. 1		1960
"A Message From Loki" *Worlds of Tomorrow*, Vol. 1 No. 6	Galaxy Pub. Corp., N.Y. [F. Pohl]	2-64
"Methuselah's Grandparents" *If*, Vol. 3 No. 3	Quinn Pub. Co. [James L. Quinn]	5-54
"Moskowitz on Kuttner" *Riverside Quarterly*, Vol. 5 No. 2	Leland Sapiro, Regina, Sask., Canada	2-72
"Music of the Absurd" [reprinted in *The Tale That Wags the God*] *Playboy*, Vol. 11 No. 10	HMH Pub. Co., Chicago	10-64
"New Drugs for Old" *Catholic Digest*, Vol. 25 No. 7	Catholic Digest, Huntington, Ind.	5-62
"A New Totemism?" *Vector*, No. 120, June 1984	British Science Fiction Assn.	1984
"On a Clear Day All You Can See Is Placards" *Warhoon*, 25	Fantasy Amateur Press Assn., N.Y. [Richard Bergeron]	11-68

BIBLIOGRAPHY *261*

Title   Publication   *Publisher [Editor]*   *Date*

"On Science Fiction Criticism"
    Riverside Quarterly, No. 3   Leland Sapiro, Regina,   8-68
                                         Sask., Canada
    SF: The Other Side of Realism   Bowling Green Univer-   1971
                                         sity Popular Press
                                         [Thomas D. Clareson]

OUR INHABITED UNIVERSE — Series of ten articles (see below)
    Thrilling Wonder Stories, Vol. 38 Standard Mags., N.Y.   6-51
    No. 2 through Vol. 41 No. 2   to 12-52
    I. "The Moon of the Sun"
        Vol. 38 No. 2   6-51
    II. "Venus, the Corpse Planet"
        Vol. 38 No. 3   8-51
    III. "The Moon, Sister of Terra"
        Vol. 39 No. 1   10-51
    IV. "Mars, the Iron Dwarf"
        Vol. 39 No. 2   12-51
    V. "The Rings of Sol"
        Vol. 39 No. 3   2-52
    VI. "The Poison Giants"
        Vol. 40 No. 1   4-52
    VII. "Systems Within a System"
        Vol. 40 No. 2   6-52
    VIII. "Pluto and Beyond"
        Vol. 40 No. 3   8-52
    IX. "Earths of Other Suns"
        Vol. 41 No. 1   10-52
    X. "A Planet in Doubt"
        Vol. 41 No. 2   12-52

"Planet Earth"
    I.G.Y. Teachers' Manual   1958

"The Playboy Panel: 1984 and Beyond" [Discussion—Blish and others]
    Playboy, Vol. 10 No. 7   HMH Pub. Co., Chi-   7,8-63
                                         cago

Title Publication	Publisher [Editor]	Date

"Poul Anderson: The Enduring Explosion" [reprinted in *The Tale That Wags the God*]
   Mag. of F.&S.F., Vol. 40 No. 4 — Mercury Press, Cornwall, Conn., & N.Y. — 4-71

"Probapossible Prolegomena to Ideareal History" [reprinted in *The Tale That Wags the God*]
   Foundation, No. 13 — SF Foundation [Peter Nicholls] — 5-78

"Pulp Magazines Satire" See "Bloody Pulp Stories"

"Science Fiction—An Uneasy Marriage"
   Book Fair — Massillon Univ., Ohio — 1962

"Science Fiction—The Critical Literature"
   S F Horizons, No. 2 — S F Horizons, Sunningdale, Berks, U.K. [Brian Aldiss & H. Harrison] — Win 65

"Science in Science Fiction: 1. The Biological Story"
   Science Fiction Quarterly, Vol. 1 No. 1 — Columbia Pub., N.Y. — 5-51

"Science in Science Fiction: 2. The Mathematical Story"
   Science Fiction Quarterly, Vol. 1 No. 2 — Columbia Pub., N.Y. — 8-51

"Science in Science Fiction: 3. The Astronomical Story"
   Science Fiction Quarterly, Vol. 1 No. 3 — Columbia Pub., N.Y. — 11-51

"Science in Science Fiction: 4. The Psychological Story"
   Science Fiction Quarterly, Vol. 1 No. 5 — Columbia Pub., N.Y. — 5-52

BIBLIOGRAPHY 263

Title   Publication   *Publisher [Editor]   Date*

"The Science in Science Fiction" (complete version) [reprinted in *The Tale That Wags the God*]
    Quicksilver, No. 2   Malcolm Edwards,   4-71
                                                 Cambridge [Malcolm Edwards]

    Vector, 69   British S. F. Assn.   8-75
                                                 Ltd., Reading, U.K.
                                                 [Christopher Fowler]

"Scientific Method and Political Action"
    Politics, Vol. 3 No. 10   Politics Pub. Co., N.Y. 11-46
                                                 [Dwight Macdonald]

"The Shadowy Figure of Roger Bacon" [see also "The Invention of Science"]
    Science World, Vol. 5 No. 6   Street & Smith Pubs., 4-59
                                                 N.Y.

"Some Propositions as to the Nature of S.F. Criticism" [from *The Issue at Hand*]
    Speculation—programme of one-day conference   14 June 70
    at Midlands Arts Centre, Birmingham, U.K.

"Sputnik and the Pharmaceutical Industry"
    Drug & Cosmetic Industries,   12-57
    Vol. 31 No. 6

"The Strange Career of Doctor Mirabilis"
    Australian Science Fiction Review,   John Bangsund, Melbourne, Australia   1-67
    No. 6

"Theodore Sturgeon's Macrocosm"
    Mag. of F.&S.F., Vol. 23 No. 3   Mercury Press, Concord, N.H., & N.Y.   9-62

"Tips to Trippers"
    Scoot, Vol. 1 No. 8   Scoot Pub. Corp., N.Y.   10-57

Title Publication	Publisher [Editor]	Date
"Toward a Technology of Pleasure" *Playboy*	HMH Pub. Co., Chicago	1966
"A Transatlantic View" *Vector*, No. 63	British S. F. Assn., Ltd., Harrow, U.K. [Malcolm Edwards]	1/2-73
"2001: A Note on the Music" *Warhoon*, No. 24	Fantasy Amateur Press Assn., N.Y. [Richard Bergeron]	8-68
"What Is 'Evidence'?" *Future Fiction*, Vol. 1 No. 6	Columbia Pub., N.Y.	3-51

INTRODUCTIONS (to works by other authors)

Publication	Publisher [Editor]	Date
Vanguard Science Fiction [magazine, edited by James Blish]		
"In the Beginning" (editorial)	Vanguard Science Fiction, N.Y.	6-58
The Happening Worlds of John Brunner		
Preface: "John Brunner: A Colleague's View"	National Univ. Pub. Kennikat Press [Joe de Bolt]	1975
The Best of John W. Campbell		
Foreword by James Blish	Sidgwick and Jackson, London	1973
Psico Scacco, by Lester Del Rey [*Pstalemate*]		
Introduction	Editrice Nord, Milan	1974
The Light Fantastic		
Introduction, "The Function of Science Fiction"	Charles Scribner's Sons, N.Y. [Harry Harrison]	1971

Publication	Publisher [Editor]	Date
Best SF: 1967 "Credo"	Berkley Books, N.Y. [Harry Harrison & Brian W. Aldiss]	1968
The Year's Best Science Fiction No. 1 "Credo"	Sphere Books, London [Harry Harrison & Brian Aldiss]	1968
La Falce Dei Cieli, by Ursula Le Guin [*The Lathe of Heaven*] Introduction	Editrice Nord, Milan	1974
Heinlein in Dimension, by Alexei Panshin "Introduction"	Advent:Publishers, Chicago	1968

POETRY

Title Publication	Publisher	Date
"An Alembic" (14 lines) *Forum*, Vol. 12 No. 4	Ball State Univ., Muncie, Ind.	Aut 71
"All Hallows Leave" (14 lines) *Forum*, Vol. 16 No. 4	Ball State Univ., Muncie, Ind.	Aut 75
"Antiphony" (14 lines) *Kinesis*, 3	Virginia Kidd, Milford, Penn.	12-70
"Atalantidon" (26 lines) *Priapus*, No. 21	John Cotton, Berk- hampstead, U.K.	Spr 71
"Aubade for Radio" (14 lines) *Forum*, Vol. 11 No. 4	Ball State Univ., Muncie, Ind.	Aut 70

Title / Publication	Publisher	Date
"Caesura" (21 lines)		
Accent, Vol. 10 No. 4	Accent, Urbana, Ill. [Kerker Quinn et al.]	Aut 50
"Caprice After Ronsard" (14 lines)		
Workshop, Vol. 1 No. 2	P a R Press, Milford, Penn.	1-69
Kinesis, 2	Virginia Kidd, Milford, Penn.	3-69
"Come Away Death" (22 lines)		
The Hopkins Review, Vol. 5 No. 1	Johns Hopkins Univ., Baltimore	Aut 51
"The Coming Forth" (25 lines)		
Beloit Poetry Journal, Vol. 7 No. 3	Beloit College, Wis.	Spr 57
"Dies Irae" (16 lines)		
Accent, Vol. 10 No. 4	Accent, Urbana, Ill.	Aut 50
Saving Worlds	Doubleday	1973
"A Djinn of the Green Djinni" (14 lines)		
Kinesis	Virginia Kidd	1970
"Dove Sta Memoria" (13 lines)		
Kinesis	Virginia Kidd	1970
"Exeunt Omnes" (12 lines)		
The Sewanee Review, Vol. 63 No. 3	Univ. of the South, Sewanee, Tenn.	Sum 55
"Grand Pause" (14 lines)		
Prairie Schooner, Vol. 46 No. 2	Univ. of Nebraska Press	Sum 72
Best Poems of 1972, Borestone Mountain Poetry Awards 1973, 25th Annual Volume	Pacific Books Pubs., Palo Alto, Calif.	1973

BIBLIOGRAPHY 269

Title Publication	Publisher	Date
"Homage to William Carlos Williams" (20 lines)		
Kinesis, 2	Virginia Kidd, Milford, Penn.	3-69
Workshop, Vol. 1 No. 2	P a R Press, Milford, Penn.	1-69
"Husbandry in Heaven" (14 lines)		
Open Places, No. 11	Dept. of English, Stephens College, Columbia, Miss.	1-72
"Huysmans Discovers the Reciprocating Engine" (14 lines)		
Counter Measures, No. 2	Bedford, Mass.	1973
"In Memoriam: Fletcher Pratt" (14 lines)		
Mag. of F.&S.F., Vol. 12 No. 1	Fantasy House, Concord, N.H., & N.Y.	1-57
The Best From Fantasy and Science Fiction, 7th Series	Doubleday	1958
"Letter From a Selenite" (14 lines)		
The Beloit Poetry Journal, Vol. 5 No. 3	Beloit College, Beloit, Wis.	Spr 55
"A Long Convalescence" (14 lines)		
Kinesis, 3	Virginia Kidd, Milford, Penn.	12-70
"Mirror Without Cloud" (12 lines)		
Workshop, Vol. 1 No. 2 (readings at the first Stony Point Poetry Workshop)	P a R Press, Milford, Penn.	1-68
Kinesis, 2	Virginia Kidd, Milford, Penn.	3-69
Second Aeon, No. 11	[Peter Finch]	No date
"Misprisions" (14 lines)		
Forum, Vol. 11 No. 4	Ball State Univ., Muncie, Ind.	Aut 70

Title Publication	Publisher	Date
"A Morning Song" (14 lines)		
Open Places, No. 11	Dept. of English, Stephens College, Columbia, Miss.	1-72
"Oryx in Phoenix" (13 lines)		
Priapus, No. 19	John Cotton, Berkhampstead	Spr 70
"The Poet Waiting for Charon"		
Beloit Poetry Journal, Vol. 2 No. 4	Beloit College, Wis.	Sum 52
"A Prayer for James Joyce" (56 words)		
Workshop, Vol. 1 No. 2	P a R Press, Milford, Penn.	1-69
Kinesis, 2	Virginia Kidd, Milford, Penn.	3-69
James Joyce Quarterly, Vol. 7 No. 4	Univ. of Tulsa, Okla.	Sum 70
"Red April"		
Beloit Poetry Journal, Vol. 2 No. 2	Beloit College, Beloit, Wis.	Win 51
"A Reprise" (14 lines)		
Open Places, No. 11	Dept. of English, Stephens College, Columbia, Miss.	1-72
"Retreat and Flourish" (14 lines)		
Kinesis, 3	Virginia Kidd, Milford, Penn.	12-70
"Scenario: The Edifice"		
Best Poems of 1975, Borestone Mountain Poetry Awards	Solana Beach, Cal.	Win 76/77
"Sennet Before Carbonek" (14 lines)		
Kinesis, 3	Virginia Kidd, Milford, Penn.	12-70

BIBLIOGRAPHY *271*

Title Publication	Publisher	Date
"Serenade for Telephone" (14 lines)		
Prairie Schooner, Vol. 44 No. 2	Univ. of Nebraska Press	Sum 70
"Sleepy Song" (12 lines)		
Workshop, Vol. 1 No. 2	P a R Press, Milford, Penn.	1-69
Kinesis, 2	Virginia Kidd, Milford, Penn.	3-69
Prairie Schooner, Vol. 44 No. 2	Univ. of Nebraska Press	Sum 70
"Song" (39 lines)		
The Hopkins Review, Vol. 5 No. 1	Johns Hopkins Univ., Baltimore	Aut 51
"A Song for Music" (18 lines)		
Poetry, Vol. 78 No. 1	Modern Poetry Association, Chicago	4-51
"Tabby Dead" (11 lines)		
Workshop, Vol. 1 No. 2	P a R Press, Milford, Penn.	1-69
Kinesis, 2	Virginia Kidd, Milford, Penn.	3-69
"Testament of Theseus" (12 lines)		
Western Review, Vol. 14 No. 3	State Univ. of Iowa City, Iowa	Spr 50
"Theory of Right Action" (14 lines)		
Workshop, Vol. 1 No. 2	P a R Press, Milford, Penn.	1-69
Kinesis, 2	Virginia Kidd, Milford, Penn.	3-69
"Theory of Tragedy" (15 lines)		
The Hopkins Review, Vol. 5 No. 1	Johns Hopkins Univ., Baltimore	Aut 51

THE TALE THAT WAGS THE GOD

Title Publication	Publisher	Date
"A True Bill" [Chancel Drama]		
Ten Tomorrows	Fawcett Pubs., Greenwich, Conn.	1973
"Two Brands for the Burning" (8 lines)		
Workshop, Vol. 1 No. 2	P a R Press, Milford, Penn.	1-69
Kinesis, 2	Virginia Kidd, Milford, Penn.	3-69
Prairie Schooner, Vol. 44 No. 2	Univ. of Nebraska Press	Sum 70
"Venice Observed 1969" (14 lines)		
Open Places, No. 11	Dept. of English, Stephens College, Columbia, Miss.	1-72

STAR TREK BOOKS

Title	Publisher	Date
STAR TREK Contents: "Charlie's Law"; "Dagger of the Mind"; "The Unreal McCoy"; "Balance of Terror"; "The Naked Time"; "Miri"; "The Conscience of the King."	Bantam Books, N.Y.	1967
Same As *Star Trek 1*	Uitgeverij Luitingh, Laren H.H. (Trans. Jan Koesen)	1975
Same As *Enterprise 1*	Williams Verlag, Alsdorff (Trans. Janis Kumbulis)	1972
STAR TREK 2 Contents: "Arena"; "A Taste of Armageddon"; "Tomorrow Is Yesterday"; "Errand of Mercy"; "Court Martial"; "Operation—Annihilate!"; "The City on the Edge of Forever"; "Space Seed."	Bantam Books, N.Y.	1968
Same As *Enterprise 2*	Williams Verlag, Alsdorff (Trans. Hans Macter)	1972

THE TALE THAT WAGS THE GOD

Title	Publisher	Date
STAR TREK 3 Contents: "Preface"; "The Trouble With Tribbles"; "The Last Gunfight"; "The Doomsday Machine"; "Assignment: Earth"; "Mirror, Mirror"; "Friday's Child"; "Amok Time."	Bantam Books, N.Y.	1969
Same As *Enterprise 3*	Williams Verlag, Alsdorff (Trans. Hans Maeter)	1972
STAR TREK 4 Contents: "Preface"; "All Our Yesterdays"; "The Devil in the Dark"; "Journey to Babel"; "The Menagerie"; "The Enterprise Incident"; "A Piece of the Action."	Bantam Books, N.Y.	1971
Same As *Enterprise 4*	Williams Verlag, Alsdorff (Trans. Hans Maeter)	1972
STAR TREK 5 Contents: "Preface"; "Whom Gods Destroy"; "The Tholian Web"; "Let That Be Your Last Battlefield"; "This Side of Paradise"; "Turnabout Intruder"; "Requiem for Methuselah"; "The Way to Eden."	Bantam Books, N.Y.	1972
Same As *Enterprise 5*	Williams Verlag, Alsdorff (Trans. Hans Maeter)	1972

BIBLIOGRAPHY

275

Title	Publisher	Date
STAR TREK 6 Contents: "Preface"; "The Savage Curtain"; "The Lights of Zetar"; "The Apple"; "By Any Other Name"; "The Cloud Minders"; "The Mark of Gideon."	Bantam Books, N.Y.	1972
Same As *Enterprise 6*	Williams Verlag, Alsdorff (Trans. Hans Maeter)	1972
STAR TREK 7 Contents: "Who Mourns for Adonais?"; "The Changeling"; "The Paradise Syndrome"; "Metamorphosis"; "The Deadly Years"; "Elaan of Troyius."	Bantam Books, N.Y. Corgi Books, London	1972 1973
STAR TREK 8 Contents: "Spock's Brain"; "The Enemy Within"; "Catspaw"; "Where No Man Has Gone Before"; "Wolf in the Fold"; "For the World Is Hollow and I Have Touched the Sky."	Bantam Books, N.Y. Bantam Books, N.Y. (8th printing) Corgi Books, London	1972 1976 1973
STAR TREK 9 Contents: "Preface"; "Return to Tomorrow"; "The Ultimate Computer"; "That Which Survives"; "Obsession"; "The Return of the Archons"; "The Immunity Syndrome."	Bantam Books, N.Y.	1973
STAR TREK 10 Contents: "Preface"; "The Alternative Factor"; "The Empath"; "The Galileo Seven"; "Is There in Truth No Beauty?"; "A Private Little War"; "The Omega Glory."	Bantam Books, N.Y. Corgi Books, London	1974 1974

Title	Publisher	Date
STAR TREK 11 Contents: "Preface"; "What Are Little Girls Made Of?"; "The Squire of Gothos"; "Wink of an Eye"; "Bread and Circuses"; "Day of the Dove"; "Plato's Stepchildren."	Bantam Books, N.Y.	1975
SPOCK MUST DIE! (A Star Trek Novel)	Bantam Books, N.Y.	1970
Same As *Enterprise 7*	Williams Verlag, Alsdorff (Trans. Hans Maeter)	1972

ENTERPRISE 1 See *Star Trek*

ENTERPRISE 2 See *Star Trek 2*

ENTERPRISE 3 See *Star Trek 3*

ENTERPRISE 4 See *Star Trek 4*

ENTERPRISE 5 See *Star Trek 5*

ENTERPRISE 6 See *Star Trek 6*

ENTERPRISE 7 See *Spock Must Die*

Title	Publisher	Date
ENTERPRISE 8 Contents: "Who Mourns for Adonais?"; "The Changeling"; "The Paradise Syndrome."	Williams Verlag, Alsdorff (Trans. Hans Maeter)	1972
ENTERPRISE 9 Contents: "Metamorphosis"; "The Deadly Years"; "Elaan of Troyius."	Williams Verlag, Alsdorff (Trans. Hans Maeter)	1972

BIBLIOGRAPHY 277

Title	Publisher	Date
ENTERPRISE 10 Contents: "Spock's Brain"; "The Enemy Within"; "Catspaw."	Williams Verlag, Alsdorff (Trans. Rosemarie Hammer)	1973
ENTERPRISE 11 Contents: "Where No Man Has Gone Before"; "Wolf in the Fold"; "For the World Is Hollow and I Have Touched the Sky."	Williams Verlag, Alsdorff (Trans. Rosemarie Hammer)	1973
ENTERPRISE 12 Contents: "Return to Tomorrow"; "The Ultimate Computer"; "That Which Survives."	Williams Verlag, Alsdorff (Trans. Iannis Kumbulis)	1973
ENTERPRISE 13 Contents: "Obsession"; "The Return of the Archons"; "The Immunity Syndrome."	Williams Verlag, Alsdorff (Trans. Iannis Kumbulis)	1973

PUBLICATION NOTES

"William Atheling Jr.: A Critic of Science Fiction," by John Foyster, appeared in *Cor Serpentis* No. 1, 1968.

"The Function of Science Fiction" appeared (as "The Tale That Wags the God") in *American Libraries*, December 1970, and in *The Light Fantastic: Mainstream Science Fiction* (ed. Harry Harrison, Scribner's, New York, 1971) under the present title.

"The Science in Science Fiction" appeared in *Quicksilver* No. 2, April 1971.

"The Arts in Science Fiction" appeared in *Vector* No. 61, September-October 1972. This version has been specially revised, and includes a review from *The Magazine of Fantasy and Science Fiction*, April 1970.

"A New Totemism?" appeared in *Vector* No. 120, June 1984.

"Probapossible Prolegomena to Ideareal History" appeared in *Foundation* No. 13, May 1978.

"Poul Anderson: The Enduring Explosion" appeared in *The Magazine of Fantasy and Science Fiction*, April 1971.

"The Literary Dreamers" appeared in *The Alien Critic*, May 1973.

"The Long Night of a Virginia Author" appeared in *Journal of Modern Literature*, Vol. 2, No. 3.

"Music of the Absurd" appeared in *Playboy*, October 1964.

"The Art of the Sneeze" appeared in *The Magazine of Fantasy and Science Fiction*, November 1982.

A small portion of "A Science Fiction Coming of Age" appeared (as "The Development of a Science Fiction Writer: II") in *Foundation* No. 2.

"In Conversation: James Blish Talks to Brian Aldiss" appeared in *Cypher* No. 10, October 1973.

ABOUT THE AUTHOR

James Blish (1921-1975) was one of the "Futurians" along with Asimov et al., is best known for his books *Cities in Flight*, *A Case of Conscience*, the Star Trek novelizations, and as a sharp-tongued critic who applied the tools of literary criticism to science fiction. He co-founded the Milford science fiction writers' workshop, and wrote science fiction criticism under the name William Atheling, Jr.

More books from James Blish and Advent are available at: http://ReAnimus.com/authors/jamesblish

ReAnimus Press
Breathing Life into Great Books

If you enjoyed this book we hope you'll tell others or write a review! We also invite you to subscribe to our newsletter to learn about our new releases and join our affiliate program (where you earn 12% of sales you recommend) at www.ReAnimus.com.

Here are more ebooks you'll enjoy from ReAnimus Press, available from ReAnimus Press's web site, Amazon.com, bn.com, etc.:

The Issue at Hand, by James Blish (as William Atheling, Jr.)

More Issues at Hand, by James Blish (as William Atheling, Jr.)

In Search of Wonder, by Damon Knight

The Tale that Wags the God, by James Blish

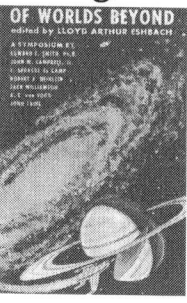

Of Worlds Beyond, by Lloyd Arthur Eshbach, ed.

by Heinlein / Taine / Williamson / van Vogt / de Camp / Smith / Campbell, ed. by Lloyd Arthur Eshbach

The Science Fiction Novel,

by Heinlein / Kornbluth / Bester / Bloch, introduced by Basil Davenport

Heinlein's Children: The Juveniles,

by Joseph T. Major

Heinlein in Dimension,

by Alexei and Cory Panshin

SF in Dimension,

by Alexei and Cory Panshin

Modern Science Fiction,

ed. by Reginald Bretnor

PITFCS (Proceedings of the Institute for Twenty-First Century Studies),

ed. by Theodore Cogswell

Footprints on Sand: A Literary Sampler,

by L. Sprague de Camp

The Hugo, Nebula, and World Fantasy Awards,

by Howard DeVore

The Universes of E. E. Smith,

by Ron Ellik and Bill Evans

Galaxy Magazine: The Dark and Light Years,

by David L. Rosheim

Have Trenchcoat—Will Travel and Others,

by E. E. 'Doc' Smith

The Encyclopedia of Science Fiction and Fantasy, Vol. 1-3,

by Donald H. Tuck

The Craft of Writing Science Fiction that Sells, by Ben Bova

How To Improve Your Speculative Fiction Openings, by Robert Qualkinbush

Staying Alive - A Writer's Guide, by Norman Spinrad

Experiment Perilous: The 'Bug Jack Barron' Papers, by Norman Spinrad

The Futurians, by Damon Knight

Anthopology 101: Reflections, Inspections and Dissections of SF Anthologies, by Bud Webster

Space Travel - A Science Fiction Writer's Guide, by Ben Bova

The Star Conquerors (Standard Edition), by Ben Bova

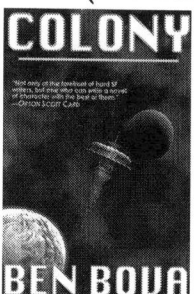

Colony, by Ben Bova

The Kinsman Saga, by Ben Bova

Vengeance of Orion, by Ben Bova

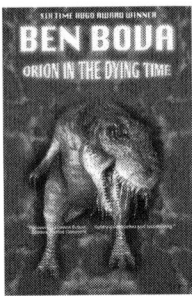

Orion in the Dying Time, by Ben Bova

Orion and the Conqueror, by Ben Bova

Orion Among the Stars, by Ben Bova

Star Watchmen, by Ben Bova

As on a Darkling Plain, by Ben Bova

The Winds of Altair, by Ben Bova

Test of Fire, by Ben Bova

The Weathermakers, by Ben Bova

The Dueling Machine, by Ben Bova

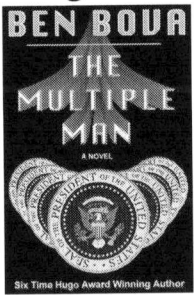

The Multiple Man, by Ben Bova

Escape!, by Ben Bova

Forward in Time, by Ben Bova

Maxwell's Demons, by Ben Bova

Twice Seven, by Ben Bova

The Astral Mirror, by Ben Bova

The Story of Light, by Ben Bova

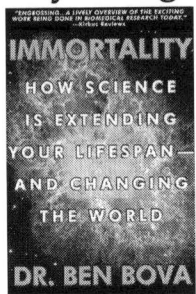

Immortality, by Ben Bova

Phoenix Without Ashes, by Harlan Ellison and Edward Bryant

Shadrach in the Furnace, by Robert Silverberg

A Guide to Barsoom, by John Flint Roy

Jewels of the Dragon, by Allen L. Wold

Crown of the Serpent, by Allen L. Wold

Lair of the Cyclops, by Allen L. Wold

The Planet Masters, by Allen L. Wold

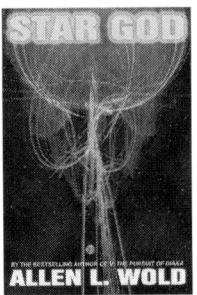

Star God, by Allen L. Wold

Bloom, by Wil McCarthy

Aggressor Six, by Wil McCarthy

Murder in the Solid State, by Wil McCarthy

Flies from the Amber, by Wil McCarthy

The Fall of Sirius, by Wil McCarthy

Woman Without a Shadow, by Karen Haber

The War Minstrels, by Karen Haber

Sister Blood, by Karen Haber

The Sweet Taste of Regret, by Karen Haber

The Science of Middle-earth, by Henry Gee

Commencement, by Roby James

Xenostorm: Rising, by Brian Clegg

The Cure for Everything, by Severna Park

Ghosts of Engines Past, by Sean McMullen

Colours of the Soul, by Sean McMullen

The Gilded Basilisk, by Chet Gottfried

Einar and the Cursed City, by Chet Gottfried

Neon Twilight, by Edward Bryant

Particle Theory, by Edward Bryant

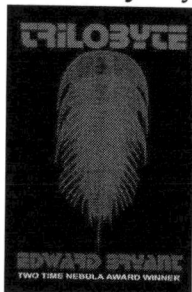

Trilobyte, by Edward Bryant

Cinnabar, by Edward Bryant

Predators and Other Stories, by Edward Bryant

Innocents Abroad (Fully Illustrated & Enhanced Collectors' Edition), by Mark Twain

Local Knowledge (A Kieran Lenahan Mystery), by Conor Daly

CV, by Damon Knight

Bug Jack Barron, by Norman Spinrad

The Void Captain's Tale, by Norman Spinrad

The Last Hurrah of the Golden Horde, by Norman Spinrad

Costigan s Needle, by Jerry Sohl

The Mars Monopoly, by Jerry Sohl

One Against Herculum, by Jerry Sohl

The Time Dissolver, by Jerry Sohl

The Altered Ego, by Jerry Sohl

The Anomaly, by Jerry Sohl

The Haploids, by Jerry Sohl

Underhanded Chess, by Jerry Sohl

Underhanded Bridge, by Jerry Sohl

Bad Karma: A True Story of Obsession and Murder, by Deborah Blum

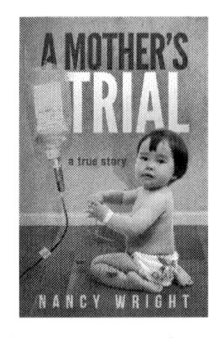

A Mother's Trial, by Nancy Wright

The Box: An Oral History of Television, 1920-1961, by Jeff Kisseloff

You Must Remember This: An Oral History of Manhattan from the 1890s to World War II, by Jeff Kisseloff

Biff America: Steep Deep & Dyslexic, by Jeffrey Bergeron (AKA Biff America)

Side Effects, by Harvey Jacobs

American Goliath, by Harvey Jacobs

By The Sea, by Henry Gee

The Sigil Trilogy (Omnibus vol.1-3), by Henry Gee

Printed in Great Britain
by Amazon